HOPE DAWNS ETERNAL

JULIE LOMOE

Norse Crone Press

HOPE DAWNS ETERNAL

Copyright © 2015 by JULIE LOMOE

Published by
NORSE CRONE PRESS
P.O. Box 363
Wynantskill, NY 12198

Cover design by The Killion Group, Inc
Interior formatting by Wild Seas Formatting
Author photo by Shannon DeCelle

ISBN 978-0-9961921-0-1 (paperback)
ISBN 978-0-9961921-1-8 (eBook)

First Edition

For Robb, Stacey, Kaya and Jasper

Prologue

I'm still wearing the fangs from my last scene when I hear the news that may very well mark the end of my life as I know it. My lips curl in a snarl, and I feel the fake blood pulling and cracking on the skin around my mouth. How dare they do this to me when I've barely begun to reach the height of my powers?

My name is Jeremy Lowell, and until today my future looked fabulous. I'm finally married to Alifair Churchill, the love of my life, and I've been planning to whisk her away to Vienna for a honeymoon. She doesn't know it yet, but I've planned a side trip to Transylvania to explore the land of my ancestors. I've been dying to turn her into a vampire, and I know she wants it too, but every time we've been on the verge of consummating our relationship in a way that takes it to a whole new level, someone or something interrupts us. In Transylvania, no one could get in our way.

But now that they're pulling the plug, those hopes are dashed, possibly forever. Chuck Winslow and Harvey Blaustein have just announced that the network is cancelling *Oak Bluff,* and that the scenes we shot today will be our last. The cast and crew are crammed into the conference room, and for the moment, everybody's stunned speechless. Huddled at my side, Alifair is gazing imploringly up at me. Her fair skin is alarmingly pale. Her deep brown eyes are brimming with tears, her full lips parted in disbelief. It's the look that always reminds me of about-to-be-martyred saints in Italian baroque paintings, the kind you see in side galleries at the Metropolitan Museum. Highly effective in scenes fraught with drama, but today she's not acting.

"We wanted all of you to be the first to know," says Chuck, the executive producer. "I realize the rumor mill has been working overtime the past few months, because the ratings haven't been what we hoped for. Harvey and I have begged and pleaded, tried to convince the higher ups that we've got a solid fan base and it's getting stronger all the time."

"We've told them the show is breaking new ground in daytime drama, taking the venerable world of soaps in a whole new direction," says Harvey, the head writer. "We practically promised them our first-born children, but no dice."

"We've got enough in the can for two more weeks, and that's it." Chuck says. He's tapping the table with his fingertips, fidgeting, looking twitchy and haggard as if he hasn't slept for weeks. "Every single one of you has been fabulous, and we wanted to give you a heads-up now, so you can pursue other opportunities."

"In the meantime, of course you can apply for unemployment," says Harvey.

At the word "unemployment," all hell breaks loose. People begin shouting questions and accusations, dialing up the drama. Men are swearing, women are crying. Actors who hate each other's guts are hugging.

Chuck stands, extends his palms in a placating gesture. "Hey, guys, don't shoot the messengers," he says. "We really gave it our best shot, and of course we'll give you all excellent references."

"One more thing," Harvey says. "I may be speaking out of turn, and this isn't official yet, but Chuck and I will be heading over to *Hope Dawns Eternal.* He'll be the show runner and I'll be the head writer. They're hoping we can inject some new blood into the show."

At the mention of blood, I feel a jolt of adrenaline.

True, the blood I've been sucking as the show's resident vampire has been fake until now, but lately I've developed an uncanny hankering for the real thing. I haven't acted on my cravings yet, but until today I was confident the time was coming soon. Now I'm not so sure. But maybe by mentioning new blood, Harvey's sending me a subtle message, telling me he'll single me out for salvation.

"What a bunch of crap!" yells Eric. He's one of the show's young studs, noted for his bulked up body and six-pack abs more than his acting ability. "They're shutting down your show and letting you take over another so you can run that one into the ground too?"

Chuck's jaw muscles clench and his face reddens. "Harvey's right – he was speaking out of turn. But he's also right about *Hope Dawns Eternal.* He and I will be taking over the show in a couple of weeks, and there's a chance we may be able to bring a few of you along with us. We'll be looking at fan favorites, as well as people who can work harmoniously as part of a team."

Harvey chimes in. "In other words, going ballistic and pitching a fit won't help your cause."

The room goes silent as the message sinks in: antagonizing the head honchos isn't going to score any brownie points, much less land a job on another show. I begin to relax, because I score high in both respects. The fans adore me, and they love me and Alifair as a couple. With her voluptuous figure, her raven hair and enormous brown eyes, she complements me perfectly in the looks department. I'm tall, on the slender side. My hair's as dark as hers, but my eyes are a piercing blue. We play off each other beautifully. Everyone says we have amazing chemistry together, and we're consistently voted favorite couple, or close to it, in the soap magazines. Chuck and Harvey would have to be crazy to split us up.

What's more, I get along swimmingly with the two showrunners. Technically speaking, it's Mark Westgate, the actor who plays me, who has such great rapport with them, but Mark's an introverted wimp, and I'm the one truly in charge. They always address me as Mark, and it's in my best interests not to enlighten them, because they'd be terrified if they knew who they're really dealing with.

Eric must have a death wish – he simply won't shut up. "I still don't understand," he says, folding his massive arms to flaunt his muscles. "If *Oak Bluff* is a failure, why would they risk letting you run another show?"

"We've done a lot of brainstorming with the people in charge of daytime programming," Harvey says. "They feel we've gone overboard with the fantasy elements – angels, ghosts, vampires, that kind of thing – and that it's too confusing for the average viewer. They offered us *Hope Dawns Eternal* on the condition we keep it more realistic, more down to earth."

My stomach lurches – that doesn't bode well. "But that's absurd," I say, doing my best to sound cool and collegial. "Fans love the supernatural element in *Oak Bluff.* The polls in the soap magazines, the emails and letters we get, are proof positive."

"You're right, Mark," says Chuck. "We've raised that point over and over, but they haven't budged. They want more cops, more law and order stuff, and we finally had to bite the bullet. But as we've said, we may be able to bring some of you along if we handle it right."

"Will we be able to play the same characters?" I ask.

"Alas, no. They were vehement about that. Any actors we cast in *Hope Dawns Eternal* will have entirely new roles."

So that's it. Effective immediately, I, Jeremy Lowell, will cease to exist, or so they believe. That last scene, the one that left me with fake blood all over my face, was my grand finale. True, I'll show up in new episodes for the next couple of weeks, and eventually in reruns, but the Jeremy fans see on TV will be a phantasm, not the real me. Mark Westgate will linger on, maybe even snag a new role on *Hope Dawns Eternal,* since brown nosing is one of his talents, but without me, he's nothing. In fact he'd be better off dead.

Feeling chilled to the bone, I rise from my chair and head for the door. I'm a vampire, not a zombie, but nonetheless, I'm a dead man walking. On the other hand, I'm positive I have powers I haven't managed to tap into yet. Maybe there's a way. . .

As I pause in the open doorway, I force a grin, fangs on full display, and channel the immortal Terminator. "I'll be back."

Chapter One

I'm Lieutenant Jonah McQuarry, and today's my first day on the set of *Sunlight and Shadow.* I've spent the past decade on *Hope Dawns Eternal,* but last month the network rang down the final curtain on the show, so this is their last soap standing. Who knows how long we'll survive?

At least I'm alive for now, fresh from a pep talk with Harvey Blaustein, the head writer. He and Chuck Winslow, the executive producer, brought me here. Or strictly speaking, they brought Mark Westgate, the actor who plays me. They have no idea I'm actually Jonah McQuarry, and I've never felt the need to enlighten them. Mark's a method actor, and few people realize how shy and introverted he really is. Over the years he's learned to channel me so deeply that by now we're virtually one and the same. I'm the persona who normally takes control in public, but now and again a little of the real Mark shows through.

Right now, for example. I'm about to shoot my first scene, and I feel like barfing. I'm afraid I'll forget my lines, my pulse is racing, and I can barely catch my breath. On the verge of a full-blown anxiety attack, I pause in the shadows beyond the set. I close my eyes, unclench my fists, and force myself to take slow, cleansing breaths until the panic subsides. These cowardly feelings aren't mine, I remind myself. They belong to Mark, and I have the power to banish them.

This is why I asked Harvey for that one-on-one to

help screw up my confidence. He jogged my memory about the way I strolled into town my first day on *Hope Dawns Eternal,* dressed in black, cool and collected like Clint Eastwood in an early spaghetti western. No one does the mysterious stranger better, he said. Piece of cake – you can nail it.

Okay, so here goes. My heart pounding, I amble from backstage dimness into the blazingly bright interior of a police station set. It's a standard cop shop, with beige walls and gunmetal gray furniture that looks a couple of decades older than the young officer seated at a standard-issue desk. He's a good-looking kid, with wavy hair nearly as dark as mine, and his short sleeves show his impressively muscled arms to maximum advantage. He's peering at a computer monitor, oblivious to my presence. I pad silently up behind him, say "Excuse me."

He jerks violently, as if zapped by a Taser, and whirls his chair around. "I didn't hear you come in," he says, trying not entirely successfully to don an impassive cop façade.

"Sorry I startled you." Actually I'm not sorry at all. You can learn a lot about people when you catch them unawares. Especially their reflexes, how they handle themselves.

"Can I help you?"

I extract my I.D. from the pocket of my black sports coat and thrust it toward his face. "I'm Lieutenant Jonah McQuarry from the Lindisfarne PD, and I'm looking into some unfinished business here – a case that went cold a few years ago."

"You're a little out of your jurisdiction, aren't you? That's Connecticut, and this is New York."

"No kidding. Thanks for telling me."

His expression hardens. Maybe I should cool it with the sarcasm – I'm not used to pulling it off. The showrunners tweaked my personality slightly when they brought me to *Sunlight and Shadow*. Harvey said I'll be a little edgier, more outgoing, than I was back in Lindisfarne. I may even get to smile and laugh once in a while. Sounds good, but it'll take some getting used to.

"I don't want to waste your time, so I'll cut right to the chase," I say. "I'm looking for a guy named Tony Giordano."

The cop tilts back in his swivel chair and clasps his hands behind his head, the better to display his impressive physique. He shoots me a glare with his dark chocolate eyes. "What do you want with him?"

"You sound defensive. That name seems to key you in."

"I guess you could say that." He rises, extends his hand for a shake, and I realize he's a few inches shorter than me. A good thing, because he's far more muscular, but my height gives me an advantage.

"I'm Detective Chris Giordano," he says. "Tony Giordano is my father."

"How about that! I guess the apple rolled quite a way from the tree. A detective who's the son of a low-level mobster."

"You'd better watch it. Don't go badmouthing my old man. He's in the construction business, and the rumors that he's a mobster are nothing but fantasy."

I shrug and shoot him the suggestion of a smirk. "Hey, whatever you say."

He clenches his jaw and his fingers twitch, on the verge of becoming fists. I realize I'd better cool it. "Sorry, maybe we got off on the wrong foot." I mean this sincerely, because I'm still adapting to my newfound edginess. Being constantly taciturn was getting old, and now apparently I'm turning into an outspoken smart ass. I kind of like the new me, but it's still a bit of a stretch.

I flash him a conciliatory smile. It feels phony – my smiles used to be few and far between. "Could you tell me where to find him?"

"You might catch him over at St. Andrew's Church. He was planning to go to a funeral there."

If this were a novel or a feature film, I'd drive to the church, one of those pseudo-Gothic piles of gray stone at least a century old, then catch sight of the funeral cortege heading off down the street, bound for the cemetery. I could catch them easily, fall in at the rear of the procession, but something about the church, the dimness beyond the open doors, might beckon me. I'd brake and pull over – but no, I'm not going there. Literally, because soaps rarely use location shots, and people are never shown driving unless something dire is about to happen – usually a fatal crash.

Instead, we'll skip a couple of hours and cut to the interior of the church, which for a change is actually a genuine location, an old deconsecrated church a couple of blocks from the studio on Manhattan's west side, in the trendy neighborhood known as Chelsea. As I step inside, a sepulchral chill envelops me, strangely refreshing after the unnatural heat of the April day. No sign of Tony Giordano – I've obviously missed the funeral, and he's probably en route to the cemetery. The cavernous space is deserted but for the lone figure in a pew near the front. Her shoulders are hunched, her head bowed in prayer. She's swathed in black, like a mourning widow in an Italian cathedral. I pad silently in my black sneakers past the guttering red votive candles and up the aisle past the rows of empty pews. As I draw close, something about the long black hair that cascades luxuriously down her back seems strangely familiar.

"Excuse me, Miss," I say softly. "I wonder if you can help me." She whirls in fright, stares at me wild-eyed.

"My god, you scared me half to death. I didn't hear you coming."

She's younger than I'd expected, and yet her brown eyes have the depth of an old soul about them. "I'm sorry," I tell her. "I didn't mean to startle you."

Her eyes widen. "Don't I know you from somewhere? There's something about your voice, your eyes – I could swear we've met before."

A lurching sensation deep in my gut tells me she may be right. "I feel that way too," I say, "but I'll be damned if I can remember where or when."

To my amazement, she breaks into song. "'The smile you were smiling, you were smiling then' – don't you just love Rodgers and Hart?"

I wrack my brain, but I draw a blank. "I guess they're from before my time."

"They were popular long before you were born. I wouldn't expect you to know them."

"Anyway, you've got a fabulous voice," I say.

"Thanks. Deep down, I've always wanted to be a cabaret singer. I love all those old chestnuts from the Great American Song Book."

"You'd be great. I can picture you lounging against a piano at the Algonquin or the Carlyle. My musical tastes don't go back that far, but do you remember that old Dionne Warwick song "Déjà vu?"

"You mean Whitney Houston's aunt? The one who was all over the media after Whitney died?"

"Yeah, that's the one. Back in the day, she made some fantastic records – especially the Bacharach and David songs like 'Walk On By.'"

"Oh, right. Now I remember."

"Cut!" We both jump at the sound of the director's shout.

Harvey shuffles into the scene. "Hey, guys, you

really nailed it at the beginning. The element of surprise and wonder was great, but then you wandered way off script after the 'where or when.' Catherine, you've got a great voice, and maybe we can use that talent sometime in the future, but Abby has never sung on the show, and this scene is hardly the time to start. And all that name dropping – singers, composers, hotels – would go over most peoples' heads. Of course I get the references, but most viewers in the heartland wouldn't, and that would turn them off big-time. Besides, the legal department would probably pitch a fit and make us get all kinds of clearances."

She blushes. "I totally understand, Harvey. I'm sorry, I don't know what got into me."

"Let's take it from the top," the director says. "We may be able to use part of that first take, but let's start from the beginning again, just in case. And this time please stick to the script. Mark, I'll need you to go back and walk up the aisle again."

And so I do. This time we both follow the script we'd memorized last night, before we met face to face. Midway through, I lean in close, gaze into her luminous brown eyes. "Maybe we knew each other in a former lifetime."

Her lips part and her eyes glow brighter. "You mean like reincarnation? Do you believe in that kind of thing?"

"Not really. But thanks to you, I have a feeling I may change my mind."

"I don't even know your name."

"I'm Jonah. Jonah McQuarry."

"Are you new in town?"

"Yes. What about you? What's your name?"

"Abby Hastings."

"Abby. Is that short for Abigail?"

She nods wordlessly, her luminous brown eyes

aglow.

"I love the name Abigail. It has an old-fashioned ring to it."

A blush creeps up her neck, and all at once her eyes grow moist with unshed tears.

"What's the matter?" I murmur. "Did I say something that upset you?"

Her blush deepens, proof positive that she's finding my presence upsetting. Our proximity is stirring unexpected feelings in me as well. "No, it's nothing you said," she replies. "I'm upset about my husband."

Looking down, noticing her ring for the first time, I feel a sharp stab of jealousy. "What about your husband?" I say.

"Our marriage has hit a rocky patch, and all because I lied to him, or rather withheld information, about something that was really important. He hates it when I'm not upfront with him."

"I can relate. I was in a similar situation with my wife. She lied to me about the paternity of our son. She thought it was for my own good, but I was really steamed. It felt as if she was driving a stake through my heart."

She gasps, and her eyes widen as she stares into mine. Suddenly I'm shaking. My vision clouds, then goes black. Something about that word, stake . . .

"Are you okay?" she asks.

"Yeah, I'm fine."

"You don't look fine. You look as pale as a ghost."

"I'm okay, honestly. I just kind of lost it there for a minute. That's been happening a lot lately, I don't know why."

She gazes at me, her eyes alight with concern. "Lost it? How do you mean?"

We're getting in too deep, too fast, and I have to

back off. "I'd rather not talk about it," I mutter.

"So," she says. "Have you split with your wife?"

"No. It took time, but we worked it out and got back together. We've got a fabulous son – want to see his picture?" I pull his picture from my wallet and hand it to her across the back of the pew.

"What an adorable baby! You must be very happy."

I long to tell her that I'm glad they're both out of the picture, but I suppress the impulse. Nevertheless, I'm feeling suddenly befuddled, and I wander off script again. "We were resolving our differences, till the writers sent my wife and child off to California and made me pull up stakes – oops, there's that word again, stakes. It makes me feel queasy. Or maybe I'm just hungry. I could use a good sirloin, or a T-bone, blood rare, with the juices dripping." I feel a sudden rush of adrenaline. "Hey, are there any good steakhouses nearby? How would you like to join me for dinner?"

"Thanks, but I really should go home and see if Mick has come back. By the way, you never told me what you were doing in town."

"I'm looking for a guy named Tony Giordano. His son the cop told me I might find him here."

Abby's blush fades to a strange pallor. "What do you want with Tony?"

"I haven't seen him for years, but we've got some unfinished business."

"Cut," the director yells. "Okay, that's a wrap."

I've blown my lines again, and he knows it. "Don't you want to do another take?" I ask.

"No, we've got what we need. You got a little off track, but we can fix that in the editing. Considering it's your first scene together, you guys had amazing chemistry. I don't want to lose that spontaneity. You generated a lot of heat, and the fans will love it."

Chapter Two

Harvey claps me on the shoulder and propels me toward his office. "That was fabulous, Mark. Piece of cake, like I said, right?"

I nod wordlessly, still wired yet wrung out from my scene with Abby.

"I knew you'd be great. Chuck and I have the utmost confidence in you; otherwise we wouldn't have brought you on board. And it should be a smooth transition. After all, you're still playing Jonah McQuarry – you didn't even have to change characters."

"True," I say. "And I really appreciate that." He has no idea how much, but then he has no idea I'm actually Jonah McQuarry, not Mark Westgate.

"Come on, Mark, have a seat," Harvey says. He plops into his chair, grabs a paper bag from his desk, and unwraps a Reuben sandwich. "You want half of this? I didn't have time to eat it earlier."

The sight and smell of that greasy heap of calories and cholesterol makes me queasy. "No thanks," I say.

He chuckles as he slides the sandwich onto a paper plate and shoves it in the microwave. "I knew you'd say that. Otherwise I wouldn't have offered, because I can easily eat the whole thing."

Over the years I've come to realize that for Harvey, food's a major stress reliever. He comes across as relaxed and easy going, but his expanding waistline tells a different story. But far be it from me to tell him he's eating himself into an early grave.

"*Sunlight and Shadow* needs someone like Jonah,"

Harvey continues. "You've got that lean and hungry look, and those piercing blue eyes women are crazy about. Most of the male leads on *Sunlight* are so bulked up, they look like they spend too much time at the gym. Lots of women are into a different esthetic, and your fan feedback has always confirmed that. We're hoping you'll help boost the ratings. God knows we need all the help we can get. They axed *Hope Dawns Eternal* and gave the time slot to that piece of dreck, *Brand New You,* because it's so much cheaper to hire a few people to sit around and yak it up on a single set. I don't need to tell you that *Sunlight and Shadow* is the last soap standing on QMA. The way the almighty bean counters see it, we're on terminal life support, and they'd like nothing better than to pull the plug."

My stomach plummets. "I wish you wouldn't talk that way, Harvey. It makes me queasy just thinking about it. Anyway, that cop Chris looked incredibly strong, and he got really ticked off when I called his father a mobster. The construction business is just a front, right? I know there are a bunch of gangsters on the show, and I admit that makes me nervous. What if they decide they don't want me around and try to kill me?" That's Mark, butting in on me, making me look like a wimp. "Shut up," I mutter under my breath.

Harvey's jaw drops. "What did you say?" He pauses. "Oh, I get it. You're using a gestalt technique to talk back to yourself. Excellent idea. You want to take it further, have a dialogue with the frightened part of you and tell him to get lost?"

I take a deep calming breath. "No thanks. I've got it under control."

Harvey extracts the Reuben from the microwave and starts chowing down, talking in between bites. "All right! That's the Mark Westgate we know and love. You've never backed down from a challenge or shied away from change. When you went from playing that vampire Jeremy Lowell on *Oak Bluff* to playing Jonah McQuarry on *Hope Dawns Eternal,* you took it in stride."

I sigh. "That's ancient history. I wish people would forget about Jeremy and let me move on."

He grabs a paper napkin and wipes pastrami grease from his chin. "I understand, Mark. Truly I do. But Jeremy Lowell is part of your legend. The fans absolutely adored you as a vampire. That role helped your career enormously."

"I realize that, but even so, I'd rather not think about Jeremy Lowell. He's been dead for ten years, and I'm fully invested in Jonah McQuarry. I don't want to get the two characters confused in my mind."

"Okay, Mark, have it your way, but I'll always have a soft spot in my heart for *Oak Bluff.* That show was my first big break, the first time I worked with Chuck. I'm still proud of it, and I'm delighted that it's become something of a cult classic. It was ahead of its time, too far-out for the network, but today, it would probably be a smash, especially if it were on cable."

"You're probably right, Harvey," I say. Actually I don't remember a thing about *Oak Bluff,* because I wasn't there. But Mark was, so I have to fake it. "There were some great characters on *Oak Bluff,* some wonderful actors. Did you bring any of them over to *Sunlight and Shadow?*"

His jaw drops. "Don't tell me you don't remember your leading lady!"

"You mean Abby Hastings?"

"Well, back then she was Alifair Churchill. But it's the same actress, Catherine Reynolds. They hired her for *Sunlight and Shadow* right after *Oak Bluff* folded." He peers at me quizzically. "How could you forget? You two had wonderful chemistry together. Mark, please don't tell me you're getting early Alzheimer's."

My stomach lurches, but I force a laugh. "No, I'm fine. You've given me so many love interests over the years that maybe I'm losing track. But I knew she seemed familiar."

"Familiar? I should think so. Jeremy Lowell and Alifair Churchill were one of the hottest couples in daytime. The fans loved you together. That's why we decided to pair you on *Sunlight.* I dropped in that bit about how you seemed familiar to each other as a nod to the audience who have been following you all these years. They like feeling in the know."

"So why didn't you tell me ahead of time?"

He gives me that Cheshire cat smile I always find so infuriating, the one he uses when actors beg him to say what's coming up in their story lines. "I didn't want to spoil the surprise. I kept Catherine in the dark as well – I wanted to capture your first reactions when the cameras were rolling. I thought it would be more powerful that way. And boy, was I right!"

The adrenaline's coursing through me, but I bite my tongue. Harvey's the main reason I'm here, after all, and arguing would be counterproductive. "You've always loved playing your cards close to the vest," I say instead.

He laughs. "Guilty as charged. But I'll make it up to you. Since you're done shooting for the day, why don't you go down the hall to the set for Tony Giordano's living room? They're just about to shoot a scene there. Don't announce yourself, because you're not officially supposed to meet yet. Just watch from the wings."

Minutes later I'm lurking in the shadows, watching from behind a phony wall as Tony Giordano paces back and forth in his luxuriously appointed living room, muttering under his breath. Following Harvey's instructions comes naturally, because eavesdropping is standard practice on soaps, and I've done it a thousand times.

Tony's been on the show forever, and although we've never met, I've caught his act on TV a few times. Officially he runs a construction company, but unofficially he's a mob boss. The casting is perfect – the dark Italian type, he'd be right at home in a Martin Scorsese movie.

There's a sharp knock, the door flies open and Chris Giordano bursts into the room. His son, the cop I met at the station. He barges right in without waiting for Tony to come to the door. Typical for soaps – imagine how boring it would be if they wasted time with people asking who's there, saying "Hold on a minute" or "Go away, I don't want to see you." And heaven forbid they should ever phone ahead. They dispense with all the nonessential crap that would slow down the action. Besides, having people just fling open doors and waltz right in makes for some interesting complications, for example when someone's caught in bed with his best friend's wife. Anyway, back to this father and son scene:

"Hey, pop," Chris says. "Got a minute?" He crosses the room toward Tony. Seeing them together, I notice the family resemblance. Chris has inherited his father's dark good looks. Tony's a little taller, but they both have the muscular build that can come only from endless hours at the gym. Tony and Christopher – suddenly I flash back to the father and son Sopranos. Damn shame about James Gandolfini – a brilliant actor, and if he hadn't carried all that excess poundage around, he might still be among the living. These two obviously don't have that problem – they're rock-solid, without an ounce of flab.

It looks as if they're about to hug, but they both back off awkwardly.

"Great to see you, son," Tony says. "Of course I've got a minute – my family always comes first, you know that. I just hope you're not here on cop business."

"No, I'm not. Not exactly, anyway. It does concern a cop, though. He's from out of town, and he doesn't have any authority here, but –"

Tony clenches his jaw and starts tapping his foot. He's obviously on the hyper side. "Goddamn it, Chris, cut to the chase. What does this guy have to do with me?"

"He says he has some unfinished business with you, something that goes back years, but he didn't want to elaborate. He just showed up at the station. No appointment, no calling ahead."

"That figures. You know we never call ahead here in Ferncliff. Wastes too much air time."

"Right. Anyway, Dad, his name is Jonah McQuarry. Lieutenant Jonah McQuarry, from Lindisfarne, Connecticut."

"Hmm, that name sounds familiar." Tony frowns, scratches his head. "Oh yeah, now I remember. He used to be FBI. He claimed I killed his brother back in Brooklyn, but there wasn't enough evidence to make a case – all circumstantial. He was royally pissed, said he'd bring me to justice if it was the last thing he did."

"So did you?"

"Did I what?"

"Did you kill his brother?"

Tony falls silent, wipes his forehead with the back of his hand. "I forget. Jesus, Chris, they just gave me the script for this backstory yesterday, and I'm not down with all the details yet. They invented this brand-new history to give them an excuse to bring that actor Mark Westgate over from the show they cancelled. They needed to give him some kind of motivation to confront me. I just hope they don't give him too many scenes, and he'd better not try to upstage me. If he does, he's right about one thing – it'll be the last thing he ever does."

I take a step back, deeper into the shadows behind the set. Jeez, Tony sounds thoroughly pissed. Nice transition, the way he segued from the script to worrying about whether I'm going to horn in on his screen time. I can't say I blame him – if I were in his shoes, I'd be worried too. But I'm a cop, and I'm pretty sure I could rein in the impulse to take drastic action. I'm not so sure about Tony. I know he's capable of killing – despite his alleged construction business, he's a mob boss, after all.

Chapter Three

By the time I finally leave the studio and step out onto the street, the sun is sinking low over New Jersey across the Hudson River. The April breeze feels like the proverbial breath of fresh air, and since I've got no plans for the evening, I decide to walk all the way back to Mark's apartment on the Upper West Side. His dog Sirius will be waiting for his evening walk, but I'm feeling frazzled after my first full day at the studio, and I need some time to decompress before coping with his manic energy.

I pause to tuck my longish hair under a Red Sox cap and don my wrap-around shades before heading over to Tenth Avenue. I turn north, and no one recognizes me as I stride uptown. By and large, New Yorkers are fairly blasé when it comes to celebrities, but there's always the occasional fruitcake, so it's better to go incognito. Mark's especially paranoid because his walk-up apartment in the west Seventies is just a couple of blocks from the Dakota, where John Lennon and Yoko Ono lived until Mark Chapman murdered John on the sidewalk right outside the building.

I won't describe the outside of Mark's place, because much as I love my fans, I love my privacy — not to mention my survival — even more, and I don't want people figuring out where I live. I can, however, describe the interior, beginning with the dingy stairwell with its scrofulous walls the color of spicy mustard. Its worn black treads, its wooden railings stained by generations of grubby hands. The apartment is rent-controlled, and the owner harbors chronic resentment over the fact that he hasn't been able to evict all the old-timers and convert it to a coop, so he isn't big on maintenance, let alone improvements.

As I climb the stairs, I hear snatches of conversations and smell the mingled aromas of dinners cooking, but in the hallway outside Mark's door, all is silent. I turn the keys of the deadbolt and the police lock, and only when I open the door do I hear Sirius panting. In the deepening shadows of the apartment, the dog is a black blur as he bounces happily in welcome. I relock the door before switching on the lights. He jumps up, plants his paws on my shoulders and begins licking my face with ardor.

Sirius is Mark's closest friend – or more accurately his only friend – and he's become mine too. He's a mixed breed, a cross between a chow chow and a German shepherd. In looks, he's more chow-like, with the deep purple tongue and the long bristly hair that led the Chinese to nickname the breed "puffy lions." He carries his extravagant tail curled high over his back. His nose is more like a shepherd's than the pushed-in pug face of the pure-bred chow, and at eighty pounds, he's far more massive. But when anyone asks, I identify him simply as a chow, because German shepherds conjure up images of police attacks and drug raids, and I don't want to scare people any more than necessary. Both breeds are fairly quiet by nature, and Mark has him trained to be even quieter, so as not to disturb the neighbors. The landlord may not even know he's there, or so Mark believes. And no one at the network knows Sirius exists.

I slip his heavy-duty choke chain over his head, clip on his leash, and grab a blue plastic poop bag. Then we head downstairs, out the door, and east to Central Park. I've already walked dozens of blocks and I'm in dire need of a stiff drink, so I make this excursion shorter than usual. Back in the apartment, with Sirius bouncing beside me, I cross to the kitchen and dump some Iams nuggets into his big stainless steel bowl.

"Downward dog," I say. He bows in the perfect yoga position, then attacks his food with relish.

As he chows down, I pour myself a double shot of Scotch and raise the glass aloft. "Here's to Abigail Hastings, the lovely lady I met today." I slug down the drink, then pour myself another.

My scene with Abby today was totally off the wall. Wandering so far off script isn't like me. And back on *Hope Dawns Eternal*, I'd never have bared my soul like that to a woman I'd just met. Why on earth did I tell her about these strange episodes of spacing out I've been having lately? I used to have a hard time baring my soul to anyone, even if I'd known them for ages. People used to get bugged at me for being so close-mouthed and poker-faced. Harvey told me they'd given my personality a minor makeover, but this goes above and beyond that.

I feel like a James Bond martini – shaken and stirred. Or no, that's shaken, not stirred. Whatever's going on, it's damned upsetting. All these years I've been keeping my emotions bottled up so tight, half the time I didn't even know what I was feeling. Now I feel things so much more acutely, and they spill out of me almost against my will. It's a period of adjustment, for sure, almost like being reborn.

By the time I realize I've drunk too much, realize I should have eaten something to balance out the Scotch, it's already too late. I sink into a stupor, and soon I'm out like the proverbial light.

Next thing I know it's almost midnight, and I find myself inexplicably back at the studios, in the corridor outside the set for *Brand New You*, the detested show that bounced *Hope Dawns Eternal* off the air. What the hell? For the life of me, I have no idea how I got here. These damned blackouts are afflicting me with increasing frequency, and they seem to last longer.

Tonight's is the worst yet, and I wonder if Abby cast some kind of spell on me. Or maybe I should blame Alifair Churchill. Harvey said the same actress played her, and that she and Jeremy Lowell were one of the hottest couples in daytime. I don't remember, of course, but maybe she's pissed off at me for forgetting.

Here she is now, wafting gracefully down the hall toward me, almost as if I'd conjured her out of thin air. Am I hallucinating? Going crazy?

"Abby!" I call out. "Is that really you? What are you doing here?" As she draws near, I reach out and clasp her hand in mine. The warmth of her flesh is no mere figment of my overwrought imagination.

She frowns. "Mark, don't you remember? You called and asked me to meet you at midnight outside the *Brand New You* studio."

"I did?" I shake my head in hopes of dislodging the plaques and tangles that seem to be strangling my brain, then toss her what I hope is a reassuring smile. "Oh yes, of course I did. And by the way, I'd prefer being called Jonah. It feels more natural since that's who I am in our scenes together. "

"Okay, I understand perfectly. And you can keep calling me Abby too. I've been Abigail Hastings for so long that sometimes I don't even answer when somebody calls me Catherine."

"Catherine? Oh, right, Harvey told me you're played by an actress named Catherine."

She gives me a quizzical look. "Yes, Catherine Reynolds – that's who I am in real life. But I prefer being Abby; I feel much more empowered that way. Anyway, why did you want to meet me here? And why at this ungodly hour? The building's totally deserted. It's downright creepy."

"Something drew me here," I say. "I don't understand it myself. It's almost as if I went into some kind of fugue state and got here on automatic pilot."

"Yeah, you looked a little disoriented just now."

"It's nothing, probably just low blood sugar. I need a bite to eat, that's all."

"Jonah, what is it with you? Every time I see you, you talk about being hungry." She shoots me a look I can only describe as lewd and lascivious. "Yet you're so slender, so different from my hulk of a husband. You're probably one of those disgusting people who can pack it away and never gain a pound. If I so much as gaze at a piece of cheesecake, I gain two."

"Another pound or two wouldn't hurt you." As I move closer, she blushes. "But you're just about perfect the way you are," I add hastily. "Not like all those anorexic models – you've got some meat on you."

She edges away, evading my gaze. "Anyway, back to the point," she says. "Why did you want to meet here, at the set for this despicable show?"

"I guess I'm just a masochist at heart. This is the show that killed off my old soap and most of the folks in Lindisfarne. Those people were like family to me. On some unconscious level, maybe something gave me the urge to check out the place when no one was around. Kind of like aversion therapy, to desensitize myself to a painful stimulus until it's extinguished. What do you say we go exploring, take a walk around the set?"

She gives the door handle a yank. "It's locked."

"No problem." I fish a set of metal lock picks from my pocket and get to work. I have no idea how they got there, but after all these years I know how to use them. In less than a minute, I've got the lock open, and I usher her in with a bow. "After you, Mademoiselle."

I follow her in and we start exploring. The studio is lit only by the lurid red glow of a couple of exit signs, but my eyes adjust to the darkness with surprising speed. The set is pretty much what I expected – a claustrophobic cube, with rows of seats jammed onto risers ascending almost to the ceiling. The people in the back row would probably have to duck to avoid being bonked on the head by the lights.

Up front are two chintzy sets – a kitchen and a stage with four identical padded chairs. I lope onto the stage and sink into one of them. "Welcome to *Brand New You*," I say. "We've got some dynamite guests for you today –"

Abby sprints to the stage, takes the seat next to me and crosses her legs to stunning effect. "Wait a minute," she says. "Your voice is much too low and mellow, and you sound too serious. You're not reporting the latest world disaster on primetime news. You should be more like this – Hi everybody! Wow, do we have an exciting show for you today! We're going to show you how to totally transform yourself in mind, body and spirit."

She's morphed instantly into a new persona, with a Cheshire cat grin, a high tinny voice and a rapid-fire delivery. I can't help laughing. "You're unbelievably perky," I say. "Your delivery reminds me of that talk show star who bombed as an anchor on evening news because she lacked the mandatory gravitas."

"Gloria Kemp. Have you heard the rumors? She may be coming to our very own network, and they're considering her for a daytime show."

Something in the pit of my stomach plummets like a stone. "I hadn't heard that," I say. "I make it a point never to read the tabloids."

"Oh, it hasn't made the tabloids yet, or even the Internet. So far it's just a buzz on the network grapevine."

"Abby, that's a mixed metaphor. How can a grapevine buzz, unless it's attracted a bunch of bees? A power line, maybe."

She punches me playfully on the arm, and I feel an

electric charge. How appropriate. "The way you talked a minute ago," I say. "Is that how they really sound?"

"The women do – even worse, actually. And they've always got these enormous phony smiles, unless they're talking about something tragic. Then they just ooze ersatz sympathy. They're such pitiful actors, it's pathetic."

"You sound as if you've actually watched the show."

"Well, yeah. Haven't you?"

"No, I haven't wanted to subject myself to such torture. Probably because *Brand New You* is in the time slot *Hope Dawns Eternal* had for decades."

She leans closer, zaps me with those enormous brown eyes. "And yet something drew you here tonight. Maybe you should check out the show. Once you see how absurd it is, you might experience some closure."

Staring at her sensuous mouth, I'm on the verge of telling her how much I want to close the distance between us with a kiss, but I manage to restrain myself. Her gaze intensifies, and I suspect she's thinking along similar lines, but she draws back. "Hey, I've got a great idea!" she says. "Why don't we go there as part of the audience?"

"No way! What if we're recognized? That would be so humiliating. On the other hand, it would be even worse if we *weren't* recognized."

"No, it wouldn't. We can go in disguise. Come on, it'll be fun. Think of it as a reconnaissance mission."

I can't help smiling. "Hmm," I say. "I suppose it could work."

"Damn right it'll work." She grins. "I know exactly the right strings to pull. I'll get on it first thing in the morning."

Chapter Four

The morning after our impromptu midnight break-in to the set of *Brand New You,* when I encounter Abby in the hall, she beckons me over and murmurs that she's managed to wangle two comp tickets for tomorrow's show. "I've got to go," she adds. "I'm shooting a scene with Mick, and I don't want him to see us hanging out together." She dashes off before I can ask what strings she pulled to get the tickets, but it's just as well. Though we met only yesterday, I feel strangely possessive of Abby. I'm already jealous of her husband, and if there's someone else I need to be jealous about, I'd just as soon not know who it is.

The next day, at one in the afternoon, we're crammed into seats in the top row, our heads only a couple of feet from the ceiling, and it feels even more claustrophobic than I'd expected. With the audience packed in around us, wedging us in on both sides, escape is impossible. Bright lights beat down on us, far brighter than the flattering lights on soap sets. Although the air conditioning is cranked up high, I'm sweating up a storm, no doubt induced by my anxiety about being recognized, and I'm afraid my spray-on tan will start to streak and run.

Thanks to Abby's shopping expedition to a couple of tacky Times Square stores last night, we're both wearing blond wigs, fake bronze tans, and Hawaiian shirts with flamboyant floral prints. Since my sky-blue eyes would be a dead giveaway, I'm wearing deep brown contact lenses and tinted aviator glasses.

"Wow, Jonah, you're too much," Abby says. "If I met

you on the street, I'd never recognize you. You look like a bleached blond surfer dude."

The image makes me smile, and I can't resist running my fingers through her fake flaxen hair. "We fit right in, don't you think?" I ask. "We could be a couple of honeymooners from one of the flyover states in the Midwest – Kansas or Nebraska – dressed in our touristy best for the Big Apple."

"Still, don't you feel a little conspicuous? There are only a couple of other guys in the audience."

"Maybe I should have come in drag."

"Sorry, Jonah, but no way could you pass as a woman. You're too –"

Her words are cut short by a burst of applause. A skinny young man in jeans and a button-down white dress shirt strides onto the set and starts working the audience, tossing off jokes and instructing us on basic talk show etiquette: smile, laugh, act enthusiastic, don't yawn or fall asleep. He puts us through a couple of practice runs, then flings out an arm to welcome the show's stars.

The audience erupts in a deafening roar. They're cheering, clapping, stomping their feet on the metal risers as the performers walk onstage. Two women sink gracefully into their chairs and arrange their legs at flattering angles. They're followed by a man wearing red and black workout clothes in a synthetic Spandex blend that shows off his buff physique and brands him as the show's fitness guru. Then the host strides to center stage, and the din of the crowd ramps up a few decibels.

"Shit!" I exclaim. "That's Gene Gentry! God, I hate that son of a bitch. I'd heard he had a new show, but I didn't realize it was this one."

"You know him? Oh, that's right, he was on *Hope Dawns Eternal,* wasn't he?"

"Yeah, he was the playboy ex-husband of the town's

richest dowager. He'd been on the show for years, but he was getting a little over the hill, and they kept downsizing his role. He was pissed, and he let everyone know it. Kept critiquing the other actors, and he picked on me in particular. Whenever we had a scene together, he'd try to goad me into forgetting my lines. Then he started sounding off about how soaps are on the verge of extinction and reality TV is the wave of the future. The director was – "

Abby grabs my arm. "Cool it, Jonah. People are staring."

She's right – three overweight biddies in the row below ours have swiveled around in their seats and are skewering me with disapproving stares. I don't want to blow our cover, so I cut my tirade short and hunker down in my seat. The relentless glare of the lights is making my head spin. If I were a menopausal woman, I'd swear I was getting a hot flash. I bury my face in my hands.

"Jonah, are you all right?" Abby whispers. "I'd say you were looking green around the gills, but that fake tan is making you look more of a bilious raw sienna color."

"I'll be okay." I raise my voice and try for a Midwestern accent, the kind they used in the movie *Fargo.* "Honey, I'm sorry, but I told you not to drag me here. This just isn't my thing." I lower my voice. "I can't stand listening to this crap. I need to zone out for a while. Give me a nudge when this abomination is over, and then we'll go check out that steakhouse you told me about earlier."

I close my eyes and focus on my breathing. Before long I'm floating in a state of limbo. Then I slip into a fantasy visualization. I'm tunneling down beneath the roots of an ancient tree deep into the earth. It's a shamanic journey, a technique I learned years ago when

Mark went to a workshop at Omega Institute up in Rhinebeck. Ideally, it's done to the hypnotic beat of Native American drums, but right now my mind is tuned to so sensitive a pitch that I can make the journey without external help. The tunnel opens into an underground cave. Candles flicker, casting eerie shadows on the walls, and I await a message from my spirit guide.

This time, the fantasy guide takes the form of a female deity with a strong resemblance to Abby. Her presence obliterates the blare and cacophony of the horrid reality show, and we spend a pleasurable hour together. I won't go into the details of the journey — they're triple-X-rated. Instead, let's cut to the restaurant a few hours later.

The Prime Cuts Steakhouse is tucked away on a side street in the heart of the Broadway theatre district, and it's decorated in the Victorian bordello style that's practically mandatory for restaurants that cater to tourists who crave enormous cuts of meat. We're in a secluded booth in the back, surrounded by dark wood, ersatz Tiffany lamps and walls of blood-red brocade. We've slugged down two bottles of Bordeaux, and we're both feeling tipsy. The lunch crowd has long since departed, and the place is practically deserted.

By now we're utterly satiated. We've gorged on gargantuan steaks, or rather I have. Abby was more restrained, and half of her sirloin is tucked away in a doggie bag for me to take home to Sirius. I could have devoured her steak as well as my own, but I didn't want to be crude or rude. Something about her brings out the gentleman in me.

Abby dips her snowy white napkin in her water glass, then reaches over and dabs at my face, zeroing in on my lips. "There, that's better," she says. "You had some steak juice on your face. Small wonder, the way you were gnawing on that bone. You looked kind of ghoulish."

"I apologize. I realize my table manners weren't the greatest, but I was ravenous."

"You really tore through that T-bone. Good thing the waiter finally went along with your ultra-rare request."

"He gave me a hard time, though. Restaurants have gotten so paranoid about serving beef blood-rare – God forbid we should come down with something terrifying like mad cow disease. But over-cooked steak is a travesty. You might as well be eating veggie burgers."

"You were so aggressive wolfing down that meat, it was almost scary."

"It may be politically incorrect, but I'm an incurable carnivore. As for the aggression, it's probably what the shrinks call displacement. Better I should chow down on a T-bone than on Gene Gentry's carotid artery."

A look of alarm flits across Abby's face. "Jonah, that image is a little too graphic for my taste. You really hate that guy, don't you."

"Hate's too wimpy a word."

"I shouldn't have made you visit the show. I should have realized how painful it would be for you."

"No, I'm glad we went, although I can't say it gave me the closure I was looking for. If anything, it made it worse. Especially seeing that scumbag Gene Gentry. He was always bragging about how he had friends in high places at the network, and toward the end, when they were cutting down on his screen time, I'm willing to bet he was badmouthing the show to the higher-ups. Maybe he screwed his way to the top, or maybe he had some dirt on one of the programming execs and threatened blackmail. Whatever it was, for some reason they eased him into a hosting gig on some crappy reality show that bombed in short order. Now it looks as if they've handed him *Brand New You* on a silver platter. God knows he doesn't deserve it; he's an execrable emcee. And it's certainly not his looks – his face was getting jowly and puffy, like Alec Baldwin or John Travolta, so he went under the knife and got shot up with Botox, and that made it even worse. Now he looks like a clone of Kenny Rogers, or an over-the-hill zombie in a bad B movie."

The waiter's hovering. To make him leave, I order another bottle of Bordeaux. I know I'm ranting, but I can't seem to shut up. "I've been obsessing about all the people I left in Lindisfarne. The network abandoned them and replaced them with these screechy so-called experts. They act so hyper, I'll bet they're coked up all the time. Or maybe they're on amphetamines."

Abby furrows her brow. "Actually, they weren't as bad as I expected. That psychologist had some good suggestions for that morbidly obese woman, although it was kind of ironic that the next segment featured a chef baking fattening desserts."

"I didn't notice. I tuned out the racket, thanks to my shamanic journey. But it's easier for you to be open minded. You've been gainfully employed on *Sunlight and Shadow* for years, so your life hasn't been disrupted like the people in Lindisfarne. They were virtually crucified, and the network's not about to resurrect them, or at least not the older ones. I guess I'm suffering from survivor's guilt, like someone who walked away from a plane crash where almost everyone else was killed."

"Don't lay a guilt trip on yourself, Jonah. You were the most charismatic, attractive man on the show. That's why the producer and the head writer brought you along when they took over *Sunlight and Shadow*. They're counting on you to breathe new life into the show."

"But it's obvious Tony resents me for horning in on his screen time, and probably some others do too. I don't blame them – I'd feel the same way if I were in their shoes – but it ratchets up the tension on the set. Besides, being brought onboard to jack up the ratings is a tremendous responsibility, and I'm not sure I'm up to the task. If they're looking for a savior, they've got the wrong guy."

"I don't know about that. When something's troubling you and you gaze thoughtfully into the distance, you've got kind of a Christ-like quality. Especially the way they light your cheekbones." She reaches out, caresses my face, then jerks her hand away as if I'm burning hot – which I definitely am. Wordlessly, I grasp her hand, bring it to my mouth and brush it with my lips.

She shivers as she meets my gaze, and we're lost in each other's eyes. Hers are infinitely deep, and I'm pulled into their bottomless darkness.

After an endless moment, she pulls away again and begins toying with her wine glass. She warms the crystal between her palms, then takes a lengthy sip. "On the other hand," she murmurs, "despite all your upright, high-falluting principles and your commitment to everything noble and good, I see a devilish side to you too. Especially when you're off camera. And you do that broody, tortured thing so well, like the archetypal romantic hero in a nineteenth century novel."

Before I can frame a response, she slams down her glass. Crimson wine sloshes onto the white tablecloth and spreads slowly, inexorably, in a bloody stain. She glances at her watch. "God, can you believe it? It's already after five. My husband has fits when I'm late, or when he doesn't know where I am."

"Relax, Abby. You haven't so much as mentioned Mick all day. Why bring him up now? Anyway, you don't owe him any explanations for how you live your life when you're off the set."

"Actually I do. And he's going to be furious if I don't

have dinner ready when he gets home."

"You mean you and Mick are involved in real life, even when you're not on the set?"

"More than involved. We're married."

All at once I'm finding it hard to breathe. "Please tell me you're speaking about your fictional relationship on the show."

Her eyes brim with sudden tears. "I wish I were. But remember my real-life name is Catherine Reynolds? Well, Mick's real name is Keith Carlton. When we first met on *Shadow and Sunlight,* they threw us into some truly steamy scenes. Long story short, we got carried away, and one crazy weekend, about a month after we met, Keith talked me into flying to Vegas for a quickie wedding. It was quite possibly the biggest mistake of my life, and not a day goes by that I don't regret it."

"So couldn't you have it annulled, or get a divorce?"

"Over my dead body, or so he tells me. I've learned not to bring it up." A look of unmistakable panic flits across her face. She scrambles out of the booth and rises to her feet, looking decidedly wobbly. "I've really got to go and throw something together for dinner."

"You mean he actually expects you to cook after a long day on the set?"

"No, only on the days I don't have any scenes. The other days he lets me get takeout."

"What is he, some kind of male chauvinist throwback? Don't you deserve better?"

But she's already fleeing, like a fairy tale maiden in flight from a dangerous predator, although from the sound of it, the villain lies in wait at home. I empty the last of my Bordeaux into my glass and slug it down, then cup her glass between my palms where her hands had been, let my lips taste the faint stain of her lipstick and savor the last of the dregs.

Chapter Five

With the careful gait of a drunk trying to look sober, I wend my way through the tables to the front of the restaurant. Outside, I stagger to the curb, hail a cab, and doze all the way uptown to Mark's apartment. The foil-lined doggy bag that holds the remains of Abby's T-bone dangles from my left hand as I exit the taxi, and a poodle on his early evening walk goes on high alert, his nostrils quivering with desire, as I make my way across the sidewalk. I smile sheepishly at she woman holding the leash.

"Steak for my dog," I mutter under my breath.

She smiles back flirtatiously. "Lucky dog. I wish I were in his place."

Upstairs, I'm barely inside the door when Sirius zeroes in on the steak, whining and snuffling excitedly at the bag. "Okay, guy, you're in luck," I say. "I brought you a special treat."

He whimpers and salivates as I dump the steak into his bowl, but I make him wait and follow the routine. He obeys when I give him the "Downward dog" command, but he's quivering with excitement, and when I give him the okay, he lunges at the meat with fearsome aggression.

As he chows down, I pour myself a double shot of Scotch and raise the glass aloft. "Here's to the enchanting Abigail Hastings," I say. "She gave me this treat for you. I hope you'll meet her one of these days." I slug down the drink even as I realize I'm making a mistake. The three bottles of wine at the steak house were more than enough.

I realize I'd better give Sirius his evening walk right now, before the Scotch kicks in, so I wrest the ravaged T-bone from the dog's jaws, shove it back in its doggie bag, and put it on a high shelf in a cupboard. "I promise I'll give this back to you right after our walk," I say as I slip on his choke chain and leash. Then I stagger down the stairs, Sirius in the lead, and we head east toward Strawberry Fields, the John Lennon memorial garden in Central Park. As usual, there are tourists milling around, sitting on benches, snapping photos of each other in front of the mosaic mandala with the word "Imagine" embedded in the center. A couple of guys are busking, singing Beatles songs with guitar cases open at their feet in hopes of handouts. The vibes are relaxed and carefree. Maybe that's how John would have wanted it, but I can't help focusing on his murder, and it makes me furious.

Maybe I'm projecting my anger or maybe people are scared of Sirius. In any case, they give us a wide berth as we wander past the mandala to a nearby path. I slump onto an empty bench and he hunkers down at my feet.

After that, everything's a blur. For the life of me, I can't even remember making it back to the apartment, much less anything else that happened in the ensuing hours. So I'll skip to the next morning at six, when I awaken to the feel of Sirius's tongue on my cheek. His biological clock is so precise, I never have to worry about setting an alarm. I'm feeling amazingly well rested and energized. Astonishing, because I consumed an enormous amount of Bordeaux at the restaurant with Abby, and then all the Scotch on top of that. I can't remember the last time I felt this good so early in the morning. As a soap star, I'm accustomed to early rising, but it's always a struggle, because I'm definitely not a morning person.

I'm probably feeling so bright-eyed and bushy-tailed

because of Abby and all the hours I spent in her company yesterday. Getting into our Midwestern costumes and characters, suffering through that ghastly taping of *Brand New You,* then whiling away the afternoon at the Prime Cuts Steakhouse. I wolfed down an enormous amount of beef, and that might have something to do with it too. As I told Abby, I'm an avowed carnivore, but I don't normally indulge myself like this. If I did, I'd pack on the pounds, and I don't want to end up looking like Henry the Eighth or one of those Victorian capitalists who put on enormous paunches as evidence of their obscene wealth. I'm known for my lean and hungry look, and I want to keep it that way.

Unfortunately, Abby seems to go for the muscle-bound body builder type, if her husband's any indication. Yet I know she's attracted to me; I can see it in her eyes and the way she blushes when we get too close. I need to tread cautiously, though, because I don't want to antagonize Mick. According to Abby, he's already bugged that I might pose a threat to his leading-man status, and all hell will break loose if I put the make on her.

I wish I could remember what happened after I got to Strawberry Fields with Sirius. We were walking past the "Imagine" mosaic, and I was ruminating about John Lennon and the man who murdered him in his prime, getting angrier and angrier. But as soon as I sat down on that bench, it's as if a fuse blew and everything went dark. Was it an alcoholic blackout? Unlikely, because I normally hold my liquor pretty well. But the rest of the night is a complete blank, except for some unsettling dreams.

Since I'm feeling so disgustingly chipper, I decide to head downtown to the studio. I'm not due on the set till nine, but I want to see how Abby's doing after our orgy of beef and Bordeaux.

Half an hour later, when I turn off Tenth Avenue onto the side street where QMA has reconfigured a row of old warehouses into studios for several shows, I stop short at the sight of three squad cars and an ambulance double-parked near the main entrance. What the hell? Curious, I stroll with studied nonchalance toward the doorway. A skinny young cop thrusts out his hand to block me. "Do you have official business here?"

"Absolutely. I'm Lieutenant Jonah McQuarry."

"Oh, okay. Sorry, Lieutenant, you can go on in. They're expecting you." He waves me through, and I head for the elevator.

When the doors slide open on the third-floor corridor, I find myself face-to-face with another police officer. "This is a crime scene," he says. "Do you have official business here?"

"The cop downstairs already asked me that."

For a surreal second, I think today's shooting has started early. But why haven't they given me the script? Then I flash on the fact that like the other one, this guy's a genuine cop. He's short and pudgy, with a pronounced pot belly, and all of the cops on *Sunlight and Shadow* are well built and buff. Besides, he's wearing a black leather duty belt laden with a gun and various state-of-the-art gadgetry. Our cops aren't nearly that generously equipped. All that hardware is expensive, not to mention unflattering, the way it breaks up the lines of their chiseled physiques.

How am I going to play this? I stand motionless, as if glued to the elevator floor, with my face an expressionless mask, as the doors begin to close. But the cop barges in between them, tripping the electric eye, and they slide open again.

"I'll ask you one more time," he says. His tone has a harder edge now. "Do you have official business here?"

I take a deep breath, then step forward, out of the

elevator. "I'm Lieutenant Jonah McQuarry. The guy downstairs said you were expecting me." I'm pulling rank, and since I've got a good six inches on him, he's having trouble staring me down.

He scowls. "That guy's a rookie, and he doesn't know everyone yet. The Lieutenant's already here. Can you show me some ID?"

I open my black sports jacket and flash my badge, then realize he probably means my network access pass, so I flash that too. "I'm on *Sunlight and Shadow,* and we're shooting a scene in a couple of hours."

His jowly face reddens. "That's not going to happen. Until further notice, this entire floor is a designated crime scene."

"So that's why all the blue-and-whites are parked outside. What's happening?"

He folds his arms and grunts.

"Jonah! Thank god you're here!" It's Abby, rounding a corner and flying full-tilt down the hall. She skids to a stop just short of throwing herself into my arms. "You're early – I guess you must have heard."

"Heard what? What's going on?" I ask.

There's a sudden flurry of activity far down the endless corridor, outside the set for *Brand New You.* The doors open and two cops emerge, followed by two med techs steering a gurney with a black body bag on top.

"Who's that on the gurney?" I'm addressing the cop, but it's Abby who blurts out the answer. "It's Gene Gentry."

"You're kidding, right?"

"Unfortunately, no."

I start toward the gurney, but the cop grabs my arm. "Let go of me," I protest. "I want to see if it's really Gentry. If this charade is an attempt to boost their ratings, it's pretty pathetic." On the other hand,

Gentry's got so much bottled up anger, he's a ticking time bomb. Maybe he stroked out. But then why the crime scene tape?

"The police aren't talking," says Abby, "but rumor has it he was murdered."

"Why doesn't that surprise me? I can think of a hell of a lot of people who'd love to see him croak."

The cop tightens his grip on my arm, and I realize I'd better stifle the sarcasm. Maybe this isn't a publicity stunt. Maybe it's the real deal.

Chuck Winslow, our executive producer, careens into view. "Jonah, Abby — I guess you've heard what happened. This is unbelievable. Poor Gene! They made us call off today's shoot, but we're having a staff meeting at eleven. Be there."

"Sorry, but that's not going to happen," says a good-looking man in a shiny gray suit. He could pass for the host of a late-night talk show, and he doesn't look sorry at all. "Not for a few hours anyway. We've got a lot of people to interview, and we'll need some privacy. Can you show us to a few rooms we can use? We can't use the *Brand New You* set; the crime scene investigators aren't finished yet."

"Of course, Lieutenant. We've got lots of rooms," says Chuck in the solicitous tone he uses to kiss up to the execs who outrank him. "Dressing rooms, meeting rooms, plus some sets. They're pretty spacious, so privacy shouldn't be a problem."

More cops materialize. They begin divvying us up, cutting us off like sheep from a herd and moving us to separate areas of the enormous sound stage. Obviously they don't want us comparing notes with each other. They're running a tight ship, I've got to admit — a lot tighter than we do on *Sunlight and Shadow* — but of course they've got a lot more personnel than we do.

Soon I'm seated across a bare table from a plain-clothes cop in an interrogation room. He's an African-American man, heavily muscled with mahogany skin. The set is claustrophobically small and minimally furnished, with walls of hospital- green tile. I've done countless scenes on similar sets, but never before have I played the suspect on the wrong side of the table.

"I'm Detective Johnson," he says.

"Lieutenant Jonah McQuarry, Lindisfarne PD." I extend a collegial hand.

He doesn't take it. Instead, he fixes me with a dark brown stare, places a pocket-size tape recorder on the table and hits the ON button. "The time is 8:35 a.m., date April 18, and I'm interviewing the actor Mark Westgate."

"I'd rather you address me as Jonah McQuarry. You can skip the 'Lieutenant' if you want."

His eyes narrow and he studies me in loaded silence. "Have it your way," he says at last. "Where were you between yesterday afternoon and this morning when you showed up at the studio?"

"I spent most of the afternoon at the Prime Cuts Steakhouse with Abby Hastings, having a late lunch. Or I guess you could call it an early dinner."

"And after that?"

My heart lurches violently. I saw the question coming, but how on earth do I dodge it? I have no memory of what happened in the hours after I walked Sirius and conked out at Strawberry Fields. "Let's see. Abby left; she said her husband was expecting her. I paid the check, and then –"

"What time was this?"

"Around five, I guess. The dinner crowd was starting to arrive."

"And you got to the restaurant when?"

"About two."

"So you and Ms. Hastings spent about three hours at the steakhouse. You must be pretty close."

"Not really. But I don't see what that has to do with –" I pause. I don't know where he's going with this, but at least he's not asking what I did later on. Maybe I can derail his line of questioning. "Ms. Hastings and I met just a couple of days ago. No, make that three days. I'm new to the show, and from what I gather, they're developing a plot line where she and I will get pretty heavily involved, so I asked her to fill me in on some of the show's history, and her relationships with other men in the cast. The leading ladies on soaps are generally involved with multiple men, but almost always sequentially. It's a kind of serial monogamy –"

He cuts me off mid-sentence. I've been blathering, filling up air time, and we both know it. "So you and Ms. Hastings left the restaurant separately. What did you do after that?"

Here it is, the moment of truth – or not. "I walked around for a few hours. Then I went back to Mark's apartment and crashed." This sounds plausible, aside from the fact that I don't mention Sirius. No need to implicate an innocent dog.

"Is there anyone who can verify your movements during that period? Did you see anyone you know?"

"I don't believe so. I realize this sounds pretty vague, but I'd had quite a bit to drink. Abby and I went through three bottles of Bordeaux – red wine, I mean."

He shoots me a glare. "I know what Bordeaux is. What about later on, after you went back to your apartment?"

I glare back. "It's Mark's apartment. I already told you. I just crash there."

"Right. So it's your crash pad, and you crashed. I get the gist. You were under the influence, and you fell asleep. Did you wake up later? Maybe go somewhere?"

That's exactly what's been plaguing me. Dim images are hovering at the edge of my consciousness, threatening to burst through, but they're probably nothing but dream fragments. Bloody ones, no doubt triggered by that enormous T-Bone steak.

I give him my coldest glare. "I slept like a log all night and woke around six. Then I showered, dressed and came to the studio."

He leans casually back in his chair. "Okay, thank you, Mr. Westgate. That'll be –"

"Don't call me that! I already told you – I'm Jonah McQuarry."

"Take your role awfully seriously, don't you, Mr. Westgate? Is this what they call method acting?"

He's deliberately needling me, hoping I'll blow my cool, but I refuse to give him the satisfaction. I rise from my chair, push it back. "Are we done here?"

"For now, yes. But don't leave town, and make sure we know how to contact you."

"I take that to mean I'm a person of interest."

"You like using cop jargon, right? Must be the character you play."

"No, it's the character I am."

"Right. Anyway, since you ask, the answer is yes. You're a person of interest."

Chapter Six

By the time Detective Johnson escorts me out of the interrogation room and toward the elevator, I'm close to blowing my stack. He's a pretty skilled interviewer, and he pushed me damn close to the edge. I managed to keep my cool, but barely. Plus I'm used to working from a script, and improv isn't my thing. Mark did a lot of improvisational theater back in the day, when he was an up-and-coming actor, but I never had the opportunity to master that particular skill set.

All in all, I think I handled the interview pretty well, but there were some glaring gaps in continuity. In daytime drama, they never show everything a character does in chronological order; that would be deadly dull. But in my own life, I'm pretty clear on the sequence of events, and the fact that I've blacked out a huge chunk of last night is highly unsettling.

Detective Johnson picked up on it, naturally. Small wonder I'm a person of interest. If I were in his shoes, I'd make me a person of interest too. Gene Gentry and I weren't exactly chummy back on *Hope Dawns Eternal*, and then they picked him to host the show that replaced it after we got the axe. Is that motive for murder? They could certainly see it that way. I don't know if they've connected all the dots yet, but if they haven't, they will. And what if someone saw me and Abby in our disguises at yesterday's taping of *Brand New You*? Even worse, we were no doubt caught in some of the crowd shots, and the cops are bound to study those. Our presence in those weird get-ups will no doubt grab their attention.

Out in the corridor, things have quieted down, but a

couple of cops are still skulking around and the crime scene tape is still up, blocking the entrance to *Brand New You*. Abby is nowhere in sight, but that's probably just as well. If we saw each other, we'd inevitably want to talk, and for now it's better if we keep our distance.

The pudgy cop is still on duty near the elevator, looking disgruntled and in need of a donut fix. Detective Johnson tells him I'm cleared to leave, and when the elevator doors finally close behind me and I'm on my way down, I let out an explosive sigh of relief.

What now? I'm not sure when or if they'll hold a staff meeting, but no doubt they'll text or email me. It's almost lunch time, but the thought of food or drink is repellant. Anyway, I'm still strangely satiated after yesterday's pig-out. I decide what I need is a few hours at MoMA – the Museum of Modern Art is always a great place to escape reality for a while.

I head uptown, then east on 53rd Street, and before long I'm lounging on a bench in one of my favorite galleries at the museum, contemplating Monet's gigantic wrap-around water lily mural and daydreaming about visiting his gardens at Giverny in the south of France, when my Galaxy beeps to signal an incoming email. It's from Chuck Winslow – they're having a meeting at four.

I kill the next few hours wandering around the museum. When I get back to the studio, the cast and crew are crammed into the police station set. There aren't enough chairs, so some are perched on desks. Others slouch near the flimsy panels that stand in for walls.

After my immersion in Monet's glorious water garden room and the dozens of other spacious galleries at MoMA, I'm still feeling preternaturally calm, and I survey the scene with an odd objectivity, like a critic awaiting the opening scene of a new off-Broadway play.

Chuck Winslow and Harvey Blaustein stand in front of a bulletin board loaded with fictional crime data, shooting each other nervous glances. The executive producer and head writer are an oddly mismatched couple. Chuck's tall and lean, always impeccably dressed, the epitome of Ivy League cool, while Harvey's on the short side, with a perpetually rumpled look and a burgeoning pot belly. They've worked together so long that they have an uncanny ability to read each other's minds and complete each other's sentences.

Compared to the clean white asceticism of the galleries at the museum, the set looks even more chintzy than usual. "Is this the best you can do for a meeting room?" I ask.

"Yeah, we didn't have a big enough conference room," Chuck replies. "I realize this isn't like the snazzy mansion sets we had back in Lindisfarne, when we had a bigger budget. We're more stripped down around here, not as pretentious."

"You've got that right," I say. "This set is pathetic."

Harvey snickers. "Sorry, Mark, you'll just have to suck it up. Don't forget who brought you here when they cancelled *Hope Dawns Eternal.* You've got Chuck and me to thank for your gig on *Sunlight and Shadow.*"

"I know, and I appreciate it, believe me." I hate it when he calls me Mark, and I hate brown nosing even more, but he's right, and I can't afford to alienate him. "Sorry, I'm just feeling edgy."

"As are we all," says Chuck. "Anyway, we're keeping the sets as stripped down as possible. The costumes too. In today's economic climate, we think it's politically incorrect and tasteless to have our characters flaunt their wealth the way they used to. Our viewers aren't part of the one percent, after all. Anyway, we don't want the production costs to go through the roof."

"They're still through the roof compared to the sets

on those crap shows like *Brand New You,"* I say.

Chuck mutters a few expletives under his breath. "Speaking of *Brand New You*, let's cut to the chase, and the reason we called this meeting."

"Yeah, it's about time," says Tony Giordano, or rather the guy who plays him. Andy Danko, I think his name is. "We've missed a whole day of shooting." His jaw is clamped tight, and he projects the coiled tension I've seen in the few episodes I watched before taking this gig.

"Chill, Tony," says Harvey. "There'll be plenty of days for shooting. Speaking of which, you get to shoot more people than anybody on this show, with the possible exception of Mick." Why isn't he calling these guys by their actors' names, the way he does with me? Maybe, like me, he's still having a hard time keeping them straight.

Mick – that's Abby's husband, and Tony's enforcer. He's looming in a doorway, massive arms crossed, making like the Incredible Hulk. What on earth does she see in him? Better to ignore him for now – I focus on Tony instead. "So this must be the infamous Tony Giordano. I've been looking forward to meeting you, but we haven't had the pleasure yet."

He sneers and fixes me with a beady brown-eyed stare. "I'd say welcome aboard, but I hate being a hypocrite."

"Cool it, guys," says Harvey. "According to the script, you aren't scheduled to meet for a week yet, so ignore each other, okay? The tension between you is great, but let's keep it on the back burner until we shoot your first scene together. It'll be fresher that way."

The culinary imagery evokes a deep rumble in my stomach. I haven't eaten in twenty-four hours, and all at once I'm ravenously hungry. "Speaking of cooking," I say, "how about if we all adjourn to the Prime Cuts

Steakhouse after the meeting? They grill a fabulous T-bone." I steal a quick glance at Abby, and she meets my eyes briefly, then blushes. I hope Mick doesn't notice.

Chuck claps his hands together sharply. "Let's get back on topic, folks. The sooner we wind this up, the sooner we can all get out of here, and I for one could use a drink."

"Yeah," Tony says. "It'll be after five by the time we get out of here. He breaks into an Alan Jackson song about how it's always five o'clock somewhere. His voice is gravely, with a credible country twang.

I can't resist chiming in: "Pour me something tall and strong."

He cracks a grin, then sobers instantly. We're supposed to be enemies, after all.

Harvey's face goes crimson. He cups his hands around his face like a megaphone and shouts. "In case you've forgotten, gang, there's been a murder here today."

"So what else is new?" says Mick from the doorway. "There's always a murder here." He's so poker-faced, it's hard to tell if he's joking or simply not with the program.

"But this one's for real," says Chuck. "I know you've all been questioned individually, but you'd probably appreciate a report on what the cops have told us so far."

The room's suddenly abuzz with anticipation, followed by silence as all eyes turn to Chuck. "Let me turn it over to the head writer you all know and love," he says. "Mr. Harvey Blaustein."

"Hey, Harvey!" It's a guy I haven't seen before, kind of small and runty with big spaniel eyes. "I'd love you a lot more if you'd write me more scenes and give me a regular contract."

"Shut up, Paul!" Chuck screams. "Jeez, what is it

with you actors? Can't you ever get out of the spotlight?" He pauses, takes a deep gulp of air, and reverts with an effort to his customary cool. "Harvey has a better sense of narrative continuity, so I'll let him take it from here."

Harvey takes a couple of steps forward. "Take it from here – hey, that's a good starting point. They did take it from here – the body, I mean." The room erupts with groans and catcalls, and he grimaces. "Sorry, that was in terrible taste. I've got a lamentable tendency to crack bad jokes when I'm nervous. Obviously, this is no laughing matter. As you no doubt know by now, Gene Gentry was found dead early this morning on the set of *Brand New You.*"

"There must be plenty of suspects," Tony says. "A lot of people could have cheerfully killed him." Exactly what I said earlier, but this time I manage to keep my mouth shut.

Abby speaks up. "Do they think somebody from this show had something to do with it? I should think they'd focus on people from *Brand New You.*"

"They're not ruling anyone out," Harvey says. "Obviously they're still in the initial stages of the investigation, but I get the feeling they're focusing especially on people from *Hope Dawns Eternal.* After all, when that show got cancelled and replaced by *Brand New You,* most of them lost their livelihood."

"Except the ones they moved over here," Tony says. He casts his eyes my way. "Like Jonah McQuarry."

Every head in the room swivels toward me, and I feel the weight of their hostile stares. "Why are you looking at me?" I say. "I'm gainfully employed here, I even have a contract. I don't have any motive."

Chris Giordano, Tony's cop son, glares at me. "You told me the other day that they made you leave your wife and child behind in Lindisfarne – that certainly gives you a motive."

I lunge toward him. "God damn it, Chris —"

Abby jumps up and grabs my arm. "Jonah, stop! Don't let him get to you. He's just trying to press your buttons."

I stop in my tracks, take a deep shuddering breath. "You're right, Abby. Thanks."

"So, Chuck," Tony says. "Did the police tell you the cause of death?"

Chuck frowns. "They won't know definitively till after the autopsy. But they say the body was practically drained of blood, and they found what appeared to be two bite marks in the neck."

Abby's face drains to a ghostly pallor. She sways, then swoons, but I manage to catch her in mid-fall. As I cradle her to my chest, I glance over at Mick. His eyes are ablaze with hatred.

Chapter Seven

I ease Abby gently into the nearest chair. She hasn't lost consciousness, but she's staring at me wild-eyed, as if she's seen a ghost, and she's still alarmingly pale. I'm pretty shaky myself. I take a few steps away – Mick's the one who needs to be at her side right now, and I've got no business getting between them. I cross my arms across my chest to hide the violent tremors in my hands. Something about Chuck's revelation hit me like a sucker punch straight to the solar plexus. Gene Gentry, dead of exsanguination with two bite marks in the neck? It sounds like the work of a vampire. Impossible, I know, but the grisly manner of death conjures up a weird atavistic energy in me. My pulse quickens and my head feels suddenly spinny. What's up with these peculiar feelings? Maybe it's low blood sugar – what with all the drama today, I've skipped both breakfast and lunch.

Abby and I aren't the only ones blindsided by Chuck's news bulletin. Around us, the room has turned to instant bedlam, like the storied lunatic asylum of old. The crew members are fairly stoic, but all the actors are in full histrionic mode. Some are keening and moaning, heads buried in hands; others are embracing each other, exclaiming in disbelief about the terrible tragedy and the bizarre manner of death. There's an overabundance of tears, as if everyone has lost a beloved friend, yet I'm willing to bet few of them knew Gene Gentry, and those who did probably detested him. But actors are good at crying on cue, and they're doing what they do best – putting on a performance.

So am I. I'm wearing my usual cool controlled

façade, but I'm not sure how long I can keep the mask in place. With all the bodies crammed into such a confined space, the temperature's climbing and the stench of fear and sweat is in the air. I need to escape, and all at once a visit to the men's room seems like an excellent idea.

A couple of decades ago, before cable TV began eating away at the network's profit margin, QMA splurged on the bathroom décor. It has a minimalist, vaguely Art Deco feel – walls of white tile, a glossy black floor and an abundance of chrome and stainless steel. I'm not in urgent need of the facilities, but the room's cool, austere seclusion provides the perfect respite from the tumultuous staff meeting. Facing the wall, I place my palms and forehead against the cool white tile, close my eyes and inhale deep gulps of fakely freshened air as my pulse slowly descends to normal.

I'm finally unzipping, ready to take care of business, when the door swings open and Tony Giordano strides in. He stops short when he sees me at the urinal. "Hey," he says. "What are you doing in here?"

Duh – talk about dim bulbs. "Taking a leak," I answer. "What does it look like?"

His mouth twists as if he's chomped down on a slice of bitter lemon. "Are you coming on to me? I didn't realize you swing that way, but somehow I'm not surprised. You've got that elegant GQ look."

His comment brings me up short, and I freeze mid-zip. "Where the hell is that coming from?"

He flashes a crooked smile. "You asked me what it looks like, and I assumed you were talking about my prick. Show me yours, I'll show you mine – it's the oldest gay come-on in the world."

"I wouldn't know – I haven't heard it since middle school." I'm not being exactly straight with him. Quite a few men have hit on me over the years, and I've heard lots of pick-up lines. I've long since learned to deal with it diplomatically; if I hadn't, I could never have survived in the entertainment industry. But there's an unsettling intensity about Tony's come-on that makes me profoundly uneasy. "I'm not interested, never have been," I tell him as I zip up my fly. All at once I've lost the urge to relieve myself.

"Guess I misunderstood." He scowls. "Anyway, we've got no business sharing a scene in a men's room. What would our fans think if they could see us now?"

"I've got no idea. This has to be a first. In daytime drama, no one ever talks about needing to take a leak. And did you ever see a scene set in a bathroom?"

He scratches his head. "Guess not."

"I didn't think so. And I can't believe you actually said the word 'prick.' That's another first."

"What about the word penis?" he asks.

"Or peeing or pissing – all the P words."

"You left out pussy," he says.

I crack up in spite of myself, then remember we're supposed to be enemies.

"So you couldn't take the heat in that meeting," Tony says. "You high-tailed it out of there when people started staring at you."

"I could care less what the other actors think about me. QMA gave me a juicy deal to lure me over to *Sunlight and Shadow.* I'm just here to do my job, which by the way is to take you down."

"Yeah, good luck with that. Lots of cops have tried to take me down over the years, and most of them are in prison or six feet under. In any case, they're off the show. Whereas I'm still here."

"Think you're immortal, do you?"

"No, that's your department." He smirks." Or at least it was, when you were a vampire. I've been authentically myself all these years, whereas you're a shape shifter. A vampire, an FBI guy, a cop – you're a flip flopper, as bad as a politician."

"That's what's known as acting. But you're talking about Mark Westgate, not me. He's the one who played the vampire. You, on the other hand, are in a rut, my man. Andy Danko and Tony Giordano are one and the same, have been for years. It can't be much of a stretch when you're just playing yourself. Speaking of which, should I call you Tony, or do you prefer Andy?"

"No one ever calls me Andy. It's a wimpy name, and Andy's a wimpy guy. I hate it."

"Okay." I bite back the impulse to tell him how much that reminds me of me and Mark. Too much information too soon. "Whatever. Anyway, you're always stumbling over your lines, like you can't remember the script."

"That's just the way – the way they write my character. I don't talk – I don't talk like that in real life."

"Oh no? You're talking like that right now."

His black eyes take on a deadly gleam, and I remind myself he has a reputation as a stone-cold killer. I'd better not push him too far, especially since there's no one else in sight. On a set, following a script, we'll probably butt heads soon enough, but this isn't the time or the place. "When I said you were in a rut, I didn't necessarily mean that as an insult," I say. "You have a lot of facets to your character, a lot of emotional range."

"Yeah, I'm complicated. I can play it tough or tender, angry or sexy. I've got more peaks and valleys to tap into. You, my man, are the one who's in a rut – just monochromatic, subtle shades of black, like a late Rothko painting."

"That's the old me. They've given me something of a personality makeover since I came here; you just haven't seen it yet. But it's strange you should mention Rothko. Before the meeting, I was at the Museum of

Modern Art, and I saw some of his work there. You're talking about that series of black canvases he did for those Texas oil millionaires, right? For a chapel? As I recall, he committed suicide soon after."

Tony frowns. "Yeah, that was a damn shame. He was depressed and alcoholic, like so many artists. But who wouldn't get depressed, filling those gigantic canvases with nothing but emptiness?"

There's more to this guy than I thought. "Filled with emptiness – hey, I like that. Kind of poetic."

"Are you a poet? You've got that lean and hungry look – the starving artist type."

"No, I'm not a poet, and I wouldn't say I'm starving – I've got a ravenous appetite, and I have to put in hours at the gym to work off the calories."

"No kidding. I'm surprised you haven't put on more muscle. Don't get me wrong, but –"

The door swings open and the runty guy bursts in – Paul, the one who asked Harvey for a contract. He rushes toward Tony. "Boss! I've been looking all over for you. I've got a message – you've got to – I mean –"

Damn! I was actually starting to enjoy this talk with Tony, realizing we might have more in common than I'd expected, when this character barges in and brings our conversation to a screeching halt. But that's typical in daytime drama. Just when people are on the verge of confiding something important, someone invariably interrupts. The writers have to throw up some obstacles to ratchet up the tension and stretch out the plot. Granted our talk about art wasn't exactly earth-shattering, Paul's interruption is nevertheless annoying.

"Chill, Paul! Focus!" Sounding as frustrated as I feel, Tony glares at the guy, who subsides instantly, a dog submitting to his alpha pack leader.

"Sorry, boss. Mick thinks you should – Is this guy bothering you? Should I get Mick?"

"No, it's okay," Tony says. "We were just having a little discussion."

"We discovered we have some artistic interests in common," I add.

Paul stares at me, bug-eyed. "Aren't you the man who rode into town like Clint Eastwood in *Pale Rider*, seeking vengeance for a long-ago transgression?"

Tony frowns. "Yeah, in tomorrow's script we're supposed to meet for the first time. If we ever get around to shooting it, that is. If it weren't for the murder, we would have shot it today. Anyway, Jonah's going to accuse me of killing his brother, and I'm going to tell him he's full of shit."

"Not in those precise words, I trust," says Paul. "Although I guess the S word is appropriate, given our current setting. But the writers would never show us in a bathroom. On the other hand, if we were on HBO –"

Tony cuts him off with a lightning-fast chop of the hand suggestive of martial arts training. "Yeah, we already covered that. So, Paul, you got something to tell me?"

"Yes, boss, I was just getting around to that. Mick wonders if you realize this gentleman used to play a vampire, back in the day, in a show that is long since deceased, on this very same network, which leads him to suspect that possibly –"

This could go on forever, I realize, so I chime in. "Tony knows, but that has nothing to do with me. That was Mark Westgate, the actor who plays me. He played the vampire Jeremy Lowell on a soap that was cancelled a decade ago. *Oak Bluff.*"

"I guess I'm too young to remember that," Paul says, triggering a sudden urge to slap him upside the head. But I restrain myself – he's too shrimpy, and it wouldn't be fair.

"Anyway, Mick suggested I should do some research

about vampires on my trusty laptop," he continues, addressing Tony now. "But he thought I should run it by you first, to see if it's okay."

Tony flashes that trademark expression that's part grin, part grimace. "Sure, Paul. Knock yourself out."

"Okay, boss, will do. I'll let you know what I find out."

"You do that," says Tony. "And while you're at it, since vampires are supposedly immortal – if they even exist – look into whether there's any possibility this Jeremy Lowell character could have gotten himself reincarnated and come back to murder Gene Gentry."

Chapter Eight

After my tête-a-tête with Tony, I'm crackling with nervous energy. A long walk is just what I need to work it off. I start heading uptown at a rapid clip, then realize Sirius could use some exercise too, so I grab a cab the rest of the way to Mark's apartment.

The big chow-shepherd mix gives me his usual greeting ritual, planting his paws on my shoulders and slurping my face with his tongue. In the bedroom, as I change into black sweats and running shoes, he whines and bounces, picking up on the signs that betoken some serious exercise. And when I take his leash off the hook in the kitchen, he goes instantly airborne, jumping and gyrating like a manic hip hop dancer. He sits on command, his purplish black tongue dripping saliva as I slip the heavy-duty pronged choke chain over his neck.

There was a chill in the air when I came in, and it's likely to get colder. I'm about to grab a windbreaker when all at once I flash on the vampire cape that hangs at the back of Mark's closet, sheathed in a dry cleaner's bag. It's the only piece of memorabilia he saved from his role as Jeremy on *Oak Bluff,* and he hasn't worn it since the show folded, but today I feel an irresistible urge to don the black wool cloak with its red satin lining. Supposedly Jeremy had supernatural powers, and if the cape contains any traces of his old mojo, I could certainly use it now. But I don't want to attract undue attention, so I drape it over my arm. I'll put it on later, after the sun sets.

With Sirius at my side, I walk the few blocks to the Dakota on Central Park West. We pause on the sidewalk in front of the massive apartment building and pay our customary silent homage to John Lennon on the spot where Mark Chapman shot him down just after getting his autograph. Then we cross the street to Strawberry Fields, the memorial swathe carved out of Central Park directly across from the Dakota and named in John's honor. Last time I was here I was too drunk to appreciate it, but it's a beautiful spot, with enormous trees, winding pathways, and benches where people can pause and contemplate the enormous black and white mosaic mandala emblazoned with the single word *Imagine.* Now, at twilight, people of all ages are paying their respects, laying down flowers and taking selfies at the edge of the circular mosaic. As Sirius and I stroll through, once again the crowd parts in our path. He's not the kind of dog who invites friendly pats.

As darkness descends, the air grows chilly, and I pull the cloak around my shoulders. The black wool smells slightly of cedar and mothballs. With my black hair, my black sweats and shoes, I'm virtually invisible, and so is Sirius. We head east, away from Strawberry Fields and its crowd of tourists, and once I'm sure no one is around, I unhook the dog's leash from his choke chain. He shoots me a questioning look, and when I say "Okay," he takes off like a shot. Mark has trained him well, and I know a whistle will bring him back to my side.

Though I'm no match for Sirius, I break into a run. We head southeast until we reach a cavernous stone underpass. You'd probably recognize it even if you're not a New Yorker. It's served as a backdrop for countless scenes in films and TV shows over the years, thanks to its shadowy, ominous look. A good all-purpose location for love scenes and murders – not to mention love scenes that turn into murders.

Do as I say, not as I do: never come here at night. The tunnel is a magnet for muggers and rapists. No doubt lots of them have seen it on CSI or Law & Order and decided to stage their own little dramatic productions, where some of the characters may not escape with their lives. Despite the danger, or maybe because of the thrill, a lot of guys come here cruising for gay sex.

Suddenly a shriek splits the air, then another. I freeze. Has someone been attacked? Should I intervene? I whistle for Sirius, and he comes bounding out of the darkness to my side.

I hear more shouts, then laughter and muffled conversation. Two men emerge from beneath the underpass. They've got their arms around each other's waists, their heads close together. They're murmuring in each other's ears – maybe sweet nothings, or maybe they're talking about me. Things aren't always what they seem, so I pivot to face them, command Sirius to sit, and drop into a fighting stance.

"Thanks for calling off your dog," says the guy on the left.

"Relax," says the one on the right. "We're not going to make any trouble."

I stand cautiously erect, hands at my sides. "Neither am I. Sorry about my dog. Was he bothering you?"

The first guy laughs nervously. "No, he just scared the shit out of us."

"He came streaking out of the darkness," says the second. "I thought he was going to attack us, but he ran right past."

"He turned on a dime when he heard your whistle," says the first. He's wearing a deep blue sports jacket with a mauve scarf, and his blond hair is artfully rumpled. He has the chiseled good looks of a young Sting. His friend is African-American, taller and more heavily muscled. Together, they have an easy way about them that suggests a regular relationship, not a casual hook-up.

"I'm Scott," says the blond guy, extending a hand. His shake is firm and confident.

"And I'm Miles," says the black guy. "Love that cape, by the way. That Dracula look never goes out of style. Did you just come from a costume party? Halloween is still six months away."

"No, actually this cape is a left-over from a daytime drama that was cancelled a decade ago. The actor who plays me kept it as a souvenir. For all I know, maybe he plans to auction it off on eBay someday."

"The red satin lining is to die for," Scott says. He strikes a pose, hips akimbo. "So you're an actor? How exciting!"

"Actually I'm Lieutenant Jonah McQuarry. Mark Westgate is the actor who plays me."

"Of course! I knew you looked familiar. Mark Westgate! I'm thrilled to meet you."

"Please, call me Jonah." Rather than explain, I give him the short form. "I prefer staying in role, even when I'm off-duty."

"I totally understand." All at once his eyes widen, and he nudges Miles in the ribs. "Hey, Jonah, didn't you play that vampire on *Oak Bluff?*"

"Yeah, Mark did. His name was Jeremy Lowell."

"I knew it! God, you were hot! I never missed an episode. Not that you're not hot now, of course. In fact, you're even more devastatingly attractive than you were back then. The years have been good to you. But then that stands to reason, since you're immortal and all."

I sway for effect, and the cape swirls dramatically. "Hate to disappoint you, but I'm an ordinary mortal. I'm just blessed with good genes, and I stay out of the sun or wear sunblock."

Miles grins. "Whatever your secret is, it's working.

Scott, I have an idea. Why don't we invite Mark – excuse me, Jonah – back to the apartment? It's not a good idea to hang out here so late at night."

"Fabulous idea!" Scott says. "My place is right over on Fifth Avenue, just a few minutes from here."

Fifth Avenue? This Scott character must be loaded. I'm curious to see his apartment, but I have the feeling they're about to proposition me, and I don't need the complications. "Sorry, guys," I say. "Thanks for the invitation, but I have to be on the set bright and early tomorrow."

"I understand," says Scott. "You need your beauty sleep. I just hope you're not turning us down because you're uneasy with gay people."

"Not at all. You can't survive in my business if you're uptight about homosexuality. I support LGBT rights and I'm glad New York has same-sex marriage. Most of our cast and crew feel the same way, and we've even got a major gay storyline going on right now. A triangle with three guys. Anyway –"

All at once Sirius growls, and the hairs of his thick black ruff stand at attention. I whirl and see two men approaching. They're still a good thirty feet away, padding toward us in silent sneakers. They pause in their tracks, heads together in conversation.

"Oh oh," says Scott. "We'd better split. Those guys are bad news – you don't want to mess with them."

I feel a jolt of adrenaline. "What kind of bad news are you talking about?"

"The worst! They're muggers, and they especially love beating on gay guys."

"Is this just hearsay? Or have you seen them in action?"

"Oh, we've seen them alright," says Scott. "They mugged us a couple of weeks ago, stole my Rolex and our iPods."

Miles chimes in. "They took us by surprise. Otherwise I could have decked them – no problem."

Scott grimaces. "And the nasty names they called us? They even called Miles the N word. God, you wouldn't believe it."

"I hope you called 911 and reported it."

"Oh, yeah, we called the cops on our land line once we got home, but nothing came of it. They took the report and told us to stay the hell out of the park."

"Sounds like good advice. Why didn't you take it?"

"We know we should," says Miles, "but something here keeps drawing us back. The lure of the forbidden, I guess."

Scott shivers theatrically. "I've got to admit, the danger's kind of a turn-on. There's a certain frisson – I don't know if you can relate."

"As a matter of fact I can." That's an understatement. I'm acutely aware of my escalating heart rate, the energy coursing through my body. Suddenly I'm spoiling for a fight. "Why don't you guys make yourselves scarce?" I say. "I can handle these dudes. And Sirius has my back."

"Why chance it?" Scott asks. "We should all get out of here – go up to my place, like I said."

"No, really." I turn to the two thugs, shoot them a stare. They're still standing frozen, like jungle cats ready to pounce. Sirius is motionless too, silent as a sphinx, and the way he fades into the darkness, they probably haven't the faintest notion how big he is. Nor do they realize that I'm the predator and they're about to become my prey.

"I'm in the mood for a good fight, and I'm sure I can take these guys," I tell my newfound friends. "Helps keep my skills sharp for the action scenes."

Scott's eyes go round. "That sounds exciting! Can we

watch? Maybe from behind those bushes over there?"

I'm fleetingly tempted – I'm used to performing before audiences, after all. But I have the feeling that whatever's about to happen, I don't want any witnesses. "No, you'd better split," I say. "You don't need to be around if things go south."

Scott puts on a campy sad clown face, extracts a business card from his pocket and hands it to me. "Okay, but here's the number for my new cell. Call me if you need anything – and I do mean anything." I stash the card in the pocket of the black hoodie under the cape.

The two thugs swagger toward us, fists clenched and arms pumped, radiating testosterone. They're bigger than I thought, with the muscular bulk that comes only with long hours of working out, probably in prison. Sirius stiffens and growls.

The one on the left steps forward. "Hey, guys, imagine meeting you here." He's slurring his words, and I realize he's sloppy drunk.

"You've got a lot of nerve showing up here again after our last little encounter," the other guy says. He appears to be equally smashed. "I see you brought a friend along – another faggot, no doubt. If you're counting on him to protect you, you're out of luck."

"Counting on him – hey, Larry, that's good," says the first. "This dude's dressed up like Count Dracula. Hey, Count, you want to bite us in the neck?"

"He'd probably rather take it in the throat," says Larry. "Or maybe the ass. Jeez, you guys make me want to puke. The thought of getting it on with that nigger – you're the scum of the earth." He hawks up some phlegm and spits, but the globule lands harmlessly on the ground.

"Funny you should mention throats," I say. "You've both got outstanding trapezius muscles, and I love the way the tendons stand out in your necks."

Larry elbows his partner in crime. "I knew it – this guy's a cocksucker, just like his friends."

Scott grabs Miles's arm. "We're going to skedaddle. Great meeting you, Jonah."

"Call me Jeremy," I say. I wave them away, then turn to confront the thugs. "I can't stand bigots and gay-bashers, but I'm all for freedom of speech. Any more venomous thoughts you feel compelled to share before we get down to business?"

They stand in stunned silence for a moment, then draw their knives. They're almost on top of me now, but I'm feeling fearless and super-heroic. An Avenger, like the Incredible Hulk. Or better still, Iron Man. It must be the vampire cape, infusing me with powers I never knew I had. At my side, Sirius rises, baring his fangs.

My vision goes blood-red. "Bring it on," I say. The words come out as a guttural snarl.

The thugs' eyes widen as I move in for the kill.

Chapter Nine

As the drunken thugs brandish their knives and my vision goes red, my animal instincts kick in, and I charge. But who am I – Jonah McQuarry or Jeremy Lowell? Or are we one and the same? It's a moot point. This is hardly the time to ponder questions of identity, because every second counts. Pure adrenaline overwhelms my conscious ego, and the next hour passes in a blur.

Picture a scene in an action movie, the kind with vertiginous jump cuts that lurch from one shot to another, so rapid-fire you can hardly tell who's killing whom. Things happen faster than the speed of thought, and your senses are so bombarded that your reactions are purely visceral. It's best if you visualize the action in the park this way, so the blood and gore won't overwhelm you.

But for me, the scene that unfolds near the underpass in Central Park is different, because I've got the starring role. I'm the eye at the center of a tornado, deadly calm as the vortex whirls around me with lightning speed. Yet at the same time, I'm watching from afar. It's as if I'm viewing the attack from a cushiony seat at the local Cineplex, or hovering over an operating table and watching myself from a near-death, out-of-body vantage point. I could describe the struggle in minute detail, but I don't want to gross you out. I'm going for a PG rating here, so all you need to know is that like all action heroes worth of the title, I come out victorious in the end.

Afterwards, as I wipe the blood from my face and

ponder the scene that just unfolded, my mind flashes back to early MTV videos. A lot of big directors in Hollywood cut their teeth and honed their skills making those videos. Guys like Tony Scott, the *Top Gun* director who took a header off the same Los Angeles bridge that had figured in his films. I can't imagine what was going through his mind as he plummeted to his death, but I wonder if he'd flipped out and started confusing fact and fiction, then realized mid-jump that this was the real deal, not one of his scripts. His last film was *Unstoppable,* that runaway train flick with Denzel Washington. Denzel survived, but for Tony, this time it was far too late to yell CUT!

But I digress. It's easier to ponder the suicide of a stranger than to confront what happened near that underpass. I've managed to wipe most of the blood off my face with Jeremy's cape, but I can still taste its coppery tang in my mouth, and I suspect the details of this double murder will leave a bitter aftertaste that lingers far beyond tonight.

Again, I'm tempted to get into more graphic detail here, because it might be therapeutic to process what happened more fully. But I'll spare you. As a soap fan, you've no doubt seen more than your share of bizarre and gruesome deaths, but they always play down the blood, and if they show the victims, they do it discreetly, deleting anything too grotesque or gory. If we were on cable, we could pull out all the stops, like they did on *The Sopranos,* but the networks are far too squeamish.

Now I know for sure: I've been shape-shifting into Jeremy Lowell. I was afraid of that, what with all those blackouts I've been having since I moved to Ferncliff. It's gotten worse since I met Abby. I suspect it may be dissociative identity disorder – what they used to call multiple personality disorder. Like that old movie, *The Three Faces of Eve.* I'm pretty familiar with this condition, because it ran rampant back in Lindisfarne.

One woman had three distinct personalities. Janet, the normal one, was usually in charge, but when she was stressed out, Penny, the wild and wanton one, took control. Annette was the third – the prim and proper school-marmish gatekeeper who tried to keep a lid on things. Janet's mother had D.I.D. too; at least on soaps, there seems to be a tendency for it to run in families.

I suspect that's what's been happening to me. There are whole blocks of time I can't account for, like the hours when someone murdered Gene Gentry. That cop had every right to be suspicious when I couldn't account for my actions during that time span. Hell, I'd be suspicious too. But this time the boundaries were torn asunder, as easily as one might rip the gauzy scrims designers use to separate scenes on stage. The fragile fabric that separated me and Jeremy dissolved, and we became one and the same as we attacked those thugs with Sirius at our side.

In the aftermath of the killings, I'm suddenly desperate for a drink. I'm not hungry – and I know exactly why – but a couple of shots of whiskey might cleanse my mouth of the taste of blood and damp down the demonic thoughts whirling through my mind. Walking Sirius home, I realize I'm in no mood for the silent solitude of Mark's apartment. No, right now I need people around me, strangers who haven't a clue about the monstrous transformation I seem to be undergoing.

In other words, what I need is McGuire's, my favorite watering hole over on Amsterdam Avenue. With Sirius trotting at my side, I jog back to the apartment. As I shrug off the cape, I notice the bloody streaks darkening the crimson lining. Stupid of me to use the satin; the stains would have been less conspicuous against the black wool. But hindsight is pointless. I stash the cape at the back of the closet, tear off my black hoodie and sweat pants, then head for the shower. With the water as hard and hot as I can stand it, I scrub myself down and throw on clean jeans, a black turtleneck and blazer.

About to leave, I realize I need more than the company of strangers. On impulse, I dial Abby's number. Too late, I remember she's probably with her husband. But just as I'm about to hang up, she answers in a husky whisper that stirs all sorts of sensations in me.

"I shouldn't have called," I say. "I wanted to invite you to meet me for a drink, but I totally forgot that of course you'd be with Mick."

"Not a problem," she says. "We have separate bedrooms, and he's so jacked up all day that he takes a lot of downers to get to sleep. He gets practically comatose."

"Not Propofol, I hope. You wouldn't want him to pull a Michael Jackson."

She laughs. "Nothing that heavy. Just fentanyl, Oxycontin, sometimes Xanax."

"That's still pretty heavy."

"Don't I know it. But he insists he knows what he's doing, and I don't dare disagree. Besides, I feel more relaxed when he's drugged up, I don't have to tiptoe around like I'm walking on eggshells. I can even play my keyboard if I keep the volume low."

"Well, I suppose that's a plus."

I give her directions to McGuire's. Half an hour later, I'm huddled in my favorite booth in the back, nursing my second Scotch, when Abby strolls toward me, holding a glass of white wine, wearing a belted black trench coat and looking every inch the femme fatale in a 1940's noir flick. My breath catches in my throat.

"Thanks for meeting me on such short notice at such an ungodly hour," I say.

"Two a.m. isn't so bad," she says. "I was wide awake anyway. Actually, I was thinking about you. I had a feeling something was up, and that you wanted to see me, and then you called. Talk about timing!"

I wonder whether she intuited anything about what happened in Central Park, but I decide to keep things vague. "That just confirms my conviction: we've got some kind of psychic connection that transcends space and time," I say.

"You may be right." She reaches out, about to stroke my cheek, then stops short and withdraws her hand. "Nice bar. I haven't been here before."

"Yeah, it's my favorite. A real downhome neighborhood bar. It hasn't changed in decades. Not like those glossy pick-up bars with their trendy designer brews."

"Just please don't tell me you own it. Ferncliff has an enormous number of bars per capita, and they're all owned by the characters on the show. It's a wonder everyone isn't an alcoholic."

I laugh. "Don't worry, I'd never get into the bar business. But you're right about Ferncliff. Everyone seems to know everyone else, and they're always hanging out in those bars and restaurants in the middle of the day, confiding deep dark secrets to each other. It was the same way back in Lindisfarne."

"And somebody's always eavesdropping."

"Naturally. But not at McGuire's. I keep a low profile, and nobody knows me here. That's why I thought it would be a good place to meet. There's something I need to tell you, in confidence."

The color rises to her cheeks, and her dark eyes dart away. She sips her wine in silence, waiting.

"You know when I said I had those memory lapses, like blackouts, where I couldn't remember whole blocks of time?"

"Yes, of course."

"Well, I've got a damned good idea what's been happening – I have dissociative identity disorder, and my alter's been coming out."

"Your alter? I suspect you're not talking about church."

"No, my alternate personality. Jeremy Lowell, to be precise. You know, the vampire Mark used to play on *Oak Bluff* a decade ago?"

Her eyes widen and her lips part. "Yes, I do know. I haven't been sleeping well, and when I do finally fall asleep, I have unsettling dreams – about us. I've realized you're right: we met before, in another lifetime."

"And I know exactly what life it was. When I was Jeremy, you were Alifair – the great love of my life."

She smiles. "I know. I've been having these flashbacks for a while, and last night it all came back to me. I was madly in love with you, but I resisted for months. They dragged the plot line out for ages, and I wanted you so badly I could barely stand it. Then you finally took that fatal bite that bound us together for all eternity."

My eyes feast on her lovely neck. "Yes, and a part of me wants to do exactly that, right here and now."

She leans closer, pulling apart the lapels of her trench coat and exposing more of her creamy white flesh. "Go ahead – I dare you!"

"You look ravishing, a veritable black swan. But I can't venture even a nip. Jeremy might come out and take over, and I couldn't be responsible for the consequences. I can do this, though." I slide over to her side of the booth, pinning her captive in the corner, and nuzzle her neck, moving from the curve of her shoulder to her ear. She shudders, then takes my face between her hands and brushes my lips with hers.

I lean into the kiss, but she pulls away, her eyes

wide with alarm. "I'm sorry, I don't know what came over me. I shouldn't have come here, and it would be crazy for us to get more deeply involved. Mick has always had a hair-trigger temper, and the body-building drugs he takes every morning make it even worse. I used to think I loved him, but I was deluding myself. His sociopathic fraternal twin was my true love." She shakes her head. "Damn, it's all so confusing! Maybe I've got dissociative identity disorder too."

I reflect a moment, then shake my head. "I seriously doubt it. Tony's girlfriend already has it, and the writers wouldn't give another character the same diagnosis. Not unless they're related, like Janet and her mother back in Lindisfarne."

"But you've got D.I.D."

"It's not in the script, though. The writers don't know about it."

"I see what you mean. But maybe Tony's girlfriend and I are related, long-lost sisters or something, and we just don't know it yet."

"That's possible, I guess. Sometimes it seems like everybody's related to everybody else in these burgs, either by blood or by marriage."

"God, this is all so convoluted. My head is spinning."

"Mine too." I inch closer again. "What do you say we get some fresh air and walk back to Mark's apartment for a nightcap? It's only a few blocks from here. You can see a sliver of Central Park from the front window, and we could watch the sunrise together."

Her eyes light up. Then after a beat she places both palms on my chest and gives me a gentle shove. "That would be total insanity. I've got to get back home and slither into bed before Mick wakes up, and he always sets the alarm for six. Anyway, Jonah, I've got to get out of this booth. It's making me claustrophobic all of a sudden."

I ease away on the bench. "There, I'm giving you more personal space. Is that better?"

"Yes, but I'm still feeling trapped – trapped in this booth, trapped in my marriage, trapped in this crazy story line I can't figure out. I need time to process everything."

She's wild-eyed, hyperventilating, clenching her hands into fists, on the verge of a full-blown panic attack. I rise, gallantly though reluctantly, before she can pummel my chest. She slides out of the booth, strides the length of the bar and shoves open the door. Without so much as a backward glance, she disappears into the night.

Chapter Ten

When Abby walks out of the bar, it's as if she sucks all the oxygen with her. I can barely catch my breath, yet I'm still thoroughly wired despite the three Scotches I've downed. Back at the apartment, I realize sleep is out of the question. Sirius is weirdly excited, eager for another walk, but his face and his thick black ruff are bristly with dried blood.

"Come on, boy. You need a quick bath," I tell him. Knowing the word, he cringes, but I order him to the tub and give him a thorough shower and shampoo, soaking myself in the process. When I turn off the tap, he shakes vigorously, drenching me even more. I towel him dry. Then, in case the rinse water is tainted with traces of blood, I change my clothes again. I shrug into Mark's black leather motorcycle jacket, slip the heavy-duty choke chain over Sirius's massive head, and we're good to go.

Outside, the night air is cooler, and the street is deserted. Out of habit, Sirius turns east toward Central Park, but I jerk his chain and he halts, then gives me a quizzical look. I pat his head and ruffle his ears. "I know you probably want to go back to check out the scene of the crime, boy. So do I, but it's not a good idea. Someone might recognize us."

We turn west instead, toward Riverside Park, where we head uptown on the path along the Hudson. We pass a few homeless people hunkered down for the night on the benches beneath the trees, a few young men in hoodies and hip hop garb, but Sirius is so intimidating that everyone gives us a wide berth. We turn back when we get to Harlem, and by the time we reach the apartment, the sky is lightening to the east.

I should grab a couple of hours of sleep, but I'm still wired despite the walk, so I decide to go to the studio, minus Sirius. No one there knows he exists, and I want to keep it that way. I give him a can of premium beef dog food and grab a cab downtown.

It's still early, barely six a.m., and I don't expect to encounter anyone, but when the elevator doors glide open, I hear voices echoing from somewhere down the hall and around the corner. I recognize our producer Chuck Winslow and our head writer Harvey Blaustein, but I can't place the third voice. Whoever he is, he's loud and manicky. I pad stealthily to the corner and listen in.

"Hey, guys, did you see the headlines? We made the front pages of both the tabloids. Here, take a look. MURDER AT SELF-HELP SHOW. That's the *Daily News*. And the *Post* is even better: BODY DRAINED BLOODLESS ON BRAND NEW YOU – VAMPIRE ON THE LOOSE?"

"Yeah, Jeff, I could hardly miss them," Chuck says. "You look like the cat who swallowed the canary, with that big Cheshire grin. You've lost your host – I should think you'd have the decency to look at least a little upset."

The manicky guy has to be Jeff Herbert, the producer of *Brand New You.* Abby mentioned him when we visited the show. I creep closer to the corner. Eavesdropping is a much overused device in soaps, but it's a time-honored way of advancing the plot. It's always amazed me how characters hold audible conversations about stuff that's better left confidential, but hey, it happens in real life too. I can't resist the chance to listen in.

"Of course I'm upset," Jeff says. "Gene's death is a major blow – he was our biggest star. But you can't buy this kind of publicity, not in a million years. Our ratings are going to skyrocket. We can always get another host."

"Yeah, I suppose so," Chuck says. "But what if he's murdered too? No one's been arrested yet – the killer is still at large."

"That's a risk we'll just have to take." Jeff damps down his voice to a conspiratorial whisper. "Or maybe we'll go with a woman host. We could promote Sheila Spencer. That would ratchet up the suspense – can you imagine the coverage if a woman's the next victim? And the killer keeps to his vampire modus operandi? We'd be the cover story in the *Enquirer,* the lead on *Entertainment Tonight."*

"Damn it, Jeff! How can you be so cold blooded?"

"Come on, Chuck, get real. A certain amount of detachment is essential if you want to make it in this business. Call it cold blooded – sang froid if you prefer the French – but I've made it this far because I don't get emotionally attached to my cast and crew. Unlike you, who hauled in all that deadwood from your old soap."

"No way are they deadwood. Especially Mark Westgate – our ratings have gone up significantly since he came over as Jonah McQuarry," Chuck says. "Anyway, unlike you, I believe in loyalty. If all goes well, I'm going to bring on his wife and baby too. That should make for some fireworks, given his growing attraction to Abby."

Holy shit! Fireworks is right. My head feels like it's about to explode, and my stomach is doing flip flops. A family reunion was always a possibility, of course, but I never thought it would actually happen. I fight back the urge to rush around the corner, grab Chuck by the shoulders, shake him up a bit and demand to know what's in the cards for me.

"Chuck, you're such a sentimental old fart," Jeff says. "Just when things are getting interesting, you want to bring back the wife and kid? God forbid you should break up the sacred nuclear family."

"Are you kidding? We break up nuclear families all the time," Harvey says. " Hell, not long ago we killed off a young guy's wife and daughter because they would have brought along too much old baggage when we moved him from *Hope Dawns Eternal* to *Sunlight and Shadow*. But that's pure fiction, not real life."

Chuck clears his throat. "Anyway, back to *Brand New You* – you were talking about promoting Sheila Spencer, but isn't she kind of abrasive? Her voice is so nasal, and her laugh sounds like a whinny. Wouldn't she get on the viewers' nerves if you give her more face time?"

"Maybe, maybe not." Jeff chortles and snorts, sounding rather horsey himself. "Frankly I can't stand the woman – she's a diva from hell. But the viewers seem to like her. She's no knockout, and she's got a few miles on her, so our target audience can relate to her. They don't feel jealous or threatened."

Harvey chimes in again. "Then maybe you should keep her where she is, as one of the panelists, rather than promoting her to a level she can't handle."

"You mean like Gloria Kemp when they promoted her from her morning gig and made her an anchor on the evening news, and she just couldn't hack it? Word has it she might be coming over to QMA daytime."

"I'll believe it when I see it," says Harvey. "Anyway, if you keep Sheila where she is, if some crazed killer is targeting your hosts, at least he won't get her."

"You're right," Jeff says. "We should probably hire a new host, someone pretty well known but expendable. Anyway, I hope the killer doesn't strike again right away. That way the tension will build. People will keep tuning in wondering if it's the last time they'll ever see someone alive. Or still better, what if it happens right while we're taping?" He chortles again.

The corridor's cool, but I'm breaking a sweat and hyperventilating. I've got to get out of here before I blow my cover and throttle that prick. Jeff Herbert doesn't give a shit about the people on that ghastly show – it's all about the ratings.

I do a stealth walk to the elevator, make it out to the street unnoticed. I've got a big scene with Abby coming up, and I'm dying to see her, talk to her, but first I've got a few hours to kill, so I decide to yield to temptation, head up to Central Park and revisit the scene of the crime.

By the time I reach the path near the underpass, I've blown off the worst of my rage, but my blood pressure still spikes when I think about Jeff Herbert. I walk on till I reach the spot where I took down those two thugs. Lingering would be idiotic – as I know all too well from my years on the force, perps often revisit the scene of the crime, and I don't want to attract suspicion if any cops are still staking out the scene. Strictly speaking, I'm not the perp, since my alter Jeremy did it, but I can't take any chances.

It's strange how benign this place feels in the light of the morning sun. There are bicyclists, a young couple holding hands, maids and mothers pushing strollers. Two gay men deep in conversation, but no sign of Scott and Miles. You'd never guess two guys were killed right around here. Not a trace – no blood stains, no crime scene tape, no bodies. It's as if the whole thing was nothing but a dream. Hell, maybe it was. Or maybe a hallucination.

Anyway, those guys were low lifes. Just thugs. Hardly even newsworthy – worth just a couple of paragraphs buried deep in the second section of the *Times,* maybe a little more in the tabloids. If the victims were young white women, that would be a different story entirely. Or if the killing happened on the set of a major show on the QMA network . . .

I stop and slump onto a bench, suddenly spent. I got it all wrong – or rather my alter, Jeremy, did. Gene Gentry was the wrong victim. He was just a flunky, like me and all the other onscreen talent at the network. He didn't have the real power. He was at the mercy of the ratings, and the big mucky mucks who call all the shots from on high. As obnoxious as Gene may have been, he didn't deserve to die.

God, my head is splitting. I can't remember the last time I went this long without sleep. But it's too late now. I've got to get back to the studio – I've got a big scene with Abby today.

Chapter Eleven

Here we are, Abby and I, in yet another bar. I grab my shot glass, throw back the amber liquid in a single gulp, and shudder convincingly. Unfortunately it's not Scotch – just diet Snapple. The bar's phony as well, one of several watering holes where the upstanding citizens of Ferncliff while away their afternoons.

Right now, Abby's proximity has me feeling pretty upstanding too. I sneak a glance at my crotch, hoping the cameras won't pick up on my growing erection, then lean in towards Abby for the climax of the scene. "Abby," I murmur, "if you ever want to talk or need a strong shoulder to cry on, I'll always be here for you."

She moves closer. Her lips just inches from mine, she gazes raptly into my eyes. "Is that a promise? Because I can't stand to be hurt again. How do I know I can trust you?" The lines are trite, but her eyes are more eloquent by far than the script.

"I swear I'd never do anything to hurt you," I say. A vertiginous feeling sweeps over me as our lips meet in a totally unscripted kiss. We slip simultaneously from our bar stools into an embrace. Reveling in the taste of her mouth, I slide my hands down to caress her butt as she grinds against me.

"Cut!" Hank, the director rushes over, arms flailing wildly, like the referee in a choreographed wrestling match that's veering away from the way it was fixed. "Stop, both of you! What the hell do you think you're doing?"

"Sorry," I say, though I'm not sorry at all. "We were just doing a little improv to get into the flow of things. I guess we got carried away."

"That's putting it mildly. You're acting positively crazed, both of you." He's red-faced, panting, and his eyes are bugging like Rodney Dangerfield's.

"Chill, man," I say. "Take it easy. You look like you're about to stroke out."

"Take it easy? You're telling me to take it easy? You've got it backwards – I'm the one who should be telling you to cool it."

Harvey Blaustein shambles onto the set and claps the director on the shoulder. "Hank, why don't you take a break and let me handle this?"

"Gladly." The director stomps off as Abby and I step back and away from our clinch.

Harvey grins. "You two have a lot of chemistry, a lot of heat, and that's exactly what we hoped for when we wrote you this story line. But this is network TV, not cable, and you have to dial it down a few notches. Besides, Abby's a married woman, and you barely know each other. You need to take it slow. We're going for a low smolder, not spontaneous combustion."

"You got that right." The low throaty voice floats out of the darkness beyond the set. Then Mick Hastings strides into the scene and bangs his massive fist onto the bar, making our glasses rattle and jump. He shoots me a glare. "What the fuck are you doing, messing with my wife? You're going to live to regret this – that is, if I decide to let you live at all."

Abby turns to face him. "Mick, it's not Jonah's fault. Anyway, it's not what it looks like."

Glowering, he folds his massive arms across his chest. "Give me a break – that's the oldest cliché in the book, and it always amounts to diddlysquat." All at once he's at Abby's side, squeezing her shoulder so hard he elicits a wince. "Come on, darling, let's get out of here."

It's borderline abusive, the way he's manhandling

her. My adrenaline skyrockets and every muscle in my body goes tense with the urge to throttle him, but I manage to restrain myself. Mick's her husband, after all. If I were in his shoes, I'd be royally pissed too.

Mick drapes his massive arm around her shoulder and pulls her close. She's tiny in his clutches. To me, they look mismatched, like Beauty and the Beast. Abby and I would make a far more attractive couple.

Everyone's thoroughly rattled. Harvey and the director huddle, speaking in hushed voices, and they decide to call a fifteen-minute break. As Abby and Mick leave the set, she looks my way and rolls her eyes. There's a world of meaning in that glance – resignation, irony, amusement and the hint of a promise that the best is yet to come.

I head outside for a quick lap around the block, then back to the set. This time, by unspoken mutual consent, Abby and I keep a respectful distance and make only fleeting eye contact. Mick is conspicuously absent; I'm betting Harvey and Hank have told him to make himself scarce. We stick to the script and surprisingly, we nail the scene in one take.

"That was fantastic," Harvey enthuses. "You played it just right – getting to know each other, with the hint of a spark, but a little awkward, trying to keep it damped down. Superb acting job, you guys."

I detect a certain irony in his tone, but I decide to take the compliment at face value. We're done for the day, actually ahead of schedule, so Abby and I head out the door and into the hallway, maintaining a judicious distance from each other. It's a good thing we're being so circumspect, because as we round a corner, we all but crash into Mick. He tenses immediately – hard to miss, with that clenched jaw and all those veins and tendons standing out on his muscular arms – and favors us with a bestial grunt.

"Hey, Mick, break a leg," Abby says as we pass each other. He acknowledges the traditional good-luck phrase with a curt nod and turns the corner. Abby and I listen till his footfalls fade to silence, then let out mutual sighs of relief.

"He's shooting a couple of big scenes this afternoon," she says. "In this same bar, with Tony and Paul. Something about their microbrewery business."

"You mean their alleged microbrewery business, right?"

"No, they're actually going to have one. It's still in the start-up phase, but Mick's told me about the set they're building. It sounds pretty cool."

"I've got to admit it's a fresh twist as a cover for mob business," I say. "It beats garbage collection. And it harks back to Prohibition, when gangsters controlled the bootleg business."

"Yeah, like *Boardwalk Empire*." She grins. "I love that show. I've got DVDs of all the seasons."

"So do I. I love the cinematography, the production values. HBO has such an enormous budget, not to mention so much more freedom to show R-rated sex and violence."

"You'd be great on a primetime cable show, Jonah." She reaches out, stops just short of touching my arm, backs away again. "I'm surprised no one's lured you away from daytime, made you an offer you can't refuse."

"Mark has gotten a few feelers over the years, but nothing ever seems to pan out."

"Same goes for Catherine. I suppose we should be thankful, though. The powers that be would never let our actors bring us along to a new show. We'd be left in limbo."

"That might not be so bad," I say. "As long as we're in limbo together."

That beautiful rosy blush rises to her cheeks, and I know we're pushing our luck. We've been keeping our distance, but just barely. Beneath all the innocent chitchat, a high-tension current is building, threatening to shock us sky high.

"I wonder what they actually thought about our little love scene back there," she says. "Hank looked so flabbergasted, I thought he was going to tell us to get a room."

"Not a bad idea." I lower my voice. "But come to think of it, I've already got one."

"Your dressing room? Be serious, Jonah. We don't dare go there. What if someone sees us? You know how people gossip around here."

"Actually, I was thinking of Mark's apartment. We've got the rest of the day free. How about we go there, where we can finally get some privacy? Since you're so concerned with appearances, we could leave separately."

Her blush deepens. "I couldn't possibly."

"Oh, come on. You could meet my dog."

She laughs. "That's the weirdest come-on I've heard in a while. I do love dogs, though. What kind is he?"

"A chow-shepherd mix." I lower my voice to a whisper. "No one here knows about him, and Mark's such a private person, he wants to keep it that way. If anyone asks while we're out walking, I don't mention his German shepherd bloodlines. I don't want to scare people, so I just call him a chow chow. They're an ancient Chinese breed, one of the oldest breeds around. They used to guard the emperors' temples, although when times got hard, sometimes people ate them. To avoid getting too attached, they kept chows outside rather than raise them as pets. That's why the breed is still rather aloof and standoffish. Some people say they act more like cats than like dogs. But once they get to know you, they're extremely loyal."

Abby laughs. "You could almost be describing Mick. He acts standoffish too, but he's extremely loyal. Over-possessive, in fact."

I nod. "Like back in the bar. I thought he was going to grab you by the hair and drag you off like a caveman."

"I know. That's the image he likes to project, and he works hard at it. He crams in as many hours as he can at the gym, and he's turned the study in our apartment into a workout room."

"I guess he wouldn't have much use for a study. No offense, Abby, but he strikes me as kind of a blockhead. Not exactly a deep thinker. He doesn't seem like your type at all – I'm surprised you married him."

She glances furtively around. "Don't insult my husband that way," she says in a stagey tone. "True, he comes across as a muscle-bound hulk, but that's just the image he has to project. He's Tony's enforcer, and intimidating people is part of his job description. Believe it or not, he's actually a very sensitive, perceptive guy."

"Thanks, Abby." Mick's voice takes me by surprise.

I pivot. He's standing three feet away. She must have seen him coming just in time to come up with that phony compliment. Even so, if looks could kill, I'd be a pulverized heap of flesh and bone. "Hey, Mick," I say. "I thought you were shooting a scene with Tony."

"They told me to take a break. They're still running some lines with him. Not that it's any of your business." As his eyes shift to Abby, his expression softens. "Lucky you were saying such positive things about me. Otherwise this could have gone south in a hurry."

How long has he been eavesdropping? Did he hear me propositioning Abby? Probably not, or he'd have gone beyond glaring to full attack mode.

Abby's face is crimson. "Mick," she stammers. "How long have you been listening?"

"Why do you ask? Were you saying something incriminating?"

"Of course not. I was just giving Jonah some background on your character, since he hasn't worked with you yet."

I can see she could use some help. "This is real life, not a script," I say. "Like Freud said, sometimes a cigar is just a cigar." Mick gives me a vacant stare, and I realize he doesn't get my allusion. "Sometimes things are exactly as they seem on the surface," I explain. "When you're eavesdropping, you don't always hear somebody's deep dark secrets. Sometimes there's nothing dramatic at all."

"I wasn't eavesdropping," Mick says. "This hallway is a common area."

Abby moves to his side and he drapes his arm around her in that proprietary fashion that raises my hackles. "Hey, honey," she murmurs. "Cool it. You've got a scene to shoot any minute now. You shouldn't be getting all hot and bothered."

"On the contrary," he says. "I'll be giving Tony some disturbing news, and this is exactly the mood I'm going for. Pent-up anger, like I can't wait to kill somebody."

Chapter Twelve

Hot and bothered – Abby's phrase perfectly mirrors my mood as I watch Mick barrel his way toward the set. Ironically, it's the same phony bar where Abby and I strayed so far off-script just over an hour ago, and Mick and Tony will probably park their butts on the very same stools. I hope they won't pick up on any pheromones still lingering in the air.

By unspoken consent, Abby and I repair to our respective dressing rooms. Calling my cubby a room is stretching it a bit, since it's barely the size of a prison cell or a bathroom in a cheap walkup apartment. It's windowless, maybe eight by ten feet, with a shabby couch, a banged-up coffee table and a makeup station with vertical rows of bulbs. As low man on the seniority pole, I've drawn the crummiest dressing room, and as yet I haven't been sufficiently motivated to go accessory shopping. Nor have I brought souvenirs from *Oak Bluff* or *Hope Dawns Eternal.* Those soaps were both cancelled, after all, and I don't want to risk jinxing my current digs with bad juju.

My little cell feels even more claustrophobic than usual. I'm done for the day, but I'm tempted to stick around in hopes of spending more time with Abby. Fortunately my superego prevails, convincing me that risking another confrontation with Mick Hastings would be foolhardy in the extreme, so I decide to split.

The thought of Mark's apartment is almost as unappealing as the dressing room, but where to go? Someplace distracting, where I can be among strangers and focus on something other than Abby and her knucklehead husband. Or even worse, that despicable prick Jeff Herbert. The thought of his vile rant still sends my adrenaline spiking,

Somewhere like the Museum of Natural History. It's only a few blocks from my apartment, but I haven't been there in ages. Once outside the studio, I stride uptown, then up the massive stone steps into the great rotunda with its towering dinosaur skeletons. For two hours I wander the dark corridors, past the gargantuan hanging whale and the dioramas, the countless taxidermic specimens of animals that once roamed America's plains and mountains. The museum is a monument to Teddy Roosevelt, his megalomania and the blood lust that inspired him and his cronies to murder hundreds of magnificent beasts and mount them so ignominiously in front of faded panoramic landscapes, imprisoned behind glass.

This gloomy mausoleum isn't exactly lightening my mood. All those dioramas are depressing enough, but even worse, I can't help ruminating about Ben Stiller and the millions of bucks he made with those *Night at the Museum* movies. He's got striking blue eyes – the color's a lot like mine – but aside from that, he's a runty little guy, and not particularly good-looking. Go figure.

I'm relieved when a guard tells me the museum will close in fifteen minutes. All the dead animals are bringing me down, and I'm eager to see my live one. I hurry home, and as I turn the key to Mark's apartment, I hear Sirius scrabbling at the door. He jumps for joy when I enter, launching himself at my chest.

"Okay, boy. Good to see you too. Now off!" He drops obediently back onto all fours. I take his choke chain and leash from the hook by the door and ease the chain over his neck, then cram some blue plastic poop bags in my pants pocket. I grab the vampire cape against the encroaching chill, and we head back downtown, through

Columbus Circle and down Seventh Avenue. Soon we reach Times Square with its blinding, ever changing signs hawking the latest TV shows, cell phones and lingerie. Had Teddy Roosevelt lived a century later, I wonder if he would have poured his money and energy into a scene like this instead of all those dead animals? Maybe he'd have become a media mogul like Walt Disney, whose stamp is all over this once tawdry tourist mecca.

My dog and I wander aimlessly through the theater district, savoring the sights and the many aromas wafting from the restaurants. When I pause longingly outside the Prime Cuts Steakhouse, Sirius sniffs the air and whines softly. I'd love to bring him inside, but no way would he pass as a service dog. As we wend our way west on the long blocks between the avenues, the sky over New Jersey morphs from spectacular shades of rosy crimson into a dusky blackish purple the shade of Sirius's tongue.

By the time we reach Chelsea, night has swallowed the last traces of purple. Somehow I find myself on the street with the sprawling old warehouses occupied by the QMA studios. I won't describe the exact location, because the network purposely keeps a low profile out of concern for the security of its high-profile stars, but it's in the high Twenties, identified only by a silvery plaque not much bigger than those favored by doctors and lawyers who practice in the city's townhouses.

I had no conscious intention of coming here, but obviously my subconscious had other ideas. Everyone's probably long gone by now, but now that I'm here I can't pass up the golden opportunity to explore the place when it's deserted.

I slip my plastic ID card into the slot beside the door. "Hey, Sirius! Want to see where I work?" He wags and dances in assent, and we head inside, then take the elevator to the third floor. Dimly lit by lurid red lights, the long corridor feels uncomfortably spooky. We pad silently down the hall till we reach an office with a warm glow emanating from the frosted glass panel in the door. Bold black letters announce the name: JEFF HERBERT.

Is the scumbag still here? If so, this is a perfect opportunity to call him on the despicable things he was saying early this morning. Sirius at my heels, I stealthily crack open the door and peer in. There he is, oblivious to the intrusion, a portly little man with thinning hair combed greasily across his scalp. He's squeezed into a swivel chair that's tilted precariously back, his feet propped on an overturned wastebasket. His desk is littered with coffee cups and the remains of a Chinese takeout dinner, and he's swigging straight from a bottle of Glenlivet Scotch.

So as to avoid freaking him out with the vampire look, I shrug off my cape and drape it over one arm, then ease open the door and step inside. "Hey, Jeff, how's it going?"

He startles violently, slams the bottle down on the desk, and spins around to face me. When he sees Sirius, his eyes widen in terror. "God damn it! You've got a hell of a nerve, barging right in without knocking." His voice is high and squeaky with fear. "Get the fuck out of here, and take that dog with you, or I'm calling security."

"No need for that. I just dropped by for a little chat."

Sirius tugs on his leash. I could make him sit, but I decide to let him do his thing and loosen up on my hold. He makes a beeline for Jeff's crotch, takes a couple of sniffs, then jumps up, puts his paws on the table, and strains toward a plate of gelatinous noodles.

Jeff's eyes are bugging out of his head. He fumbles for his cell phone. "That's it – I'm calling security. I'm serious!"

I grab the phone out of his hand and point to the dog. "No, *he's* Sirius."

"What the fuck are you talking about?"

"The dog – he's Sirius. That's his name – like the dog star near Orion's belt." I let Sirius chow down on the noodles, then yank on the choke chain and order him to lie down. No point in letting the creep stroke out before I can even talk to him. "How about that?" I say. "A chow chow, chowing down. Good line for a song lyric, don't you think? Kind of catchy."

"Okay, let's cut to the chase," he says. "Who the fuck are you, and what do you want? I'll give you five minutes; then I really am calling security. There's a panic button under my desk."

Maybe he's bluffing, but I can't afford to find out, so I decide to cool it. "Okay if I sit down?" Without waiting for an answer, I ease myself into a chair. "I'm Jonah McQuarry. I just started working on *Sunlight and Shadow*. Sorry if I startled you just now."

Tension flows slowly from his body, leaving him limp. "You did give me a start, charging in without knocking."

"We do that a lot in daytime drama. It saves time, keeps things crisp."

He glances ostentatiously at his Rolex. "Speaking of time, what are you doing here so late? It's almost ten. Your show must have wrapped hours ago."

"I had a hunch I might find you here." Actually I had no such notion, but I'm enjoying watching him squirm. "I thought we should have a little chat, as Heidi Klum used to say in the scene before she kicked someone off the show."

He fakes a laugh. "*Project Runway?* Great show, but it's got nothing to do with me."

"Well, maybe this will. I overheard you talking to Chuck Winslow and Harvey Blaustein this morning."

His face pales, and he backs his chair away from mine. "That was a private conversation. You had no business eavesdropping."

"Come on, Jeff. Don't you realize eavesdropping is standard operating procedure on soaps? Come to think of it, maybe you don't. On *Brand New You,* everything's out in plain sight, with everyone shrieking and laughing hysterically and the audience jammed into those tiny seats, obeying the cue cards and hoping they'll get some merch at the end of the show. It's pathetic."

"It's what people want. Our ratings prove it – they're climbing every week."

"That's only because you had a murder on your set. People love the titillation of real-life crime. Watching your show, they've got the thrill of being vicariously involved, but with none of the risks. But your attitude toward your talent really bugs me. I heard what you said about Sheila Spencer – talking about her like a piece of dirt under your heel that you could grind into the ground. Totally disposable. It's a disgusting way to think."

"I'm the showrunner. It's my creation, and I can think about it any damn way I please. I can hire and fire at will."

"But you've got to kowtow to the guys at the top of the ant hill. They're the ones who call the shots. The director of daytime programming, for example. I know you answer to him."

"True, but he's in my corner a hundred percent. He's relying on me to jack up the daytime ratings. If the numbers for *Brand New You* keeps climbing, he's going to give me another show to produce. You and your cronies on that outdated soap have a limited life expectancy. You're on terminal life support."

My stomach lurches, and my adrenaline skyrockets. "I don't believe you! The network's committed to

Sunlight and Shadow. They want to carry on the venerable tradition of daytime drama. Chuck and Harvey told us they heard it from the guy at the top."

"Ah, but his days are numbered too. He's outlived his usefulness, been here for decades. He's practically antediluvian. They need fresh blood – that's why they're bringing in Gloria Kemp for a new show."

"Is that true?" I ask. The acid's attacking my stomach, rising in my gorge. "I'd heard the rumor, but I wasn't sure whether to believe it."

"You better believe it. She's coming to QMA next month, and her show is taking over your time slot. You'll be running an hour earlier."

That's the time slot *Hope Dawns Eternal* occupied for decades. Where do they come off, jerking us around like this? All at once I'm panting for breath, and my pulse is hammering, blood rocketing through my body. This must be what athletes on steroids mean when they talk about roid rage – an over-the-top anger spinning out of control.

Sensing my shift in energy, Sirius focuses on Jeff, bares his teeth and growls. The red veil descends, and I spring into action.

Chapter Thirteen

Déjà vu all over again. As I slake my thirst in long slow gulps from the puncture wounds in Jeff Herbert's neck, I flash back to the night in Central Park when I offed those two thugs, or rather when Jeremy did. But there's a critical difference. That night I saw everything from my own vantage point as I hovered over the action. But this time it's not like watching a movie. It's more like an off-off Broadway play in a tiny black box theatre, and I'm close enough to feel the heat radiating from Jeff's body, smell the coppery tang of blood and the foul stench of his bowels and bladder letting go.

Sirius is in his element, crouched by my side, slurping blood from the puncture wounds he made close to mine. In between swallows, he strains at his leash, longing to explore the stinky mess that's spreading on the floor below Jeff's butt. There are few things dogs love better than sniffing shit. Except for fucking, of course, but Mark had his dog neutered at an early age, so Sirius probably doesn't know what he's missing. I'm keeping a tight grip on his leash, because he likes to lick my mouth, and even the faintest suggestion of human waste on his tongue would disgust me.

I'm probably grossing you out, so I'll spare you any more gory details and cut to the aftermath. Sirius is lying on the floor near the corpse, fastidiously cleaning his paws, when all at once he bristles and begins growling softly. A moment later, I hear the sound of the door latch clicking open, and Abby is standing in the doorway, framed by the lurid red lights in the hall.

"Jonah, are you in here?" she whispers.

"Yes, it's me. Hang on a minute while I grab the dog." Sirius is already standing, eager to sniff the newcomer. He's stopped growling, but I have no idea how feasting on human blood may affect him, so I grab his collar.

Abby cracks open the door. "Eeuw, what's that stink?"

"Abby, what are you doing here?"

"For some reason I had the strangest feeling I'd find you here, and that you needed me. But you haven't answered my question. This place smells vile. Did the dog take a crap?"

"Sirius? Of course not. He has better manners than that. But you haven't answered mine either. What on earth gave you the idea I'd be here?"

She's silent for a long moment. "It's hard to explain," she finally says. Her eyes are averted and she's acting strangely dodgy. "Call it a sixth sense. Why try to explain? It's just one more proof of our psychic connection."

"I guess you're right." I pull on my cape, then stride toward the door, spreading my arms in hopes the voluminous garment will keep her out and shield her from the sight of Jeff's body splayed on the floor. But there's no stopping her. In a moment her body is against mine, and I'm encircling her in my arms. She snuggles into my chest, and I feel the pounding of her heart against mine. She's breathing heavily.

We embrace in silence. Then she pulls away. "This place smells like an abattoir," she says.

"How would you know? Have you ever been to a slaughter house?" I'm stalling for time, longing to share in the satisfaction of the kill but afraid of her reaction. How should I play it? I'm feeling simultaneously guilty and gleeful.

Sirius tugs at his leash, wriggles between us and

thrusts his nose into her crotch. I give his choke chain a jerk. "Bad dog!"

"That's okay," she says. "He just wants to get acquainted." She crouches down and scratches behind his ears. He responds by licking her lips with his long purplish tongue.

She pulls away. "Sorry, but that's a bit much." Rising, she brushes her mouth with the back of her hand, stares in horror as it comes away smeared with blood. In the red light of the hallway, it looks almost black. She stifles a scream. "Is that what I think it is? He didn't bite me. But that salty taste –"

"It's blood." I furl my cape, affording her a clear view of the body sprawled on the floor.

She gasps. "Oh my God, that's Jeff Herbert! Did Sirius bite him?"

"Yes, but I bit him first. Or I should say Jeremy did. But I might as well admit it, we're one and the same. I was walking Sirius, and something drew me back to the studio. I was prowling around up here, I had no idea Jeff was going to be in his office, but I decided it was the perfect time to confront him about all the crap he's pulling with *Brand New You.* He was spouting such disgusting shit, I went ballistic, and that's when Jeremy came out. Then Sirius joined in. I'm ashamed to say we both sated ourselves with blood."

"He probably had it coming." She takes a couple of tentative steps toward the corpse. "Is he dead?"

"Beyond the shadow of a doubt. I checked."

"Can I see?"

"If you want. There's not that much to see. Just a few bite marks."

She crouches down, extends her hand, but stops just short of touching the throat. "Those marks are so subtle, so neat. There's hardly any blood."

"Well, Jeremy had tons of practice back on *Oak Bluff.*"

"Yes, but he was just following a script, and they used fake blood. He never actually bit anybody."

"How would you know? Oh, right, you were his lady love on the show."

"Not me, but Alifair Churchill. I hadn't even come into being yet, but on some level maybe I was watching, almost as if I was a part of her. Like you and Jeremy."

"I suppose that's possible. But if Jeremy didn't actually drink blood, how did he get so expert so suddenly? It feels as if he's been doing it all his life." All at once a flash goes off in my head, brilliant as a cartoon light bulb. "Or lives."

Abby's face goes pale. "Lives? You think he's a genuine vampire? That he's lived multiple lives?"

"Probably not. But maybe Mark has."

"Mark Westgate? But he's such a wimpy, introverted guy. He doesn't seem like the vampire type." She flashes an impish grin. "But then again, you never know."

I trail my fingers down her cheek. "It seems far-fetched, but it's conceivable. I'm a skeptic by nature, but I'm trying to keep an open mind and entertain all the hypotheses. I'm not ruling anything out."

"Jeff looks so peaceful. No signs of a struggle." She shivers delicately. "But he looks pale as a ghost."

"Yes, Sirius and I pretty well drained him. Anyway, the world's a better place without him. You should have heard the despicable things he said about the cast of *Brand New You.* He put down Sheila Spencer's looks, even had the gall to suggest the show would benefit if she were murdered too, because the press coverage would boost the ratings. He didn't give a damn about any of them as people. To him they were just commodities."

Abby's mouth twists in distaste. "I always thought he was disgusting – a male chauvinist pig and a fat sweaty slob to boot. He was always leering at me in the halls, dropping not so subtle hints that he'd like to get it on with me. Yecch!"

"I didn't realize that."

"He managed to keep it under wraps when men were around – probably scared someone would punch his lights out if they saw him hitting on a woman."

"That confirms it – the guy was a total prick. Contemptuous of everyone he could pull rank on, although he was a consummate brown noser with the higher ups. Anyway, listening to him badmouthing his cast and bragging about all the pull he has, all of a sudden I snapped and everything went red, just like those other times I was telling you about."

"You mean when you were talking about dissociative identity disorder?"

"Right. Jeremy came out and took over, just like last night in the park."

"Last night in the park? What are you talking about"

Damn, that was a serious screw-up. The bond between us is so powerful that I keep forgetting there's still a lot we haven't told each other. "I'll tell you another time," I say.

"Okay. But you have to promise. We need to be totally truthful with each other."

"I agree."

She's studying me intently, her eyes aglow and her lips parted, looking as turned on as I feel. I lean forward, cup her face in my hands. We come together in a passionate kiss. I caress her neck, her shoulders.

She's trembling, taking deep, ragged breaths, but all at once she breaks away. "This isn't right. That man is lying dead, drained of blood, right next to us, and I'm feeling as horny as hell. How perverse is that?"

"I don't see it as perverse, Abby. The presence of death makes us savor life that much more keenly. All our senses are heightened."

Color floods her cheeks. "Mine certainly are. And I know it's wrong to speak ill of the dead, but I sincerely believe the world is better off without Jeff Herbert. I feel this weird sense of satisfaction. Happiness, even."

"The Germans have a great word for that. *Schadenfreude* – taking pleasure in the misfortune of others. In Wagner's Ring Cycle, for example –"

Abby gives my arm a squeeze. "I love listening to you expound on the arts, Jonah, but shouldn't we get out of here, while the place is still deserted? Morning's only a few hours away, and people could start trickling in any time now. You're already a person of interest in Gene Gentry's murder. The last thing you need is for someone to see you here."

"You're right, we'd better split. We should leave separately, though. You first – I'll just look to make sure the coast is clear. Then I'll stay and do some damage control. As soon as they discover Jeff's body, forensics will be all over this place, but I figure I've got a couple of hours."

Sirius, who's been taking an after-dinner snooze, jumps to his feet as I move to the door. Wrapping my hand in the cape to avoid leaving prints, I grab the handle, crack the door and peer out into the hall, which is eerily empty. "All clear," I whisper, and we both step out into the corridor, followed by Sirius. No sooner is he out the door than he shifts to full alert status, his fur bristling and a low growl rumbling in his throat.

"Hey, Jonah. Abby. Imagine meeting you here at this ungodly hour. What's with the dog?" The voice echoing down the hall is unmistakably Tony's. I whirl barely in time to catch a fleeting glimpse of his black-clad form, disappearing around a corner.

Chapter Fourteen

Sirius is straining at his leash, pumped to take off in hot pursuit of Tony, but I order him to sit. Bad enough we've been seen, but at least Tony has no knowledge of the carnage that lies behind Jeff Herbert's door. He'll know soon enough, along with everyone else, but there's no point in giving him an exclusive preview.

The dog whimpers. The blood feast has made him edgy. He's panting, saliva dripping from his jowls, his thick ruff of black hair bristling. A veritable puffy lion, he'd have made a truly intimidating temple guardian back in the Ming dynasty in China. Right now he's guarding me, Abby, and Jeff Herbert's flaccid, bloodless corpse. But I don't want Sirius scaring Tony, much less attacking him. I have no desire to confront the man, no idea what I'd say to him if we were face to face.

Abby clutches my arm. "Jonah, I want to stay with you. I can help you clean up. Or maybe between the two of us, we can hide the body somehow."

"I don't think we can pull that off – too much risk of being seen. Besides, Jeff's death makes a statement. The world needs to know what a shit he was. Come to think of it, maybe I'll write a little missive on the computer and leave it with the body. Good riddance to bad rubbish, that kind of thing."

"I could help with that."

"No, don't put yourself at risk. This has nothing to do with you, Abby. I don't want you implicating yourself."

Her eyes are aglow with a fiery energy. "It has

everything to do with me, Jonah. It felt almost as if you were sending me a message, and I knew I had to come to you at this precise place and time. We've got a psychic connection that makes us stronger together than we can ever be on our own."

"I feel that too, but I don't want to take you down with me. You need to get back to Mick before he wakes up. Besides, I need some time alone, time to sort things out in my mind. All hell's going to break loose in a few hours, and I want to be ready." I clasp both her arms, pull her close.

As we kiss, she thrusts her tongue deep into my mouth, then licks my lips."Mmm, you taste yummy."

I mirror the gesture, and she moans. "So do you," I murmur. "But watch out – I wouldn't want you acquiring a taste for blood." I pull away, spin her toward the door and give her a gentle nudge, then watch as she walks down the corridor. Soon she's enveloped in darkness.

Once I hear the soft hiss of the elevator doors closing, I turn to the laptop on Jeff's desk, but my thoughts are far too chaotic to write anything comprehensible. Anyway, it's an asinine idea. No point in leaving a cyber trail when the physical evidence is already more than damning enough. I head further up the hall in search of cleaning supplies. The utility closet's locked, unfortunately, so I have to make do with wads of paper towels from the men's room, soaked and doused in liquid soap from the dispenser. I spend the next hour swabbing down Jeff's office as best I can, taking special care with the surfaces Abby and I might conceivably have touched, the doorknobs in particular, but leaving Jeff's body untouched. It's probably an exercise in futility, because the forensic techs will no doubt find plenty of telltale traces I've missed, especially the dog hair. Mark's a stickler about keeping his private life private, and I know he hasn't told anyone about Sirius.

Even so, compulsively cleansing away the forensic evidence is probably pointless, because Tony Giordano can place us at the scene. He got a good look at us, even called us by name and commented on the dog, and he won't think twice about ratting us out.

If I had any sense at all, I'd high tail it down to the Port Authority and hop an early bus heading west. I could probably pull off a decent disguise, change buses a few times, but what would I do for cash? Before I split, I'd have to find an ATM across town where a cash withdrawal wouldn't incriminate me. And what about Sirius? They wouldn't allow him on a bus. More important, what about Abby? They might arrest her as an accomplice. And what about my career, and the identity – or identities – Mark has built all these years? Without it, I'd be nothing.

Besides, this particular story line is the most challenging one I've ever encountered, and I'm dying to see how it will turn out. I may not like the ending, but what the hell. I've made it through innumerable dicey situations before, and I've always come through alive, though sometimes the worse for wear. Chances are I'll make it through this crisis too. What the hell – I decide to stay.

The dog and I make it out of the building unseen, then make the long trek uptown to Mark's apartment. I open a can of Science Diet for Sirius, but he gives it a disdainful sniff and turns away. He's probably still satiated by our recent feast, but I hope his burgeoning taste for human blood hasn't spoiled him for more pedestrian fare. I've got to rein in Jeremy, put an end to these killings now, before he takes total control.

I hang Jeremy's cape at the rear of the closet, then treat myself to a long soaking bath and an oversized goblet of Cabernet Noir. Sleep eludes me, but I'm still wired, so I decide to walk all the way downtown to the studio. I'm looking and feeling so clean and spiffy, I can almost believe the events of a few hours ago were nothing but a nightmare.

No such luck. At nine sharp, when I round the corner and head toward the studio, I feel as if I'm walking smack dab into the middle of a movie I've already seen. The three squad cars, the ambulance, the cop guarding the door. A different cop this time, a bigger guy with a muscular build, but I pull the same bit I used last time with the rookie, and lo and behold, it works.

When the elevator doors slide open at the third floor, I recognize the cop – the short pudgy guy who confronted me the morning Gene Gentry's body was found. This time no introductions are needed – his eyes flash in instant recognition, and his hands move toward his belt, weighted down with weaponry.

I raise my palms in surrender. "Imagine meeting you here," I say with feigned confusion. "I didn't expect you back so soon. What's happening?"

"Why don't you tell me?"

"I haven't the foggiest. I'm just here to shoot a couple of scenes." Cautiously, I start easing my way past him. "Now if you'll excuse me – "

"Hold it right there." He waylays me with a beefy arm, talks into his intercom. "He's here, Detective Johnson. The guy you wanted to talk to, Jonah McQuarry."

This sounds less than auspicious. Sure enough, the African American plain clothes detective shows up in less than a minute. He shepherds me into a vacant dressing room and gives me a cursory report of Jeff Herbert's death, then starts grilling me. He questions me exhaustively about my whereabouts last night, coming at the same territory from different angles, no doubt hoping to trip me up with inconsistencies. He can't find any, because my explanations are boringly repetitive. I was alone in Mark's apartment, took a long walk. Saw no one, spoke to no one. Pretty pathetic, I've got to admit. I don't mention Sirius – I'm still worried the dog hair will prove problematic.

The whole time, I'm thinking about Tony Giordano. Has he told the cops about our late-night encounter yet? Evidently not – if he had, I'd probably be under arrest already. Maybe he's not even here, doesn't have any scenes today, doesn't know about the murder. Yeah, right – fat chance of that, the way news travels around here.

It's obvious Detective Johnson is underwhelmed with my story, but like a dog worrying a bone, he refuses to let go. He keeps rolling his swivel chair closer and closer to mine, invading my personal space, and it takes all the acting chops I can muster to project the proper attitude of polite concern and unflappable cool.

Finally, after what seems like an eternity, he shoves back his chair and stands. "That's it for now," he says, "but don't even think about leaving town. We need to know where to reach you at all times. Like I told you when the first murder went down, you're a person of interest. Now more than ever."

Free at last, I stroll with studied nonchalance down the corridor to the set of *Sunlight and Shadow*. People are milling around, murmuring to each other in stagy whispers. When they catch sight of me, their eyes widen. Then they turn their backs and huddle closer to each other, closing ranks and shutting me out.

"Hey, I'm not contagious," I say. "How's it going? Have the police questioned all of you too?"

"Not all of us," Mick Hastings says. "I guess they're focusing first on the people they consider prime suspects." He smirks, then turns and mutters sotto voce in Tony's ear, evoking a muted chuckle of complicity. Tony claps Mick on the back and they stroll off down the corridor and out of sight around a corner. I feel a pang of anxiety and an acute urge to talk to Abby, but she's nowhere in sight – a good thing, because I'm feeling so edgy I might well blow our cover.

Tony and Mick are best buds, so it's a virtual certainty Tony's telling him about our encounter in the wee hours of the morning, if he hasn't done so already. I half expect them to be back any minute with a couple of cops ready to read me my rights and cuff me, but they don't return. I kill time chatting with Paul Devane and some other cast members, who tell me the day's shooting will go on pretty much as scheduled. Chuck and Harvey haven't called any meetings yet; evidently they've decided to make like ostriches and pretend everything is business as usual.

Out of nowhere, a hand claps me on the shoulder, and my body goes tense. I wheel to face Tony. His black eyes are drilling into mine, and he gives me a reptilian smile. "Let's you and me have a little chat," he says as he takes my arm and steers me away from the others.

Whatever he's got in mind, it's better he says it out of earshot of the others. "I don't know about you, but I could use some fresh air," I say. "Why don't we get some coffee from that deli down the street?"

"Sounds good to me."

Lost in our own thoughts, we're silent as we trudge down the block to the corner. A cold north wind is whipping down Tenth Avenue, chilling the back of my neck as we walk toward the deli. The silence between us is becoming oppressive, so I decide to break it. "What's up?" I ask. "Why do you want to talk?"

He smirks. "Pretty obvious, isn't it?"

"You tell me. I gather you haven't told the cops about our little encounter last night."

"No, I haven't. If I had, they'd be all over you by now."

"What about Mick? I saw you guys having a tête-a-tête back there."

"I haven't told him either. No one else knows I saw you and Abby last night, not to mention that dog. Right at the scene of the crime, although I didn't know it at the time. I thought you were just having a rendezvous. Mick wouldn't be pleased, you know. Your life would be worth squat if he found out."

"So why haven't you ratted me out? It can't just be out of the goodness of your heart." The proverbial light bulb goes off in my head. "What were you doing at the studio at three in the morning? Having an assignation of your own? Something you want me to keep quiet?"

His smile is as warm and comfy as a crocodile's. "No, nothing like that. Sometimes I sleep in my dressing room, that's all. It's got a couch that converts to a king-sized bed, some exercise equipment and a few other amenities I've acquired over the years."

Nothing like rubbing my nose in it. I resist getting into a pissing contest over dressing room size and status. "But there has to be a quid pro quo," I say instead. "Something you want from me in return for your silence. In daytime drama there always is."

"Yeah, but this isn't fiction – it's real life. I don't have script writers feeding me my motivation, and the details haven't come into focus yet. But I'm pretty well convinced you're a vampire."

"Come on, Tony, that's ridiculous. I'll admit some pretty strange stuff has been going on, and I don't have a handle on it yet, but I'm no vampire."

"Don't be so sure. I believe you have supernatural powers, powers you may not even realize you possess yet. As this plot plays out, I may want you to share those powers with me."

"I don't understand. How could I do that?"

He grins. "You could turn me into a vampire too."

Chapter Fifteen

I've got two scenes to shoot this morning, both of them with Paul Devane, Tony's computer whiz. Simple talking heads stuff. Nothing too emotionally demanding, fortunately, because it takes everything I've got to maintain the unflappable cool that's part of my professional façade. No scenes with Abby, and she's nowhere around. Wise decision on her part, because the combustible chemistry between us would be damn near impossible to hide.

I sleepwalk through my lines with Paul, somehow managing to nail them on the first take. As always, he's hypomanic, self-conscious and easily flustered – his standard persona, but amped up a few degrees, and I sense my close proximity is driving him close to panic. When the director calls it a wrap, he breathes a giant sigh of relief and scuttles away.

I'm making everyone edgy today. Their body language is painfully obvious – the averted eyes, the way they turn quickly away when they see me approaching, the huddled confabs with their cohorts. The morning after Gene Gentry's death, there was an atmosphere of excited titillation, but now everyone looks just plain terrified. Chuck still hasn't called any meetings, so I decide to split. I'd love to take Sirius for a long walk in the park – but no, that's a crappy idea. No doubt the crime techs have found some mysterious dog hair by now, and I can't risk being seen with him.

I'm pondering which museum to go to when Tony materializes at my side and fixes his dark eyes on me. "Done for the day?" he asks. "How about joining me for a drink?" His tone suggests that refusal isn't an option. In any case, I've got nothing to lose. He's the only one I can discuss the situation with, aside from Abby, and I don't want her pulled into this mess any more than she already is.

"Why not?" I reply. "Have you been to McGuire's?"

"No, I don't know it."

"It's kind of a funky pub up on Amsterdam Avenue. It hasn't been gentrified yet, and it's frequented by old timers who've patronized the place forever. Chances are no one will recognize us there."

He claps me on the back. "Okay, you're on. Let's go."

Half an hour later we're ensconced in my regular booth in back, slugging down Scotch. Midafternoon, the place is deserted except for a handful of hardcore drinkers at the bar, all of them looking oblivious to the world around them.

"Classy place," Tony says with a sardonic grin.

"Yeah, I like it. Reminds me of bars I used to hang out in before I'd landed my first role. Helps keep me humble." It also conjures up Abby in that forties-noir trench coat she wore here the other night, but I keep that image to myself.

He guffaws. "Humble? That's the last adjective I'd pick to describe you."

"I could care less about your impressions of me or my favorite watering hole. Let's dispense with the chit chat, Tony. Why do you really want to see me?" I slouch back into the corner of the booth, feigning nonchalance, certain he's decided to extort something to buy his silence about what he saw last night.

His dark eyes drill into mine as he slugs down more Scotch. "Like I said this morning, maybe one of these days I'll want you to turn me into a vampire."

I stare back at him. "Sorry, Tony, no can do. That's

outside my area of expertise."

"Why not? You're a vampire, right? Doesn't that come with the territory?"

"You're the one who insists on calling me a vampire. I still don't believe I am."

"Well, maybe not you, but your alter, and deep down you're one and the same. I'd be willing to bet that if you went to a shrink, he'd diagnose you with dissociative identity disorder."

"You've got some nerve, flinging around psychiatric diagnoses. What makes you such an authority?"

"A former girlfriend of mine had D.I.D. It caused major problems, so I had Paul do some research on the Internet and bring me up to speed on the subject."

I stifle the impulse to crack wise about Tony's literacy or lack of it, but he picks up on something in my expression. "Believe it or not, I do read on occasion, but I've got better things to do with my time." He shrugs. "Anyway, that's beside the point – we're here to talk about you. The cops wouldn't make it official, but word has it this was another vampire-style hit. More than ever, they're looking at you as a suspect, and I've got to admit I'm kind of jealous. Over the years I've been responsible for more hits than anyone else on this show, either directly or indirectly. They've tried to pin quite a few murders on me, but they've never been able to make the charges stick. The evidence was purely circumstantial."

"You mean like my brother's murder, right?"

"Oh no, you don't. You're not going to get me to cop to that one. But these vampire killings are going to wreak havoc with my reputation. It's bad for my image when some anonymous killer is getting all the credit and I'm not even a suspect."

"In other words, you're the guy with the most notches in your belt, and you don't want anyone upstaging you."

"Yeah, and especially the guy knocking off those losers on *Brand New You.* Their ratings have taken off like a rocket since Gene Gentry's murder, and once Jeff Herbert's death hits the headlines, they'll be in the stratosphere."

"But wasn't Herbert the main creative force behind the show, the guy who really had a bug up his ass about making it work? Without him, the show could very well fold."

He flashes his crooked grin. "No way, they'll keep it on life support till they bleed it dry. Then once the murders are old news, they'll kill it off. And don't forget Art Balinger, Jeff's's production partner. Until now he's kept a low profile and stuck pretty much to number crunching, but I bet he'll step forward now. He's got too much invested in *Brand New You* to put it out of its misery."

"Just before I went ballistic, Herbert told me they have another show in the works, ready to replace *Sunlight and Shadow* if our ratings don't improve."

He clenches his jaw, and his obsidian eyes blaze with anger. "So between that and Gloria Kemp's new show, they'd be killing off the last of the great daytime dramas on QMA? That'll happen over my dead body."

"Don't talk like that, Tony. Put a negative postulate into words and it takes on amazing power. The negativity can grow exponentially till it sucks everything into a deadly vortex, like a black hole. Better to visualize something positive."

"Don't give me that Norman Vincent Peale crap. It makes me want to puke."

"Okay, I'll spare you for now. But you shouldn't be so cynical. There's a lot to some of this New Agey stuff."

"I suppose you believe in reincarnation too."

"Absolutely. I'm convinced we've all lived multiple

lives going back hundreds or even thousands of years. If you connect with someone on a deep soul level, it's virtually certain you were bound to them in a previous existence, and you have unfinished karma to work out with them."

"Like you and Abby, right?"

The non sequitur brings me up short, and I signal the waiter for another Scotch. "My relationship with Abby is purely professional," I say.

"Bullshit! I've seen the way you two look at each other – you can hardly keep your hands off each other. I was watching from backstage when you shot that scene yesterday – I thought it was going to end in spontaneous combustion. I wanted to tell you to get a room, but then I guess you did – Jeff Herbert's office. Weird place to consummate a mutual attraction, in a room with a fresh corpse, but hey, who am I to say?"

"That's not why we were there. Not that it's any of your business, but she had a feeling she'd find me there and that I might need her."

"More of that karmic connection stuff, huh? Or maybe it was the scent of blood. Wasn't she your paramour, back on *Oak Bluff*? You turned her into a vampire, didn't you? Just like you could turn me."

"That wasn't me, it was Jeremy Lowell. And it was just part of the script. It wasn't real."

"But these murders are definitely real – Gene Gentry and now Jeff Herbert. Maybe that's why I'm so intrigued. You know how it feels to kill, and I want that feeling too. The actual blood and gore, not just the illusion."

"You don't want it, Tony, believe me. Even though my alter was the one draining the blood from those victims, on some level I was present too, if only as a voyeur, and I didn't take any pleasure in it."

"Ah, but maybe I would. All these years I've been a

killer, even though I kill only for the most honorable of reasons, like protecting my family or bringing down criminals too heinous to live. But I don't know how it feels to truly kill, to feel someone's life ebb away at the touch of my."

The devilish gleam in his eyes is unnerving. Forget about that extra Scotch – it's time to hightail it out of here. "Speaking of fangs," I say, "I've got to get home and walk my dog."

"Great looking dog, but kind of spooky looking. What breed is he?"

I nearly tell Tony that Sirius is a chow-shepherd mix, but I don't want him conjuring up visions of vicious police dogs. "Chow," I say instead, as I slide out of the booth and rise.

"Hey, wait a minute, Jonah. It's too early for 'ciao.'"

I force a grin. "Not that kind of ciao. Chow as in chow chow. You asked about his breed."

"Oh, right. Anyway, I should split too, but one more thing. I know we're supposed to hate each other's guts, but that's just the script the writers have given us. I'm not your enemy and you're not mine – not really. Our true enemies are the guys who want to put us out of business and send us to the unemployment line. Like the late unlamented Jeff Herbert, and his partner Art Balinger. Maybe Gloria Kemp. Then there's the head of daytime. It goes all the way up the food chain."

At the mention of food, my stomach growls. The satiation of last night's blood feast has worn off, and I realize I'm ravenous. As soon as I ditch Tony, I decide, I'll call Abby and ask her to meet me at the Prime Cuts Steakhouse. Or on second thought, maybe Mark's apartment, where we could finally get the privacy we crave.

"Think it over," Tony says. "You and me, working together – we could take those suckers down."

Chapter Sixteen

It's edging toward dinner hour, and Abby is probably home with her lout of a husband. Calling her is idiotic, I know – what if Mick overhears? I decide to text her instead.

Within a minute, she calls me back. She's gasping for breath, and the sound instantly quickens my heart beat. "Abby, are you okay?" I ask.

"I'm fine. You caught me out running."

"Outrunning whom? Is someone chasing you? Mick, maybe?"

She laughs. "You're kidding, right?"

"Of course." Actually I'm dead serious. Mick Hastings hates my guts, and he's not someone to mess with.

"You can rest easy, Jonah. Mick is out of town for a few days, so for once in my life I'm utterly free and untethered."

Is she propositioning me? It almost sounds that way, and it sounds more promising still when she agrees to dinner at Mark's apartment. I stop at Gristedes for a couple of filets mignons and the fixings, give Sirius a quick walk, then head back to the apartment to await her arrival.

When the intercom buzzer sounds an hour later, Sirius springs to his feet, quivering all over. I realize that as reclusive as Mark is, chances are no one has ever come here before, so the dog may never have heard the sound. I stab the intercom button and a tinny voice issues forth. "Jonah, it's Abby. Can you buzz me in?"

Sirius cocks his head, perks his ears and starts wagging.

"Come on up, Abby." I press the button that unlocks the door to the lobby. "Sorry, I forgot to tell you it's a walk-up. I'm on the third floor, apartment 3A. Make a left when you get to the landing."

As we listen for her footsteps in the hall, Sirius pants, and the drool drips from his tongue. "I know how you feel, boy," I murmur. When she rings the bell, I peer through the little glass fisheye in the door to confirm it's her, then grab the dog's collar, open the dead bolt and the Fox police lock and crack the door open. "Welcome to my humble abode."

Sirius is dancing with excitement. "Sirius, down," I say. Instantly he executes a play bow, then sinks to the floor.

"Wow, what a perfect downward dog. Have you been teaching him Yoga?"

"No, he comes by it naturally. The pose is named for dogs, after all. Not vice versa." Crouching, she scratches behind his ears, and he fervently licks her hand. She rises, and we stare into each other's eyes as silence stretches between us.

"I could use a drink," I say. "How about you?" I usher her into the kitchen and toward the wine rack on the counter. "Mark's quite the wine connoisseur. Unless you prefer the hard stuff. He's out of Scotch, so I think I'll go for some bourbon. He favors Knob Creek, if that's good for you."

She smiles. "That sounds perfect."

I pour us both doubles, neat. "Here's looking at you, kid," I say in my best Bogart voice as we clink glasses. We take healthy swigs, then head for the sofa, where we sit a cautious couple of feet apart.

"This is ridiculous," she says. "Why do I feel like some kind of ingénue on a first date? I've even got butterflies."

Something stirs deep inside me as I wonder exactly where in her body those butterflies are. "Maybe it's because we've never been so totally alone together before."

"Except for Jeff Herbert's office."

"But his corpse was in the room, so that kind of put a damper on things. I know what you mean, though – I feel awkward too. Maybe it was a mistake, inviting you here."

"No, I'm glad I came. I wanted to see where you live, and I love getting the chance to see your dog again."

Sirius has planted himself at her feet, and he's gazing adoringly up at her. "Looks like he loves seeing you too," I say.

She leans over and strokes his long black hair, and he responds by rolling over onto his back and wriggling in delight. She starts massaging his belly, and when she touches the ticklish spot on his chest, his left hind leg thumps out a steady rhythm. "Lucky dog," I say. "I wish I were in his place."

She turns to me and her lips part in a sensual smile. "That can be arranged."

I slide closer and drape my arm around her shoulder, then lean into her and brush her neck with my lips. A rosy blush creeps into her cheeks. She shivers, then tenses and pulls away. "You know, Jonah, this could be a colossal mistake. We could be getting in over our heads."

"I know. I was wrong to invite you here. I feel as if I'm caught up in some crazy whirlwind I don't understand, and I can't control the spin. I don't want to pull you down with me."

"Maybe I want to be caught up in the whirlwind with you. 'Down and down I go, round and round I go –'" She launches into "That Old Black Magic" in a smoky alto that gives me the chills.

"I love your voice. You sound a little like Diana Krall."

"Thanks. I'll admit I fantasize about singing cabaret, maybe in the Oak Room at the Algonquin Hotel."

"I remember you told me that in the first scene we shot together."

She grins. "Right, and Harvey chewed us out for going off script."

"Anyway, you'd make a great chanteuse. And you'd look fantastic lounging atop a baby grand."

"Forget about lounging. If there's a piano, I'd rather be playing it."

By now we've both downed our whiskeys, and we're feeling a little tipsy, although the booze is only partly to blame. We start trading snatches of our favorite standards – Gershwin, Porter, Ellington. "You've got a sexy baritone," she says, as I pour another round. "I could sing with you all night."

"Do you and Mick like singing together?"

She scrunches up her face. On her, the grimace looks charming. "No, he's totally tone deaf."

"Too bad. So you said he's out of town. For how long, exactly?"

"A week or two. He's not sure."

"Where did he go?"

"New Mexico, somewhere near Taos. Keith Carlton wants to get away, possibly even quit. He doesn't have any scenes to shoot for a couple of weeks, and Mick's pretty pissed about it."

"They're giving me a week off too, but that's no big deal. It happens to everybody."

"I know, but he's afraid they're downsizing his role, focusing too much on the kids – all those teens and twenty-somethings."

Her words make me wince. "Not to mention the

actual children, the preadolescents. For once I agree with him. I realize they want to draw in a younger demographic, but they're taking it too far."

"I agree. Anyway, Keith says if they think he's over the hill, he might as well take to the hills, so he wants to look at some land out there. Mick's not happy about it, and neither am I. I've been feeling pretty over the hill myself."

"He's not over the hill, and neither are you." I stroke her cheek, let my fingers trail through her long black hair. "To me you're absolutely perfect. In the prime of life."

I let my hand slide lightly onto her breast. She shivers, and her lips part invitingly. Then, maddeningly, she draws away. "I'll turn forty next year. It's all downhill from here."

"I don't believe that. I'm forty-six, and I feel as if my best years are still ahead of me."

"Easy for you to say. When it comes to acting, the double standard is vicious. Men can be sex symbols into their sixties, even beyond. Look at Clint Eastwood."

"Yeah, he won the genetic lottery – he's got great bone structure. But he doesn't do romantic roles anymore."

"But there are still plenty of good roles out there for older guys. For women, not so much." All at once her eyes widen. "Jonah, I just realized – now that you're a vampire, maybe you won't go on aging. You'll stay as devastatingly attractive as you are right now."

"You flatter me. But I'm not a vampire, and I don't believe in immortality."

"Why not?" She smiles. "It happens all the time on soaps. Say an actor wants to quit. He's convinced he can become a superstar on the big screen, so they kill him off. Then lo and behold, a few months later, or maybe even years later, if he doesn't make it in Hollywood, they bring him back to life."

"That's just fantasy, Abby. It doesn't happen like that in real life."

"So who's to say what's real life and what isn't? The boundaries get pretty blurry sometimes, don't you think?"

I lean forward, about to kiss her, then take her lower lip between my teeth and bite. She squeals and pulls away. "Jonah, stop! What's gotten into you?"

"Damned if I know." I back away. We're both breathing heavily. "I'm sorry," I say. "I'd never do anything to hurt you. That was meant as a love nip."

"It felt like more than that. Jonah, I believe you when you say you'd never hurt me. At least not intentionally. But you should know – I'm not into that Fifty Shades S&M stuff."

"Nor am I – not that I've ever read that garbage." Her brow is furrowed with worry, her dark eyes full of questions, and I realize I'd better back off. "You were telling me about Mick," I say. "Do you really think Keith will quit? That would mean the end for your hubby."

"He says it's pretty serious." At the sound of his name, Sirius comes over and begins nuzzling her lap. She rubs his head, runs her hands through his thick mane of hair. "Not you, baby – I'm talking about someone not nearly as nice. Anyway, Keith flew out to New Mexico to look at some land. He has this dream of quitting the show, buying a few horses and moving there permanently. He's checking out Arizona too. So far I'm the only one Mick's told, and he's sworn me to secrecy."

"How's Mick taking it?"

"Not well. He's been on *Sunlight and Shadow* longer than I have, and the fans adore him. Being out of the limelight is going to kill him."

"How about you? Since the two of you are married,

both in the show and in real life, he'll probably want you to come along."

"Forget about it." She shudders. "The thought of moving out to the middle of a desert full of rattlesnakes and scorpions freaks me out. I'd be miserable. I'm just hoping this Wild West scenario turns out to be a passing fantasy."

"If he leaves, they'll have to write him out of the show, unless they recast him."

"Keith doesn't want that, and he's such a mainstay that he'll probably get his way. Chances are they'll write a story line that sends him off for an indefinite stay in some out-of-state prison, or maybe put him in a coma in a faraway nursing facility."

"Yeah, those are tried and true plot devices. Or they could always kill him off but have the body disappear. Knock him out, dump him in the river and have him swept downstream. Kind of a cliché, but that way they can always bring him back if Keith gets bored playing cowboy."

"I've got to admit I'd be relieved if he leaves. Ten years is a long time to be stuck with someone so possessive. And he's not exactly the most scintillating guy in the world. When it comes to music, theatre, anything in the arts, forget it. He'd much rather be spending all day at the gym, building up his beloved body."

"He does have an impressive physique. You've got to spend endless hours working out to get that massively ripped."

"It takes more than just time. He's upfront about the downers he takes, because it's blatantly obvious, but he denies taking body-building drugs, although I'm positive he is. Better living through chemistry."

"I remember you told me about that. Steroids, testosterone, that kind of thing. Right?"

"Yes, and human growth hormones. You know – the whole Lance Armstrong trip."

"That stuff is bad news. It can really wreak havoc on your system, not to mention triggering unpredictable outburst of rage."

"I'm well aware of that, Jonah. And his anger seems to be getting more intense – especially since you arrived on the scene."

"I know. He's not exactly subtle."

"Promise you'll stay clear of him."

"I can't very well promise that – it depends on what the writers have in mind for us. But don't worry, I can handle him."

Sirius stretches, then rises and heads for the kitchen, whining. "He's telling us something," Abby says.

"Yes, he's reminding me it's high time I cooked those filets mignons. They've probably marinated long enough."

As I rise, my Galaxy trills its jazzy incoming call message. "Damn!" I exclaim. "Who could be bugging me at this hour?" I rummage in my pocket, pull out the phone and check the screen. The number is unfamiliar.

"I'd better take it," I tell Abby, who's shooting me an inquisitive look. "Practically no one has this number. Probably someone dialed it by mistake, but I should make sure."

"Is this Mark Westgate?" The female voice is low and melodious.

"Who wants to know?"

She laughs. "This is Gloria Kemp."

"You're putting me on. Really, who is this?"

"It's really me. Chuck Winslow gave me your private number. I'm sorry to call so late, but I need to talk to you. Is this a good time? Am I interrupting anything?"

The voice has the middle Atlantic non-accent cultivated by TV reporters. Could it really be Gloria Kemp, my arch-nemesis? The woman who may well destroy daytime drama? Curiosity gets the better of me. "I'm kind of busy," I say, "but I guess I can spare a few minutes."

As I stroll toward the bedroom with Sirius dogging my steps, I grin at Abby and hold up my hand in a five-minute sign. Silently I mouth the name – Gloria Kemp – but I can tell she doesn't get it.

By the time I hang up and return to the living room, Abby is gone.

Chapter Seventeen

I check the kitchen, the bathroom – nothing. Abby is definitely gone. My talk with Gloria ran longer than I expected, and I must have lost track of time. My watch reads 9:30. Let's see, when did Gloria call? My Galaxy tells me it was 9:05 – nearly half an hour. Small wonder Abby was annoyed. Still, walking out seems a bit over the top.

I'm willing to bet she was eavesdropping. That's practically de rigueur on soaps, so deeply ingrained in most of us that we tend to carry the habit into our off-screen lives. Anyway, how could she help it? The bedroom door was wide open, and I made no effort to lower my voice. It's not as if I had anything to hide, but Abby must have heard my enthusiasm when Gloria convinced me she was truly who she claimed, the warmth in my tone as we chatted about the latest goings-on at the network. She certainly heard me confirm the name and location of the restaurant where I'll meet Gloria for lunch tomorrow. Before her new show starts, she wants to pick my brain about what's been going on at QMA. Especially the murders, of course. She didn't broach the topic, but she's a journalist, so how could she resist? The place is vegetarian, totally off my radar screen, but Gloria's on some kind of purification diet to slim down for her new show.

At the thought of lunch, my stomach growls. By now I'm truly ravenous, and those filets mignons in the kitchen are singing their siren song. In hopes that Abby is still nearby and that I can talk her into coming back, I jab her contact number on my Galaxy, but the call goes straight to voice mail.

"Abby, I'm sorry I lost track of time," I say. "I'm about to cook those filets, and I hope you'll come back and join me." Too proud to beg, I leave it at that. But speaking of begging, Sirius is bouncing around my legs, looking at me, then at the kitchen, and emitting little yelps.

I lean down and let him lick my face. "Okay, you lucky dog. Abby's probably pissed and I doubt if she'll come back, so I'll share with you. You deserve it – I know you'd never abandon me the way she did. But it'll be awhile. I need to preheat the broiler. Then I'll shove them right up under the flame, so they're seared on the outside, bloody rare on the inside."

I retrieve the steaks in their Pyrex dish from the high shelf where I've stashed them out of Sirius's reach, and turn them in the marinade. As the wine-dark liquid drips from the meat, he sniffs, licks his lips, and whines piteously.

"You're right, guy. These are going to be fabulous. In fact they'll probably be even more fabulous if we eat them right now. The hell with cooking."

I settle down onto the floor, cross my legs, and place the dish in front of me. "Sirius, sit," I say. Quivering with expectation, he obeys, and we pause for a few beats. Then I give him the release command: "Okay." He lunges for his filet and I follow suit. Our faces and hands dripping with bloody juices, we wolf down the meat.

By one the next afternoon, waiting for Gloria Kemp at the vegetarian place, I'm ravenous again. Those filets mignons were only about ten ounces each, not nearly enough to sate the carnivore blood lust that so suddenly overwhelmed me. The menu here is utterly devoid of meat. I should know – I've had half an hour to study it.

I've damped down my hunger pangs with a juice concoction the color of pea soup. Called Emerald Ecstasy, it combines collards, kale, spinach, arugula, parsley and basil. Not half bad, actually, especially since I ordered it spiked with a double shot of Grey Goose vodka. I hope Gloria won't be able to smell the liquor on my breath.

I was totally blind-sided last night when she called to invite me to lunch. Purely professional, she said: she was feeling guilty about bumping *Sunlight and Shadow* back from its usual time slot to make way for her new talk show. Why me, I asked, but she played it coy. "I'd rather tell you in person," she said. "It'll be my treat. I hope you don't mind vegetarian. I'm trying to lose a few pounds before the show starts next week."

"No problem," I said. I didn't mention the steaks marinating in the kitchen, or the delectable woman coming to a boil in the living room as I ignored her and chatted with Gloria. After devouring the steak, I called Abby repeatedly, left increasingly abject messages, but she never returned my calls. I can't say I blame her.

So here I am, sipping Emerald Ecstasy and hoping I'll recognize Gloria when she walks in. It's been over a year since a rival network bounced her from her prime time news anchor gig, and I generally avoid network news anyway – I prefer getting my news online from *The Huffington Post* or *The Daily Beast*. As I recall, she had auburn hair styled in a no-nonsense page.

"Hi, Mark, I'm delighted to meet you. I've been a fan forever." A smashing redhead is grinning down at me, extending her hand for a shake.

"Thanks so much," I say, enfolding her hand in both of mine. "My fans mean the world to me." I'm being sincere – my career would have been in the toilet years ago if it weren't for my fans, and I always make a point of treating them graciously, whether they call me Mark,

Jonah or Jeremy.

The redhead removes her tinted glasses and fixes me with brilliant green eyes. Her grin widens. "You don't recognize me, do you?"

Shit! I hate it when people pull this guessing game, because I almost invariably flunk. I meet hundreds, maybe thousands, of people every year, and if they meet me again they somehow expect me to miraculously conjure up all the whos, whens and wheres. "You look familiar, but you'll have to remind me," I say.

"Ha! Gotcha! I'm your lunch date. Gloria Kemp."

I rise and offer my hand. Her shake is warm but businesslike. "Delighted to meet you, Gloria," I say. "Sorry, I should have recognized you. Especially your voice, after our talk last night."

"Don't apologize. I changed my voice just now. I've been playing around with disguises these past few months while I've been out of the public eye. I enjoy going incognito." She runs her fingers through her mass of flaming curls. "This is what my hair looks like when I let it go wild and don't dye it. And this green is my natural eye color — they used to make me wear blue contacts."

"You look much better au naturel," I say. No need to tell her I've got only the vaguest notion of what she looked like before.

"Emerald Ecstasy," I say as we take our seats.

"Pardon me?"

"That's what I'm drinking." I don't mention the vodka, nor do I say the name is better suited to her eyes than to the drink. That would be far too smarmy.

She scans the menu, orders the Crimson Crescendo. "And add a shot of Stoli," she tells the waiter.

"The vodka makes the beet juice more palatable," she says once he's gone. "Though the pomegranate, cranberry and strawberry help too. They juice everything to order here. Are you into juicing?"

"Mark has a juicer, but I'm not really into it. It takes too long, and I don't have the patience."

She tilts her head, gives me a quizzical stare. "Don't tell me you're one of those actors who refers to himself in the third person?"

"No, I find people who do that unbearably affected." She thinks I'm Mark Westgate, I realize. That's who she invited to lunch, after all. I decide I'd better play along, at least for now. "This morning I was shooting a scene as Jonah, and they'll want me back by three. I've played Jonah for so long, I tend to immerse myself in his role. It's easier if I stay in character all day."

"I totally understand. When I'm working, I stay in role all day too."

"In role? Aren't you just being yourself?"

She laughs. "The self you see on TV isn't necessarily my real self. It's a persona I don on demand. The Gloria who's pert and perky – that's what everyone expects, so that's what I give them. At least I did until they made me a primetime anchor; then they told me to curb my enthusiasm and dial it down a couple of notches. I tried, but I didn't feel authentic, and the audience could tell. The powers that be said I lacked the gravitas to handle world news. In retrospect, they were right to let me go."

"Let you go? I thought you made the decision to quit."

She giggles. "That was the official story, but no, after the first six months the die was cast. I was relieved, actually, and I was amazed how much better I felt once the gig was over. Immersing myself in all the woes of the world day after day was absolutely horrible. I didn't fully realize it at the time, but I was heading toward full-blown clinical depression. But now that I've had all those months of R and R, I've realized being a lady of leisure doesn't suit me. I've been climbing the walls, and when QMA offered me this new show, I jumped at the opportunity."

I lean across the table and gaze into her eyes. "This is all very fascinating, but I'm curious — why did you invite me to lunch? You said you felt guilty about bumping us out of the time slot we've had forever, but I still don't know why you picked me in particular."

A blush creeps from her neck to her cheeks, and I wonder for the first time if she's here to hit on me. The possibility has a certain appeal. I hold her gaze, waiting.

"Your Crimson Crescendo, Madame." Her cheeks blush deeper still as the waiter places an enormous goblet in front of her. She raises her glass, takes a tentative sip. "Mmm, delicious," she pronounces, as I raise my glass to hers. We clink a silent toast.

"Emerald and crimson," she says with a giggle. "What a brilliant combination. Very Christmasy."

"Yes, the complementary colors really vibrate against each other." I lean forward, rest my chin on my tented fingers and zero in on her eyes once more. They're a remarkable green, the green of a summer's day.

"So why did I choose you to talk to," she says, picking up on the conversational thread I'd almost forgotten. "Out of all the men on the show, you're the most fundamentally decent. There are several romantic leading man types, but they're all morally compromised, if not downright criminal. You're the only one I feel I can truly trust. And you're a wonderful listener. So much empathy, it's marvelous. The way you've been there for Abby when she's needed someone to talk to — "

"Hold it right there, Gloria. That's just the way the writers are spinning my character. Believe me, I'm not all sweetness and light."

"Oh, I know. You're a man of many facets, many

moods. I remember when you played that vampire, Jeremy Lowell – god, you were hot." Her eyes are aglow, her lips parted. Then suddenly she shivers and shrinks back away from me, her arms folded defensively across her chest. "Listen to me – I sound like a star-struck fan."

"That's okay. That's what I thought you were when you first came in."

"Whereas actually I came here to talk about our respective shows, and how they interface. And I'll admit I'm a little freaked out by those recent murders of people associated with *Brand New You*. If somebody's targeting afternoon talk shows, what if I'm next in their line of fire?"

"I doubt you will be. You seem like one of those inherently good people it's impossible to hate, let alone kill."

"Oh, you'd be surprised. This business is so full of backbiting and animosity, no one is exempt." She leans forward, her eyes aglow. "Mark, what do you think of those stories that the victims were drained of blood, vampire-style? Is that the truth, or is it just rumors?"

I pause, unsure how much to reveal. Her eyes are so wide, so brimming with sincerity and concern, that I'm tempted to unburden myself completely. "I can see why you've got such a great reputation as an interviewer," I say. "It's hard to resist that penetrating gaze of yours. But you probably know as much about it as I do, which is approximately zilch."

"But you must be an expert on vampires, having played one so effectively."

"Not really. I was just following the script they gave me."

She leans back, takes another sip of her Crimson Crescendo. "Okay, have it your way. But remember I cut my teeth as an investigative reporter long before I became a TV star, and when I sense a good story, I'm like a dog with a bone. I don't give up."

"I get it, Gloria. Tell you what, I'll give you a scoop, on condition you keep it to yourself for now. I'm a prime suspect in the murders of Gene Gentry and Jeff Herbert. A person of interest, as they say."

Her eyes widen even more, and her jaw drops. "No! I don't believe it!"

"It's ridiculous, I know. But you're bound to hear the rumor sooner or later, so I thought I should be the first to tell you."

"Thanks for sharing that, Mark. I know it can't be easy, being so forthcoming about something that touches you so personally."

I crack up laughing. "Forget it, Gloria. I'm not going to succumb to your charms as an interviewer. Save that sympathy shtick for the cancer victims and the 500-pound women."

"Touché." She giggles. "Okay, I'll back off, but I'd like to keep the lines of communication open. I'd like you to be my informal liaison, keep me abreast of what's going on. And I can do the same for you."

"That's an intriguing proposition, but are you sure? There are people who might suit your purposes better. I've only been on the show a couple of weeks, and a lot of people still see me as an interloper."

"I'm sure plenty of people see me that way too." She reaches across the table, covers my hand with hers. "Come on, Mark. I'm not asking for much – I just need someone I can talk to at QMA. Someone who's not involved with my show, but who's close enough to know what's going on. Someone I can dish the dirt with, who I can take into my confidence. We could meet maybe once a week after work, have dinner."

"Would it always have to be here?"

She takes another sip of her Crimson Crescendo, scrunches up her lips in distaste. "God, no. Once the show's underway, I'll need something more substantial to keep my energy up – a good steak, for example."

"In that case, you're on." I take out my Galaxy and bring up the calendar. "How's Tuesday?"

But her attention has wandered. She's looking somewhere over my shoulder, and I swivel to follow her gaze.

Abby is standing behind me. Her dark eyes shoot daggers.

Chapter Eighteen

I spring from my chair, feeling totally flummoxed. "Abby! What a surprise! I'd like you to meet Gloria Kemp."

Abby forces a patently phony smile and gives Gloria's outstretched hand a perfunctory shake. "So, Gloria. What an honor to meet the woman who's about to take over the time slot *Sunlight and Shadow* has had for thirty years."

Gloria responds with a grin that projects ingenuous delight and promises instant friendship. I'm dazzled by all those brilliant white teeth. She hasn't yet favored me with that smile, and I realize she's shifted into her on-camera persona. "Delighted to meet you, Ms. – " She pauses, glances at me, and I fill the awkward silence with the proper introductions.

Gloria graciously invites Abby to join us for lunch, but she declines, citing her need to get back to the studio. I know she's lying – she doesn't have any scenes today, or for the rest of the week, for that matter – but I don't call her bluff, and I'm relieved when she flounces away.

"What a beautiful woman," Gloria says. "I take it she's your love interest on the show?"

I pull my best poker face. "No, not yet anyway. She's married to someone else."

"Ah, but there's something between you, I can tell. It probably won't be long. The two of you make a great-looking couple, and isn't that what soaps are all about? Love triangles?"

"Among other things."

I manage to steer the conversation in a more neutral direction. The next couple of hours pass in a pleasant blur, fueled by more Stoli-spiked Emerald Ecstasies, Crimson Crescendos and mysterious vegan concoctions. We find a lot to talk about, yet all the while I'm conscious of keeping myself in check. Gloria's an investigative journalist, after all. She told me she still likes to scout out big stories – and I've got a doozy.

When we say our goodbyes outside the restaurant, she still doesn't know I'm Jonah, not Mark. Against my better judgment, we agree to meet next week. Then I speed-dial Abby's number, but the call goes straight to voice mail. Just as well, because I'm feeling pretty pissed at her, and if we got to talking, I'd probably chew her out for coming on so hostile at lunch. Instead I leave a terse, value-neutral message asking her to call. Abby's a married woman, after all. She shouldn't be coming off all jealous and possessive because I'm having a strictly professional lunch date.

All at once I remember: I've got an entire week ahead of me, free and clear. When Abby said Mick had two weeks off, I told her it was no big deal, that it happens all the time. But my situation is different. It's worrisome that Chuck and Harvey are giving me time off so soon after I got here, and that Chuck told me only two days ago. I wonder if it has anything to do with the murders on *Brand New You,* and if they're getting their orders from the higher-ups.

What the hell am I going to do for a whole week away from the set? At the thought of all those empty days yawning ahead, I feel a sharp pang of anxiety. Even worse, what if the powers-that-be order me killed off? Chuck and Harvey have had my back for years, and I trust them more than anyone else I know, but in this business, that's not saying much. I haven't a clue what they have in mind for my story line, and what with all the brouhaha about the recent murders, and me being a person of interest, they may decide I'm more of a liability than an asset. Or the people over their heads may give them an ultimatum.

On the other hand, the press, and especially the online blogs and gossip columns, are having a field day with the story. No arrests have been made, and the weird nature of the killings has made for juicy headlines. Vampires stalking talk shows, bloody-awful daytime drama – there are countless ways to spin the murders of Gene Gentry and Jeff Herbert. *Brand New You* ratings are skyrocketing, and since our show comes on right after, that has to be boosting our ratings too. If Chuck and Harvey boot anyone off the show, that would arouse suspicion, wouldn't it? Or would it simply create more of the buzz their bosses crave?

It's barely an hour since lunch, and already my stomach is in an uproar. Too many goddamn vegetables, and all those soybeans masquerading as meat. Once they power their way through my intestines, I'm not going to be fit for polite company. Farting is one of the many bodily functions you won't hear about in daytime drama, and it's not exactly welcome in real life either. I wonder if Gloria is having similar problems right about now.

At the thought of Gloria, more pleasurable bodily sensations start kicking in. Next week's dinner date seems a long way away. I'm tempted to call, invite her to get together tomorrow – but no, that's a terrible idea. She's delightful company, but she's far too clever and inquisitive, and she has a way of parting her lips and widening those huge green eyes that invites the sharing of true confessions. As for Abby, she's trouble too, what with that beefy behemoth of a husband who'd love nothing better than to tear me limb from limb. Best to keep clear of both women for now, and of everyone else, for that matter. Sirius is plenty of company, and one of his many virtues is his inability to talk.

Unfortunately, his hair speaks volumes, and the crime scene techs are bound to have bagged some of those long black strands at the crime scene. Aside from Abby and Tony, probably no one at the show knows of his existence. But what about people in the apartment, people who've seen me walking him around the neighborhood? I have no idea if the police have zeroed in on Mark's building yet, but it's only a matter of time. So how can I walk Sirius? His very presence could incriminate me. No more strolls along Riverside Drive, no ambling through Central Park – especially not Central Park. I've been checking the papers, and the deaths of those two thugs seem to have dropped off the radar. But even if we wait till well past the midnight hour, we're bound to encounter someone. After all, this is Manhattan, the city that never sleeps.

Maybe it's time to split, get out of town for a few days. God knows I need to clear my head. Complete and utter solitude would do me a world of good. No one to impress, no one looking over my shoulder or ordering me around. I flash back to the Zen Mountain Monastery up in the Catskills, west of Woodstock. Mark went there one weekend a couple of years ago. As I recall, he liked the code of silence, the anonymity, but the hours of sitting zazen, cross-legged on a black cushion on the floor, not to mention the Spartan diet consisting primarily of brown rice, drove him up the wall. I'm not that ascetic, and anyway they probably don't allow dogs.

Then there was that cabin up in the Adirondacks, the one that belonged to an actor who said Mark could use it any time. He went there last fall to ogle the foliage. The place was out in the middle of nowhere, a scaled down version of those old Victorian lodges well-off Manhattanites built as retreats from the summer heat, sequestered in a pine forest on the edge of a smallish lake. Yes, that would do very nicely, but can I find it? Mark's so obsessively well organized, he probably has the directions on file in that cabinet next to his desk. I could rent a car . . .

A couple of hours later I'm cruising west over the George Washington Bridge in a Prius, Sirius riding shotgun by my side. We head north on the Palisades Parkway, then onto the Thruway, and I feel the tension draining away with every mile. I've brought a handful of Mark's jazz CDs, and Coltrane is wailing his heart out on *A Love Supreme.* Sirius looks dubious; his ears are swiveling and he's whining a little, but he settles down when I crack the window and he sniffs the country air.

It's almost midnight by the time we reach the cabin. I walk Sirius, find the key right where I had a hunch it would be, beneath a rock under one of the pines that ring the yard. Once inside, I make a beeline for the liquor cabinet in the kitchen, grab a bottle of bourbon, plop onto a saggy sofa and take a few swigs. Within a few minutes, I'm out, and for the next nine hours, I sleep the proverbial sleep of the dead.

I awaken to the rough wet warmth of Sirius's tongue caressing my face. The sun is streaming in like butterscotch, as Joni Mitchell would say, but this is no Chelsea morning. Instead I'm up here in the middle of nowhere. Still, I'm feeling more rested than I have for ages, and Sirius is bouncing and whimpering, begging for a walk, so we set out to explore the property. He stays close to my side until he realizes I've left him unleashed, then gives me an incredulous stare and bolts off into the woods.

At this point I could launch into a long digression about the wonders of the untamed wilderness, the pristine beauty of the spring-fed lake, and the songs of birds celebrating the coming of spring, but to be honest, that kind of descriptive writing bores me. If I forced myself to wax poetic about the great outdoors, I'd probably either put myself to sleep or drive myself to drink. Besides, when have you ever seen people on soaps just hanging out ogling the landscape? So I'll leave you to fill in the details. Everybody's spent time in the woods, so use your imagination.

Since describing Mother Nature doesn't do that much for me, I'll fast-forward to four days later. It's another sunny spring day, and I'm climbing the walls, bored out of my mind. Sirius is in heaven, but how many squirrels can you chase before you become weary of the hunt? An infinite number, apparently, though no doubt it's the same handful of squirrels over and over again. He never catches them, but that doesn't dampen his enthusiasm, and he keeps on trying.

Now I know for sure: unlike Thoreau, I'm not a solitary cabin-in-the-woods kind of guy. I've lived in cities all my life, and I've always had plenty of people around. I ask you: how many scenes have you seen in soaps where a single character just sits around and does nothing, or takes a quiet, uneventful walk in the country? Once in a while you might get a soliloquy, where a character muses aloud, Shakespeare style, but it never lasts more than a minute. Or they might read a letter out loud if it contains information that advances the plot, but that's about it. You never see someone meditating or doing their morning yoga routine, not unless someone bursts in and interrupts them after a few seconds. The writers and directors can't abide wasting air time with solitary silence.

Neither can I, as it turns out, even if it's the kind of fresh spring mountain air that poets love to rhapsodize about. The first day was fine, I got to relax and chill out, but one day is more than enough. In prison, the worst thing they can do is put someone in solitary confinement, cut them off from all but the most minimal human contact. You get your meals shoved through a metal slot in the door, and if you behave yourself, you might get fifteen closely supervised minutes in a walled recreation yard ringed with barbed wire. It's nothing like the jails you see on *Sunlight and Shadow* and kindred soaps, where there's plenty of space between the bars, the better to show the actors' faces, and visitors can waltz in and out at will. They call it stir crazy for a reason. If I'm stuck in this cabin for one more single solitary day, I'll go stark raving mad.

Now if Abby were here, that would be another ball game entirely. I know she's off this week, and presumably Mick is still out in New Mexico. Or maybe I should give Gloria a call – I have the feeling she'd come running, probably in a black chauffeur-driven car with discreetly tinted windows. But no, I promised myself I'd stay clear of her. She's too smart, too savvy a reporter, and I have a hunch her lust for a juicy scoop would trump any lust she might harbor for me.

No, Abby is a better choice. True, she's got that enormous thug of a husband who hates my guts, but Mick Hastings is away in the not so wild west, and even if Keith Carlton, the actor who portrays him, decides to come back early, I'd rather face off with Mick than have Gloria feature me in an exposé on national TV.

For the first time since I left the city, I switch on my Galaxy, but of course there's no signal. Hardly surprising, out here in the boonies. Resisting the urge to smash my phone and grind it into the floor, I decide to drive down out of the woods until I can find a signal and reach Abby. I go to the cabin door and whistle for Sirius, who comes bounding joyfully out of the woods. As always, he's up for anything.

"Hey, boy," I say. "Want to go for a car ride?"

He barks ecstatically, races to the car and starts pawing the door.

"Sirius, down! No scratching – this car is a rental."

He obeys and sinks into a sit, but he's panting and trembling with excitement. I give him a good scratch behind the ears. "Hey, dog, how would you like a visitor? Remember Abby?"

He probably has no idea what I'm talking about, but his ears perk up and he gives me that expectant, bright-eyed stare he uses when he thinks I'm going to feed him some people food. I open the door of the Prius and he jumps in.

"So," I say as I start the engine. "Maybe all that squirrel chasing was only occupational therapy. Maybe you're just like me – we've both got a bad case of cabin fever."

God, I hope Abby picks up.

Chapter Nineteen

What a difference a day makes! It's the next morning, Abby is by my side, and all at once this lakeside hideaway in the North Country is the most romantic spot in the world. Overtly, nothing's changed – the towering pines, so dark a green that they're almost black, surrounding the rustic cabin, the lake sparkling in the morning sun – but I'm seeing things in a whole new light.

Maybe it's just that I'm seeing them through Abby's eyes. She's been rhapsodizing about the place since she pulled up in her rented Focus hatchback an hour ago, and her enthusiasm is infectious. We've been strolling hand in hand like young lovers, with Sirius running delirious circles around us as I show her the sights I've been too oblivious to notice over the past four days. There's a certain awkwardness between us, and so far we've kept to innocuous small talk. We've sidestepped the big questions: what about Mick? What about those murders and the police investigation? And above all: is this the day we become lovers at last?

She pulls her hand away. "We need to talk," she says, and the edge in her voice tells me this may not be the day after all. I remind myself it's probably better that way. I must have been out of my mind to invite her here. Making love would take things to a whole new level and unleash passion I'm not at all sure I could control. What if Jeremy took over and blood lust triumphed over the good old-fashioned romantic variety?

"You're right, we should talk," I say. "Let's go sit by

the water." I lead her down to a little clearing that overlooks the lake. We sink into two well-weathered Adirondack chairs that have probably been here for decades.

She turns to me, her eyes narrowed. "So, Jonah. It seems like you really hit it off with Gloria."

I sigh in relief. Right now, Gloria seems like the least of my worries. "We found we had a lot of things to talk about," I say with a smile. "I felt weird about hobnobbing with the enemy, but she's really not all that bad."

"It looked to me as if the two of you had a lot of chemistry going. She's a very attractive woman."

I laugh. "Funny, she said almost the exact same thing about us after you left. She asked if you were my love interest on the show, and when I said not yet, she said it probably wouldn't take long. I told her you were married, and she asked me if it wasn't true that love triangles are what soaps are all about."

A blush creeps up her neck and into her cheeks. "So what did you tell her?"

"I said soaps are about lots of things, not just romantic conflicts. Then I changed the subject. But speaking of love triangles, what's happening with Mick? Have you talked with him?"

"A couple of times. But you know Mick. He's so terse, and he's not big on phone conversations. Actually it was kind of frustrating. You'd think by this time I'd be able to read him – he's my husband, after all – but he's so damn uncommunicative, it drives me up the wall. Keith Carlton's just as bad, and when I mention Keith, Mick goes ballistic."

"That's kind of counterproductive. If Keith weren't playing him, Mick wouldn't exist."

"I know. Just as I wouldn't exist if Catherine Reynolds stopped playing me. Mick's terrified Keith may actually quit. If he does, it would be curtains for Mick."

"When's he coming back from New Mexico?"

"He's scheduled to resume shooting in eight days, so he'll have to be back by then, but Keith wants to take another week. He says there's some more land he still wants to look at."

"So he's really serious about moving out there?"

"Maybe, but with Keith you never know – he's as tight-lipped as Mick. This could just be a ploy to drive up his price when they negotiate a new contract."

"But Mick must have told you. You're his wife, after all."

She frowns. "What can I say? He's got major trust issues. And Keith's even worse – he doesn't tell Catherine anything. Believe it or not, their supposedly real-life marriage is even worse than mine with Mick. That's why we've virtually taken over our actors. But can we change the subject?"

"Sure, what do you want to talk about – the murder investigation? We might as well get it over with. What's happening? Have they made any progress?"

"Not that I'm aware of, but I wouldn't know. I've been away from the studio, and I've gone out of the way to avoid looking at any newspapers. I've even managed to stay off Facebook and the Internet."

"Me too. But it's easier up here in the boonies, where I don't really have a choice."

She drags her chair closer to mine. Her expression is softer now. "I don't think I could stand the isolation. At least in the city I had plenty of distractions. I played the piano a lot, meandered around Barney's and Bloomingdales, walked in Central Park. I love this time of year, when everything's leafing out and coming into bloom. The azaleas, the apple and cherry trees – they're magnificent."

"You mean you can actually tell an apple tree from a cherry tree? I'm impressed." I move my chair so that we're sitting knee to knee.

"Well, not really. I'm just guessing. I haven't spent that much time out in nature. Anyway, the city's full of blossoming trees right now, mostly in shades of pink and white. It feels really festive compared to this place. All these pines are magnificent, but it feels a little gloomy and lugubrious."

"More than a little, I'm afraid. With every day that passes, I'm finding it more and more oppressive." I lean forward and take both her hands in mine. The soft warmth of the contact sends an electric charge coursing through my body.

"Small wonder," she says. "It's so shady. Have you spent much time out in the sun, or gone out on the water?"

"No, I'm not big on sunlight. I'm more of a night owl by nature, and I don't want to get premature wrinkles."

"Neither do I. I love the sun, but with my fair skin, I burn rather than tan, so I always slather on sunscreen. Look at the lake, the way the water's sparkling. I suppose it's way too early for swimming, though."

"Yes, I followed Sirius down to the shore because he wanted to check out the water. But he's not a water dog by nature, and he was in and out in less than a minute. Then he shook himself off all over me. I got soaked."

She laughs. "I'd love to have seen that. You'd look pretty hot in wet jeans." She rises, and I follow suit. She pulls her hands away from mine, runs them lightly over my hips. All at once we're in each other's arms, locked in a wordless dance. She rises onto her toes, grinds her body against mine, making me gasp. We're both breathing harder now. I cup her face in my hands, lean down to kiss her – and Sirius crashes against us with so much force, he practically knocks us off our feet.

I whirl. "Down, Sirius! Bad dog!" I turn to Abby. "I'm sorry, I don't know what's gotten into him. I've never seen him act like this before. Are you okay?"

"I'm fine. But maybe he thought I was attacking you, and wanted to protect his master."

I glare at Sirius. He's bouncing and wagging, smiling wolfishly. "No, I think he just wants to play. This probably looks like some new kind of game to him."

She laughs. "Or maybe he's jealous. Far be it from me to come between a man and his best friend."

"He'll just have to get used to it." I reach for her again, but she tenses at my touch. The moment has passed, and we both feel it.

She steps back, widening the distance between us, and busies herself by running her fingers through the thick ruff of hair on the dog's neck. He twists his head back and starts licking her hand with his purplish black tongue. She giggles. "Ooh, that feels so sensual."

I stifle a sudden urge to caress the smooth skin of her throat with my own tongue, to savor the scent and taste of her. Or better still, to kiss and nibble her neck. No, wait – that's dangerously blurring the boundaries. I step back, away from her.

She frowns. "Jonah, what's wrong? Why are you so uptight all of a sudden?"

"I'm afraid coaxing you to come up here was a mistake."

"Why on earth would you say that? I didn't need any coaxing, I came of my own free will."

"I know, but I'm not sure if I can trust my own impulses."

Abby gives Sirius a final scratch behind the ears, picks up a pine cone and tosses it toward the woods. "Go on, boy. Go play and give us some privacy." He races off after the prize, and a startled squirrel scrambles across his path. As he takes off in hot pursuit, she moves toward me and twines her arms around my neck. My breath quickens as I inhale the intoxicating scent of her. "Speaking of impulses," she murmurs, "why keep fighting them? Let's stop second-guessing ourselves and go inside."

"I'd love to, but first let me explain. I want you –"

She presses her body to mine. "That's obvious."

I feel myself hardening, and I groan. "It's not sexual impulses I'm worried about, it's what's been happening when feelings trump reason and I lose control."

"You mean when Jeremy takes over."

"Exactly."

"But that's about anger and rage. I'm talking about love –" She bites off the word, blushes furiously.

I grin. "Don't tell me you're embarrassed about using the L word."

Her skin takes on an even rosier hue. "I was talking about love as an emotion in a general sense, not about us in particular."

"Whatever. You know, you're even more beautiful when you blush. The way your blood rushes to your skin – but that's exactly what I'm afraid of. Admiring the curve of your neck a little while ago, it was all I could do not to take a bite."

"A little love nip? What's the big deal?"

"The other night in my apartment, when I bit down on your lip, you practically freaked out. Told me you weren't into S&M."

She smiles. "I've been thinking it over, and I realize I overreacted. I wouldn't know whether I'm into S&M or not, since I've never tried it. But I trust you not to hurt me."

"I hope I deserve your trust." Eying her neck again, I feel a pang of hunger. "Abby, I haven't eaten today," I say. "I just realized I've got a ravenous appetite."

Her stomach gurgles loudly, and we both crack up laughing. She glances at her watch. "Nearly three o'clock. No wonder my tummy's raising a ruckus. I'm ravenous too."

"Sorry, I'm a terrible host. The thought of lunch totally slipped my mind."

She grabs my hand. "Let's go inside and rustle up some grub."

"I'm afraid there's not much grub to rustle."

At the sight of us heading for the house, Sirius comes bounding out of the woods and greets us with ecstatic yips.

I sigh. "Damn, I'm out of dog food."

"Maybe we should go shopping," Abby says. "How far is the nearest store?"

"There's a store about ten miles away," I say. "They have the bare basics – dog food, corned beef hash, beef jerky, stuff like that."

She refrains from saying "Eeuw," but she scrunches up her face in distaste.

"Or if we drive to Loon Lake, I understand there are a few decent stores. A gourmet deli, a bakery, a liquor store. They cater to the tourist trade. I haven't been there, but we could check it out.

"Fantastic! Let's go," she says.

Minutes later we're in the Prius, heading for Loon Lake. Perched precariously on the back seat, Sirius isn't happy that Abby's usurped the shotgun position at my side, but he compensates by craning forward and licking our necks.

By five, we're back in the Adirondack chairs, watching the sun set over the lake and gorging on Brie, Stilton, pate and assorted delicacies, washing them down with wines from Finger Lakes vineyards. Before long we're thoroughly sated, not to mention soused. As dusk deepens into darkness, mosquitos descend on us. We swat them away ineffectually.

Dusky forms skitter above. "I wonder what kind of birds those are," Abby mumbles. By now we're both sleepy, slurring our words.

"Actually, they're bats," I say.

She shudders. "Ugh, how creepy. They carry rabies, don't they? What if they bite us?"

"Don't worry, they're just interested in wolfing down insects. They're actually doing us a favor. They won't bite – you're thinking of vampire bats, from South America."

"But the mosquitos are still biting, and I'm getting cold," she says. "Let's go inside and build a fire in the fireplace."

"Sounds good to me."

When I shove myself out of my chair, everything goes suddenly spinny, and it's a struggle to regain my balance. "Jeez, how much did we drink?"

She wobbles to her feet. Swaying, she counts the empty bottles on the grass. "Four bottles – that's at least two too many. I'm afraid I'm going to be sick."

"Try not to think about it. Let's go inside, and you can lie down and take a nap on the sofa while I build a fire."

We stagger back to the house as Sirius runs circles around us. Once inside, Abby collapses onto the enormous ramshackle sofa by the fireplace. Within minutes she's asleep and softly snoring. I find a scruffy old Hudson Bay blanket to shield her from the chill, but as I'm draping it over her, I'm overcome by the urge to lie down beside her. It's a tight fit, but it works if we snuggle together, spoon-fashion. She murmurs softly as I climb over and slide my body against hers, then wrap my arms around her. Who needs a fire? Together, we're generating plenty of heat. Slowly, I sink into the stuporous slumber of the well and truly drunk.

Later – how much later, I have no idea – I startle awake to the sound of Sirius's hysterical barking. The inky black of midnight surrounds us, penetrated only by the brilliant beam of a flashlight shining in my eyes, blinding me.

"Abby, my darling wife." Mick's voice is soft, almost a whisper. "I knew I'd find you here."

Chapter Twenty

I rip off the blanket and scramble off the sofa. It's a tricky maneuver, since I'm wedged in tight behind Abby, but I manage to make it to my feet.

"Hold it right there." Mick's voice is venomous. "Don't move or I'll shoot." He's pointing a gun at us, and it gleams in the beam of the flashlight. Is it an unloaded prop gun from the set? Somehow I doubt it, and I have no desire to find out.

With Sirius growling at her feet, Abby grabs the blanket and screens her body with the scratchy wool, then sits up. She's still fully dressed in her jeans and fleece pullover, but even so, the misguided gesture of modesty is somehow incriminating. "It's not what it looks like," she says.

Mick forces a strangled laugh. "Give me a break, Abby. I'm not buying that old cliché. It's been done to death."

"It happens to be true," she retorts. "I was exhausted and I fell asleep. I didn't even realize Jonah was next to me."

"She's right," I say. "Don't blame Abby. She was sound asleep when I lay down next to her."

Crouching, he lays the flashlight on the floor. With the beam illuminating him from below, he's a dead ringer for Frankenstein's monster. "So you seized the opportunity to take advantage of her."

"He did no such thing," she says. "We were just talking, and we had a little too much to drink. We were sampling wines from the Finger Lakes, and we wanted to try one from each vineyard. We got totally zonked. I felt like I was about to barf, so Jonah suggested I come in and lie down."

Mick shoots me a glare. "That's pretty sophomoric. You think this is some kind of frat house? Maybe you put a couple of roofies in the wine for good measure. I wouldn't put it past you to hit on Abby when she's practically comatose."

I've never heard Mick string this many sentences together. He's obviously wound up tight; the veins in his massive neck are bulging, and he's gnashing his teeth, but at least he's lowered the gun.

"I'm not comatose." Abby shakes her head as if to clear away the cobwebs. "In fact I'm feeling much better. That nap did me a lot of good."

Mick scowls. "How nice for you. Now maybe you've sobered up enough to tell me what the fuck you're doing up here with this creep in the middle of nowhere."

"I invited her," I say. "I was getting cabin fever, and I realized I wasn't cut out for the role of Thoreau."

His scowl intensifies, and I realize he probably doesn't have the foggiest idea who Thoreau is. I consider enlightening him, just to prolong the conversation in hopes he'll cool down, but a mini-lecture about a Transcendentalist philosopher in a cabin on Walden Pond probably wouldn't go down too well. Abby's told me he's sensitive about his lack of education, and I don't want to provoke him.

"You told me you weren't coming back for at least another week." Abby's voice is full of reproach.

"That's what Keith was planning, but Chuck Winslow called and told him they were willing to up the ante and sweeten his contract, so he decided to come back early. We start shooting on Monday."

Abby forces a smile. "That's great, but why didn't you tell me?"

"I wanted to surprise you. Obviously I succeeded."

"You certainly did. I didn't even hear you drive up," she says.

"I didn't exactly want to announce myself, so I parked the truck near the road and walked up the driveway."

She frowns. "How did you know where to find me?"

Mick clamps his giant paw of a hand on her shoulder and squeezes. "What's with the third degree? I'm the one who should be asking the questions, not you."

Wincing, Abby tries to wriggle out from under his grasp. He tightens his grip, and she emits a little yelp. Sirius growls and moves protectively to her side.

Mick takes a step back, then recovers and stands firm. "Get that damn mutt out of here."

He's obviously afraid of Sirius, and for good reason, but that's not necessarily a good thing. The hand holding the gun is trembling, and I wouldn't put it past him to shoot the dog. "Sirius, come," I command in my best alpha male voice. "Down."

Sirius comes to my side and subsides to the floor, but his hackles are up, his black hair bristling, and he's still growling. "Don't worry, that's just an act. He won't hurt you," I say, though I'm not at all sure what Sirius will do. After all, his chow ancestors were bred as temple guardians over thousands of years, and his German shepherd bloodlines make him an even more formidable aggressor.

"You still haven't explained how you found me," Abby says.

"Piece of cake. Paul Devane tailed you to the rental agency and stuck one of those little GPS gizmos on the underside of your car while you were finishing up the paperwork. I should think you could have sprung for something snazzier than a Ford. It's not good for your image."

"I wasn't thinking about my image. I haven't driven in a while, and I was afraid my skills were rusty. I wanted a sensible car that wouldn't intimidate me."

"No, you wanted something nondescript so you could stay anonymous."

Abby scowls. "That too. On the rare occasions I have time off, I like to fly under the radar. Anyway, how dare you spy on me? Our marriage has always been based on trust."

"Trust? Don't be ridiculous. I used to trust you, but you've been practically drooling over Jonah ever since he came on the show. Tony saw it too – he was the one who suggested we have Paul tail you."

"I might have known," Abby says. "Tony's always the one who comes up with the ideas." She's right, but this isn't exactly the brightest thing to say at such a fraught moment.

Sure enough, Mick goes red in the face and clenches his jaw even tighter. "I suspected you'd get it on with Jonah the minute I left town, and you proved me right."

"But Mick, nothing has happened between us. I haven't slept with Jonah, I swear it."

"You call this nothing? Spooning on the sofa, sound asleep? Don't give me that bullshit – obviously you've slept with him."

"Not the way you mean it!"

I can't resist chiming in. "Abby's right. It's a matter of semantics. The writers always have characters talking about sleeping with people, when what they really mean is having sex, which we didn't. It's a euphemism, so in a sense we did sleep together, but only literally, not figuratively. In other words–"

"God damn it, McQuarry, put a sock in it. You're sounding as bad as Devane. I can't stand that kind of pretentious gobbledegook."

I remind myself of the twelve-step slogan – *keep it simple, stupid.* With Mick, big words and run-on sentences are like a red flag to a bull. "Sorry," I say. "I swear on my father's grave, nothing happened between Abby and me."

"You don't have a father to swear on."

"I certainly do. He was a cop, and a great one."

"Whatever. Anyway, Abby's my lawfully wedded wife, and I'm taking her back to the city." He tightens his grip on her shoulder and starts steering her toward the door.

"Mick, no! I don't want to go with you!" She jerks away, catching him off guard, and rushes toward me. I open my arms to enfold her, but Mick pounces first, wrapping his massive arms around her waist and squeezing hard, like a lion bringing down prey. His right hand still clutches the gun.

"Let me go!" she shrieks.

"Like hell I will. You'll do what I say, you slut!"

Still screaming, she struggles frantically, trying to break free, but he's far too strong. Can I take him down? A muscle-bound gym rat, he outweighs me by a good fifty pounds, but I've got no choice.

The second I lunge, so does Sirius. I put a lock on Mick's right forearm, try to wrestle the gun from his hand. He shakes me off. Instantly Sirius sinks his fangs into his other arm, just above the wrist. Blood spurts out in an arc, and as it soaks my hand, the tangy scent reaches my nostrils. An adrenaline rush surges through me, with a strength more powerful than any I've known before.

Mick is screaming bloody murder, waving his gun around. In the glare of the fallen flashlight, his eyes burn with rage. "I'm going to kill you, motherfucker," he yells. The gun clicks as he cocks it. For a split second, his eyes dart between me and Sirius. He wants to kill us both, but who will he shoot first?

That second of uncertainty is all we need. Moving as one, Sirius and I tackle Mick and bring him to the floor. Across the room, Abby is screaming, and I realize there's no need to traumatize her by letting her witness what the dog and I are about to do. I fumble for the flashlight, click the switch. The room plunges into darkness.

Sirius and I don't need light. Touch, scent and taste are more than enough.

Chapter Twenty-One

I'll spare you a graphic description of what transpires next. You'd need night-vision goggles to see anything anyway, because the cabin's interior is swallowed up in darkness. I know there's a new moon because I saw its silvery crescent last night, but its feeble light is curtained by the dense black of the pines that surround the clearing on three sides. The darkness within the cabin is impenetrable.

I can, however, give you a sense of the soundtrack – first and foremost, Mick's screams. The word blood-curdling comes to mind, but the arterial blood that jets from his neck is much too warm and fresh to curdle. As I hunker down to drink, his screams gradually weaken, and before long they're replaced by groans and gurgles.

Sirius growls and whimpers with excitement. His furry body presses against my side as he slurps at the spurting blood, but then he realizes he'd better respect my alpha male status. In the pitch blackness I feel him shift away, back to the wound his fangs have already made in Mick's forearm. His prey utters a strangled scream and flails his arm in a frantic effort to shake off the dog, but his struggles only incite Sirius further. He growls in the guttural tone he uses when he's playing with one of his stuffed animal toys. I reach out to touch him, and sure enough, he's worrying at the arm, shaking it back and forth in glee, crouching in the classic downward- dog Yoga position. All the puppyish play I've found so delightful has actually been basic training for a genuine kill.

By now Abby's screams have escalated into full-blown hysteria. "Stop! Enough!" she shrieks. "You're killing him!"

"I've got no choice. He was going to shoot us."

"But Jonah, you do have a choice. You've won the fight, you can let him live."

"So he can get away and kill us later? Sorry, Abby. I don't think so."

"Please, Jonah!" Her screams segue into broken sobs. "You don't have to do this. I'm begging you – please stop. Call off your dog."

But Sirius is hunkered down, emitting slurping and sucking sounds. I'm as powerless to call him off as I am to call off the primordial hunter who's taken possession of my own psyche. "I can't stop," I mutter. "I've surrendered to a higher power."

"Bullshit! This isn't some goddamn AA meeting. You don't have to surrender your own power – it's not too late to reclaim it."

"You're wrong, Abby. It's far too late. I think you should go, get out of this cabin while you still can. Forget you were ever here, forget Mick was here. You didn't see anything, didn't hear anything."

"You're asking me to help cover up a murder?"

"It's not murder, it's self-defense. The guy was waving a cocked gun in my face, about to shoot me at pointblank range."

"And sucking the blood from his body – you call that self-defense too?"

"No. I don't know. But whatever it is, you should get out of here. I may be a lost cause, Abby, but you're not. I don't want to implicate you in all this craziness and drag you down with me. Please, just leave. Go back to the city, and I'll call you tomorrow."

"But what are you going to do?"

"About Mick? I don't know yet, but whatever it is,

you should stay out of it. The less you know, the better."

Mick is groaning now, gasping in deep agonal breaths that signal death is near at hand. Abby hears it too. She gropes her way across the room, kneels at my side and extends her hands, fumbling in the darkness like a blind person until she feels his face. Then she leans down, and I know she's kissing him, but where? The forehead? The lips? In the inky blackness of the room, it's impossible to tell. I reach over and touch her hair, then let my hand wander down to her shoulder.

She jerks away. "Don't touch me!" Her shriek is shrill, terrified.

I withdraw my hand. "Abby, it's okay. I'm not going to hurt you. I'd never hurt you in a million years, you know that."

"No, I don't know that, and neither do you. You have no idea what you're capable of. You're a ravening beast, as bad as Sirius." Her scream climbs suddenly higher. "Yecch! He licked my arm. He's going to kill me too!"

"No, he's not. He heard you call his name, that's all." I pray I'm right. Actually, I have no idea what Sirius might be capable of. Once he's sated himself on human blood, will he move on to flesh? What if the cover of darkness heightens his aggression?

Abby gasps. "Eeuw, now he's licking my hand. Jonah, make him stop!"

"Is he nipping you?"

"No, but he's slobbering like crazy. I can feel his drool on my skin. Or what if it's blood? Mick's blood? Oh God." She dissolves into broken sobs.

I grope blindly till my hand closes on the flashlight. "You'd better close your eyes," I tell her. "I'm going to turn on the light and see what's going on."

"Okay. Maybe it's not too late to save him."

Yeah, right. Dream on, Abby. I'm getting pretty

skilled at taking life, but I don't have the power to raise the dead. Silently I flip the switch and shine the beam on Mick's motionless body. He's well and truly dead, I can see at a glance. Even so, I place my fingers on his neck, checking for a pulse, but I feel no movement, only warmth and wetness. Still, the sight of his corpse is less gruesome than I'd expected. There's surprisingly little blood – Sirius and I have been fairly fastidious in our feasting. Sated, the dog lies quietly, licking his paws.

Abby is cowering on the floor, cradling her head in her hands and awaiting my verdict. "Mick has abandoned his earthly body," I say softly. "You can look if you like, and say your goodbyes."

She crawls closer and kneels at his side. Bending over, her long dark hair curtaining her face, she has the classic beauty of a Madonna in a Renaissance painting of the Pieta, mourning over the body of the fallen Christ. Her fingers linger near his eyelids, then close them gently over his glassy brown eyes.

"Would you like some time alone with him?" I ask.

She nods wordlessly, her dark eyes brimming with tears, then leans down so closely that her hair falls atop his face, his chest. I flash on another art historical image – Eduard Munch's vampire woman leaning over her handsome young victim. Abby would be a ravishingly beautiful vampire. I wonder if I possess the power to transform her.

But no, that's insane. All the hot blood I've been drinking has addled my brain. Suddenly desperate for fresh air, I grab Sirius by the collar. "Come on, boy. Let's go out!"

He jumps up and rockets toward the door and out of my grasp. By the time I reach the threshold, he's vanished into the night. His name's on the tip of my tongue, but I bite back the urge to call him. There's an infinitesimal chance someone might hear. Besides, running may bleed off some of his manic energy. I wish I could dash through the woods along with him, but I've got unfinished business inside the cabin.

Hunkering down on the porch, I listen to Abby's voice within. She's talking quietly, soothingly, the way a mother might murmur a bedtime story to a sleepy child. I know she's saying farewell to Mick, but I have no desire to make out the words. When she beseeched me to save him, her pleas were coming straight from the heart. True, she bitched about his possessiveness, his lousy communication skills. Clearly she was bored, maybe even ready to leave him, but doesn't every marriage go through its problem periods? Faced with his imminent death, maybe she realized that on some level, she still loves him. If she's telling him so, I don't want to hear it. Waiting, I stare at the cold sliver of crescent moon hanging over the pines.

She begins to sing – "Golden Slumbers," from the end of the Beatles' *Abbey Road.* Her rich contralto sends shivers through me. I could listen all night, but her siren song could hypnotize me into immobility, and I don't dare wait for daylight.

I decide to let her finish the lullaby – Paul's song is a short one, after all – but then I cross the threshold back into the range of the flickering flashlight. "Abby, it's time for you to go, while we still have the cover of darkness."

She leans over to kiss Mick one more time, gently on the forehead, then rises and walks silently past me, out the door and into the clearing. At the sound of her car door slamming, Sirius begins barking somewhere far in the distance. A minute later he comes careening out of the woods and takes off in hot pursuit of her car, but she's driving too fast, taking the curves of the long dirt driveway at breakneck speed. As I watch the red taillights recede, then disappear beyond the pines, he trots back to me, sits at my side, then tilts his head to the sky and lets loose with a mournful howl.

Chapter Twenty-Two

Something howls back in answer to Sirius, and the hair at the back of my neck goes as erect as the hair of his ruff. Is it a coyote? A wolf? Someone's pet hound dog? Definitely canine, in any event, and I'd sooner encounter a wild beast than a dog with a human master who might decide to investigate the foreign noises in the night.

"Quiet! Damn it, Sirius. I hope you haven't blown our cover." He does his cute bit, cocking his head and trying to understand. "We've got to get out of here," I tell him. "And we've got to do something with the body. Want to go for a car ride?"

He bounces enthusiastically over to the Prius. I open the front door on the shotgun side, he jumps in, and I shut it, then climb into the driver's seat. The car's fairly compact, and I decide to check out Mick's truck to see if it might serve better as an impromptu hearse for his final journey. We drive out toward the road, and sure enough, there it is, parked on the driveway shoulder a couple of hundred feet from the blacktop.

One look, and I know the truck's out of the question. In the glare of my headlights, the cherry-red finish and high-polish chrome bumpers and hubcaps scream out for attention. It's a Chevy, jacked up on gigantic wheels, great for a custom car show at a state fair, or maybe a Fourth of July parade with a bunch of kids waving from the flatbed, trailing balloons out over the tailgate. For discreetly transporting a corpse, not so much.

Besides, given the truck's height, loading the body would be a challenge. Not insurmountable – I could find some boards and rope, maybe make a ramp – but I've got to get this done before dawn, and there's no time for tinkering. The Prius will have to do.

The next hour goes by in a blur. I drive back to the house, consider tying Sirius on a line off the porch, but I don't want him howling again, so I put on his choke chain and leash. We lope down the driveway and climb into the truck. Mick has left it facing the road, unlocked, with the key in the ignition. Either he was being incredibly careless with his pimped-up ride, or he was counting on a quick getaway with Abby. We roar back to the house. I leave Sirius in the truck with the windows cracked to keep him out of temptation's way for the next phase of the operation.

I snatch a heavy vinyl tarp from atop the wood pile, then rush inside and grab the blanket from the bed. I wrap Mick up like a mummy and drag the bundle out to the car. Hoisting him into the back seat is the hardest part, but rigor hasn't set yet, so he's still fairly flexible. I try rolling him down onto the floor behind the front seats, but he's too massively built, and he only fits halfway.

I adjust the tarp for optimal coverage, then check out the garden shed for relevant tools. I grab a shovel, a heavy metal mattock, a saw, some rope – anything that might conceivably come in handy, though I still have no idea where we're going or exactly what I'll do when we get there. I arrange the paraphernalia carefully over the tarp, then go to retrieve Sirius from the truck. He's sitting tall and proud in the driver's seat, looking every inch the master of all he surveys, but he happily jumps down to join me in the other vehicle, and we're finally on our way.

I hate getting back on the main road, but the Prius is hardly an off-road vehicle, so there's really no choice. I head north, higher into the mountains, heedless of route numbers or directions, zigzagging on twisty back roads until I see the sky lightening slightly to the east. So far I've seen no other vehicles, but my luck can't hold out forever, especially once daylight comes. By now we're high in the Adirondack state forest. For the past half hour I've seen no houses, no signs of human habitation.

Exhausted, desperate for a break, I pull over at a narrow parking area to stretch my legs and take a piss. As I stop, Sirius whines, eager to join me, but I order him to wait. Once I'm outside, the roar of rushing water assaults my ears. I cross to the gravel's edge and onto what seems to be an unmarked trail. Beneath a blanket of fallen pine needles, I hit an unexpected patch of mud, go into a skid and land painfully on my ass. Reaching out to feel my way back to standing, I plant my hand where earth should be, but it encounters thin air. In the semidarkness before dawn, I peer over what turns out to be a sheer drop-off to a jumble of gigantic jagged rocks and a cascading stream swollen with spring run-off from the melting mountain snow.

In general, I pride myself on my coordination, and if I could slip and fall near an unmarked drop-off, so could Mick. Talk about providential bathroom breaks! I send a silent prayer of thanksgiving to whatever force of nature drew me to this perfect place. I hurry back to the car and wrestle the bundled up body unceremoniously out onto the ground and toward the edge. I grab the tarp and blanket by the edges, give them a yank. The corpse rolls free and comes to rest on the muddy patch where I took my pratfall. I dig in my left heel, let that leg take all my weight, then wedge my right boot under Mick's back and give him a cautious nudge. But the massive body doesn't budge, so I kneel down in the mud and shove with both hands, then scramble back away from the edge as the corpse rolls off the cliff.

His fall is soundless, swallowed by the roar of the mountain stream, and I don't even hear him land. Naturally, I need to look, to verify where he's fallen, so I creep cautiously to the edge and peer down. In the dusky rose light of dawn, he's splayed, limbs akimbo, on the jagged rocks mere inches from the stream. If he hadn't died by exsanguination, this fall would definitely have done the job. There's still plenty of unmelted snow pack in these mountains to add to the spring runoff, so maybe the stream will continue to rise, carry the body downstream and batter it against the rocks. Maybe animal predators will discover it and feast on the carcass. Or carrion-eating birds – crows or turkey vultures. If Mother Nature cooperates, maybe Mick will become one with the elements before anyone discovers the body. If not – well, it's best not to speculate.

Abby's farewell lullaby to Mick comes to mind. *Golden slumbers fill your eyes*, I sing softly as I unzip my fly and add my contribution to the swollen stream.

As I head back to the car, Sirius starts barking in the imperious tone that tells me he wants a walk and he wants it now. To the east, the darkness is giving way to a flaming crimson, heralding a sunrise that's coming much too soon. *Red sky in the morning, sailors take warning.* The old rhyme doesn't bode well for the day ahead. So far, the road has been blessedly free of fellow travelers, but our luck can't hold forever.

I stash the filthy blanket and tarp in the trunk, then climb into the driver's seat and fire up the engine. Sirius clambers over the console and plants his paws on my thigh, whimpering urgently. "Sorry, boy, but you'll have to hold it awhile," I tell him as I peel back onto the blacktop. "We've got to get as far away as possible, as fast as possible. This is a crime scene now, and we don't want anyone spotting us anywhere near it."

He licks my face in reply, then begins nuzzling and sniffing my hands. No doubt they're bringing back pungent scent memories of the night's adventures – enticing to Sirius, maybe, but we're both in dire need of a bath before we get back to civilization. I'm driving higher into the mountains, desperate to put maximum mileage between me, the cliff and the body smashed on the rocks below, but as we crest a hill and the red ball of the rising sun hits me blindingly in the eyes, I realize I have to turn back and do some damage control. The cabin needs a thorough cleaning before I close it down, and I've got to do something about Mick's truck. Then I've got to hightail it out of there. For all I know, Abby could sic the cops on me, or Tony could decide to come looking for Mick, so I can't afford to linger. Then I have to drive back to the city and return the rental car. With any luck, I'll have a few hours left over to get my mind and body in good enough shape to report to the set bright and early tomorrow morning. Much as I'd love to take off for parts unknown, going AWOL would arouse all kinds of suspicions.

A few miles up the road, I see a narrow parking area a lot like the one where Mick took his final fall, so I pull over and stop. As I give Sirius his long overdue walk, I turn on my Galaxy and check for messages, but I can't get a signal. Just as well – if I could, no doubt some electronic eye in the sky could pinpoint my location, so it's best I stay incommunicado. I click off the device and stash it in my jacket pocket.

Sirius takes care of business, then tugs at his leash to inform me he wants to go exploring. I give him a few minutes to lift his leg and leave his signature on the trees that border the area. Back in the Prius, I make a tight U-turn and head back downhill toward the cabin. There I spend the morning cleaning, packing up everything I brought in, doing my best to make it look as if no one's been there in ages. If I could wave a magic wand to bring back the dust and cobwebs we disturbed by our presence, I'd gladly do that too, but all in all, thanks to the shop vac I found in the mudroom and a lot of elbow grease, it looks pretty good – not even a trace of dog hair. I drag a grungy old braided rug out of the bedroom to cover the faint stains that might otherwise betray last night's struggle and decide that will have to do.

Have you ever seen people clean house on daytime dramas? I'm talking about serious deep cleaning, not just the casual sweep of a rag. Now and then people throw drinks or shatter priceless antique vases when they're sufficiently enraged, but if there's not a maid around to clean up the mess, they just let it be and things miraculously return to normal by the next scene. What beleaguered housewife or stay-at-home mom wants to watch other people doing housework? None, except in the commercials that show blissfully happy women touching up their already immaculate homes with the latest products the soaps are hyping. No, housework is too tedious to show on screen.

Once I'm confident the cabin will pass muster, I confront the problem of Mick's truck. Parked in the clearing, it's as conspicuous as the proverbial elephant in a room, but where can I stash it? All at once I flash on the mountain bikes I saw leaning against the wall in the mudroom. What if I put one of them in the truck bed, drive it a few miles away and hide it somewhere, then bicycle back to the cabin? That could work, but where should I leave it? I'll figure that out once I hit the road. I lock Sirius in the cabin, grab a bike and toss it into the pickup.

This time I drive downhill, slowing when I encounter a dirt road with a sign that reads *Private No Trespassing*. I cruise past, and a quarter mile later, I see a similar road, then another. They probably lead to lake houses and cabins. With any luck, they'll be as isolated as the one I'm leaving behind, and since April in the Adirondacks is a muddy mess, there's a good chance they'll still be shut down for the winter. If anyone's in residence, I can just tell them I'm lost, apologize and leave.

I choose a driveway with a particularly antagonistic sign that reads *No trespassers – We stand our ground* , bordered by crude paintings of guns and rifles and flanked by Harley Davidson signs. No one in their right mind would wander in uninvited, and that's exactly what makes it an attractive place to hide an enormous and ostentatious truck. Halfway up the drive, I stop the truck and stealth-walk the rest of the way. As I'd hoped, the place appears deserted. It's also dilapidated. Clearly the owners haven't had the time, money or energy to maintain it. I drive the truck in and park it next to a prefab metal garage where it won't be readily visible from the drive. With a chamois cloth I found on the floor behind the seat, I wipe down all the shiny surfaces, the steering wheel, and finally the keys. I leave them in the ignition, smiling as I imagine the delighted reaction of the resident biker dude when he rolls in to open his cabin for the season. I have a hunch I won't have to worry about Mick's truck turning up as evidence.

The mountain bike ride back up the road is brutal. I've never been big on bicycling, and I don't have the right conditioning, so my leg muscles are screaming in pain by the time I get back. Thankfully I didn't encounter any cars on the way, so no one witnessed my pitiful uphill battle.

By the time I take to the road with Sirius, I'm profoundly exhausted, and once we're finally back on the Northway and headed for Manhattan, I can barely stay awake. I'm on cruise control, and my mind is on automatic pilot, but by chugalugging a few cans of Red Bull and taking a few strategic rest stops, I figure I can make it back to Mark's apartment by nine o'clock.

For the final few hours on the Thruway, I fantasize about taking a long hot bath, downing a couple of drinks and falling into bed. But when I turn onto my street at long last, I realize I'll have to jettison those plans, because I don't dare stop, let alone enter the building. At least a dozen women are milling around on the sidewalk next to the stoop, shouting and waving signs. And all of the signs are about me.

Chapter Twenty-Three

Talk about mayhem! The women outside Mark's building are facing off in two camps, shouting and thrusting the signs in their opponents' faces. A frumpy lady in sweats brandishes one that says "I love Jonah McQuarry!" in fluorescent orange. At her side, a twenty-something woman in goth black waves a sign saying "Vampires rule!" in crimson letters that mimic dripping blood. Their opponents wield signs emblazoned with sentiments like "Jonah's a killer!", "R.I.P. Gene Gentry" and "Long Live *Brand New You.*"

A couple of paparazzi types are egging them on like fans at a football game, and three men with professional shoulder supports are shooting video for TV. On one camera I catch sight of the familiar QMA logo. Clearly the media coverage is inciting the women to act ever more outrageous in hopes of maybe grabbing a few fleeting seconds of fame on the evening news. Torn between conflicting impulses – staying to watch or stomping on the gas for a quick getaway – I take the middle ground. I avert my head, scrunch down in my seat as far as I can, and cruise slowly by, praying none of them look my way. If anyone recognizes me, they'll swarm all over my car for sure. Fortunately Sirius is riding shotgun in the passenger seat, helping to hide me from view.

He knows the crowd doesn't belong there, and he wants to protect his turf. A growl rumbles deep in his throat. "Shh, quiet, boy," I hiss. Fortunately he complies, and soon we're well down the block and out of range. In any case, the fans don't know about Mark's dog. At least I hope they don't. But there's no telling what they know by now. They never knew where he lives either. Mark's fanatic about keeping his private life private, and until now he's been remarkably successful at flying under the radar. But obviously those days are gone. I can hardly blame the ladies and gentlemen of the press for zeroing in on a story as juicy as the murders at QMA, but that doesn't mean I like it. I especially don't like the fact that the network sent their very own cameraman to camp outside Mark's building. For all I know, someone at QMA is responsible for leaking confidential information that should be nobody's damn business.

So forget about going back to the apartment, at least for now. After my self-imposed exile in that cabin in the pines, I'm not ready to confront even my fans, let alone the media or all the people who hate my guts. Reporting to the set tomorrow is all the stress I can handle. In the meantime, like a diver surfacing from the depths, I need to take it slow, to decompress and readjust to the rhythms of the city. A walk in Central Park would be a good way of easing the transition, but someone would surely recognize me and blow my cover. But where can I go?

The thought of Central Park brings back flashbacks of the two thugs I killed. And the two guys I was defending – I wonder how they're doing? Come to think of it, one of them gave me his card. As I recall, I stashed it in my hoodie, then stuck it in my wallet when I got home.

Eureka! It's still there, stuffed behind some insurance cards. Heavyweight ecru linen card stock with the name Scott Van Vliet, a phone number and e-mail address. Nothing about his line of work, but as I recall, he lived on Fifth Avenue. A definite possibility, but first I check my phone for messages in the foolish hope that Abby may have called. No such luck. Gloria has left a couple of messages, but a relentlessly inquisitive reporter is the last thing I need right now. Okay, Scott it is. The fates are in my favor, and he picks up.

An hour later I'm lounging on a white leather sofa in a lavish apartment high over Fifth Avenue overlooking Central Park. In the darkness outside the windows, lights twinkle from the buildings on Central Park West. Inside, everything is awash in white, with a few accents of chrome and black. The style is lush, with a retro art deco feel, and Scott is dressed to match, in a black velvet smoking jacket, white silk shirt open at the collar, and white linen slacks. That night in the park, with his tousled blond hair and chiseled features, he reminded me of a young Sting, but tonight, with his hair slicked back, he looks more like David Bowie in his incarnation as the "Thin White Duke."

Everything is immaculate, except for a few strands of black dog hair that already litter the floor. "I'm sorry, but Sirius is a serious shedder," I say.

"Love the alliteration. Try saying it over and over fast, like 'Peter Piper picked a peck of pickled peppers.'" Scott laughs. "Don't worry about it, the housekeeper will be here in the morning."

Just like the soaps. I wonder if Scott ever does his own cleaning. Probably not. "I love your place," I say. "I can just picture Fred and Ginger twirling around on the white tiled floor. Maybe a party in progress, with lots of champagne and Cole Porter at the piano."

"You've got it exactly! I love throwing parties here, and people are always saying it makes them feel like actors in a thirties movie. Except for the smoking, of course. I don't allow smoking, except for quality cannabis. Anyway, I'm delighted you're here. Remember that night in the park, when I said you could call on me if you ever need anything?"

"I do, and that's why I decided to take you up on it. I

really appreciate your letting me come over on the spur of the moment like this."

"No problemo. Mi casa es su casa. So I assume you're looking for someplace you can hide out for a while?"

I pause, weighing my words. How much does he know? What's been in the papers? "I wouldn't call it hiding out, exactly," I say. "I'm due back at the studio tomorrow. Anyway, I've got no reason to hide. But when I drove past my building, the place was under siege from a bunch of women waving signs, and I wasn't in the mood to forge my way through the mob."

He sighs dramatically. "I can imagine. It must get terribly tiresome having to fend off fans all the time."

"Not all of them were fans. Some of the signs were downright hostile. The pros and cons were pretty evenly divided, and they were definitely at loggerheads with each other. But speaking of fans, are you in the entertainment business? I'm guessing maybe a model?"

"No, I took a stab at that, but the competition was too vicious. I'm an interior designer by trade."

"You must be very successful."

He flashes a sardonic smile. "Not terribly. I didn't earn this apartment, in case you're wondering. I inherited it from my grandmother. It's been in the Van Vliet family for almost a century."

"Oh, I see. I admit I was wondering." I stifle a yawn, then another. "Sorry, but this sofa is so damn comfortable, I'm finally starting to relax and unwind. I feel like I haven't slept in days."

"Really? What have you been up to, Jonah?" He giggles. "Nothing too naughty, I trust."

If he only knew. I force a light hearted laugh that morphs into another yawn. "Nothing worth mentioning." I sink deeper into the soft white leather and stretch luxuriously.

"Have you Googled yourself lately?" He puts a salacious spin on the word Google. "There's a lot of buzz about you online. You should check it out."

"I haven't been online in days. I learned long ago that getting caught up in social media is a colossal waste of time." He's openly ogling my crotch, and I realize I'd better not get too comfortable. I sit up straight and compose my body into a less languorous pose. "You mentioned you've got a spare bedroom I can use? I think now's the time, before I fall asleep on your sofa."

"Of course, Jonah. How thoughtless of me. You've got to get your beauty rest so you'll be gorgeous for the cameras tomorrow, and I shouldn't keep you up. Although I'd love to *get* you up, but –" He dissolves into another fit of giggling, then struggles back into some semblance of composure. "Allow me to guide you and that magnificent beast of yours to your lair."

In contrast to the blazing whiteness of the living area, the bedroom walls and ceiling are painted black. The drapes and carpet are deep purple, almost an exact match for Sirius's tongue, and enormous gilt-framed mirrors hang on three walls. There's a huge mirror suspended over the king-sized bed, with an elaborately carved gilded wood frame that would look perfect surrounding one of the baroque masterpieces at the Metropolitan Museum a couple of blocks away. It's so obviously weighty that it feels rather ominous, and I hope it's anchored securely.

"I see you're ogling the décor," Scott says. "Miles made all the design choices for this room, and it's his esthetic, not mine. I'm always kidding him that it looks like the kind of Las Vegas suite where they comp their most high-rolling guests. But over the years we've learned that one of the keys to a long-lasting relationship is knowing when to compromise in matters of taste."

What are some of the other keys? I'm tempted to ask, about this and a lot of other things, but I'm too exhausted to prolong the conversation, so I simply ask, "Where is Miles, by the way?"

"Oh, he's up at our farm in Columbia County. We've got a couple of small herds of goats and sheep. We're getting into artisanal cheese making."

I have no desire to go there, either literally or conversationally, so I let loose with a conspicuous yawn.

Scott picks up on my hint. "Sweet dreams," he says. He closes the door as he leaves.

Too tired to undress, I kick off my sneakers and collapse onto the king-sized bed. Sirius climbs up and snuggles in beside me, his muzzle in my arm pit. Within minutes I drift off into oblivious darkness.

I'm deep in a dream when the wet slurping of Sirius's tongue jolts me awake. Sunlight floods the room, so blazingly bright that I scrunch my eyes shut and take cover beneath the sheets, then squint at my watch. Almost ten. Shit! I should have been at the studio two hours ago. On the other hand, I haven't slept this soundly in ages. Scott was right – I needed my beauty sleep.

He's left a set of keys on the counter with a note inviting me and Sirius to enjoy his hospitality for as long as we like. There's fresh coffee and orange juice, a bag of croissants and scones from Gristedes, and premium dog food, both canned and dry. Since I'm already unforgivably late, I decide I might as well indulge myself as well as my dog. Then I shower and dress, give Sirius a quick walk east to Park Avenue and back, stash him in the bedroom – his shedding won't be so obvious with all that black – and grab a cab to QMA.

It's quarter after eleven when I skulk into the studio. I make a beeline for my dressing room, but when

I'm almost at the door, Tony Giordano materializes from the open doorway of his own room and blocks my way. He's totally wired, his black eyes ablaze, his fists clenched. Adrenaline rockets through my body and my muscles tense for a fight. But it doesn't happen. With a visible effort, he reins himself in.

"What the hell are you doing here?" he mutters through clenched teeth.

I take a step forward. "I work here, remember? Don't tell me your memory's gotten that bad – I've only been gone a week."

"That's not what I meant. I mean Mick –" He bites off the words midsentence and his eyes dart to one side – a guilty look if ever I saw one.

"What's wrong, Tony? You look nervous. What about Mick?"

"He's, uh, I mean, he's supposed to be back today, and he hasn't shown up yet. That's not like him."

I take a deep calming breath. Something's seriously off here. Aside from the fact that Mick's shattered body is lying on a bunch of rocks beside a stream in the Adirondacks, that is. Can Tony possibly know? It doesn't take much acting skill to don a look of confusion. "I thought Mick was still out west somewhere. I heard the guy who plays him was prospecting for land. I didn't realize he was due back so soon. In fact I heard he was thinking of quitting."

Tony grimaces. "That was just a rumor, a trial balloon Carlton launched to see if he could get a better contract this time around. And he succeeded – that's why he was going to come back early. Not that it's any of your business."

"Come on, Tony, around here everything is everybody else's business. Our very existence thrives on rumors. Where would our plot lines be without them?"

"I guess you've got a point."

He's looking a little more relaxed, losing that coiled-spring tension, and it occurs to me he might be my best bet for catching up on what's been going on while I've been off in the boonies. "I'm famished," I say. "What do you say we grab a bite to eat? Maybe you can fill me in on what's been happening while I've been away from the set."

"You mean like whether you're still the prime suspect in the vampire murders? Okay, since you put it that way, why not? A bite sounds good."

Chapter Twenty-Four

I check the shooting schedule, learn I'm not needed till three o'clock, and Tony and I grab a cab to McGuire's. By high noon we're ensconced in the back booth, where it's so dark you'd never guess the sun is at its zenith. I'm slugging down a double shot of Knob Creek, and Tony's nursing a Scotch while we wait for our burgers.

He narrows his eyes. "Hey, Jonah, take it easy with that bourbon. It's supposed to be a sipping whiskey, and you're belting it back like you're in the desert, dying of thirst. I'm done for the day, but you've got a scene to shoot in three hours."

"I'm well aware of that. With Abby. Have you seen her, by the way?"

"Yeah, she was here to shoot a scene with Mick. She was shocked when she found out he hadn't shown up. She waited around for about an hour, then she left. She seemed pretty pissed off."

Way to go, Abby. I'm glad you can keep your acting chops in a crisis. "I should think they'd have arrived together," I say, trying for a tone of nonchalance. "Seeing as they're so blissfully married and all."

He smirks. "I don't know about blissful. But then you'd know more about that than I would."

"What's that supposed to mean?"

"Come on, Jonah, cut the crap. It's obvious you and Abby have the hots for each other. Everyone on the set can see it – most of all Mick. It's been driving him up the wall. That's why he –" Tony breaks off abruptly.

"That's why he what? Go on, Tony." Goading him

like this is like teasing a coiled rattlesnake, but I'm hoping the risk is worth it.

"Okay, Jonah, I'll be straight with you. If our esteemed writers were calling the shots, they'd drag this story line out for days, maybe weeks, but I don't have that luxury. If Mick's in trouble, I need to know now, so I can get him out of it ASAP." He leans forward across the pockmarked table and fixes his beady serpent eyes on mine. "You know where he is, don't you." He signals the server for a refill, then leans back and gives me that trademark stare, the same one he's used thousands of times in the pregnant pause just before they cut to commercial.

Alas, there's no commercial forthcoming, but the waitress is the next best thing. As she sets down Tony's Scotch, I ask for another Knob Creek. Single this time – I can't afford to get smashed.

Tony folds his arms. "Enough stage business. I asked you a question, Jonah. Where's Mick?"

I fold my own arms, mirroring his gesture, a trick that supposedly builds empathy. "I haven't the foggiest idea."

The trick doesn't work. He's not buying it. "You're lying," he says.

"Why would I?"

He unfolds his arms, bangs both fists on the table. Our glasses jump, but fortunately they're not full enough to spill. "Careful, Tony," I say. "You wouldn't want to waste good whiskey."

His ruddy face darkens, and he starts to rise. "You're pushing it, Jonah. Watch out."

Actually that's exactly what I'm doing – watching his reactions, his body language, in hopes of eliciting some useful information. Treating him like a suspect in an interrogation room, except that this booth is a lot more cramped and claustrophobic. I don't mirror his rage. Instead I wait, silent, till he subsides.

It feels like forever, but he finally cracks. "Okay, it's like this. I know Mick went to the Adirondacks, to confront you and get Abby back."

It's a killer punch to my solar plexus, and I know it shows in my face. He smirks. "What's wrong, Jonah? You look white as a ghost all of a sudden. The kitchen's kind of slow with those burgers, aren't they? Missing your blood fix?"

"I won't dignify that with a response. And I can't imagine why you're talking about the Adirondacks."

"Okay, I'll spell it out for you. You know Paul Devane, right?"

"You mean the shrimpy little guy who talks in circles?"

"That's the one. He might seem like a space cadet, but believe it or not, he's a decent private investigator, and a whiz when it comes to the Internet. Occasionally he does research for me, and I've had him checking you out. As a favor to Mick, since he's so insanely jealous and insecure about Abby, I had Devane investigate her as well. Long story short, he tracked her to that cabin where you were holed up in the Adirondacks, and I alerted Mick so he could go cut short your little rendezvous at Lake Woebegone. "

"You're confused, Tony – you're thinking of Minnesota and Garrison Keillor."

"Duh. You think I don't know that? Believe it or not, I listen to public radio now and then. I'm not stupid."

"I never said you were. Anyway, I don't know what makes you think I'd go to the Adirondacks. Being marooned out in some godforsaken wilderness sounds like the epitome of hell to me. Since I wrapped my scenes last week, I haven't been out of Manhattan."

"What if I told you I have concrete evidence that proves otherwise?"

What if he does? Maybe he's thinking about the GPS Mick said Devane planted on Abby's rental car, but that wouldn't prove I was present at her destination. What else could it be? I've got a gazillion questions I'm dying to ask, but the less I say, the less likely I am to shove my foot in my mouth.

Tony flashes a crooked grin. "Come on, Jonah. You've got to be curious what I've got on you. Trust me, it's more than enough evidence to bring you down."

He's probably bluffing, hoping I'll cave and confess, but I refuse to give him the satisfaction. "Then why don't you just go to the police with it?" I ask. "You'd be a hero, with your name splashed all over the media. The exposure would be incredible."

"It's not exposure I'm after. It's the thrill of the hunt, the suspense of stringing out the story line until you simply can't stand it any longer. Until you give me what I want."

"And what might that be? Don't tell me you're still obsessing over that vampire nonsense."

At the sound of the V word, Tony's eyes take on a demonic glint. Or maybe it's the scent and sight of the bloody red juices oozing from the gigantic burgers the waitress is setting before us that's calling forth that gleam. I grab my burger and he grabs his. As we bury our teeth in the first succulent bites, we groan in unison, then laugh. By unspoken consent, we call a temporary truce, the better to indulge our carnivorous instincts.

By the time Tony proposes a postprandial brandy, I'm at risk of being seriously late, so I tell him I'll take a rain check, slap a couple of twenties on the table and make my getaway. I catch a cab on Amsterdam Avenue, and the driver careens downtown as if he's auditioning for a gig as a stunt man in an action flick. By the time I make it to the studio, my innards are in an uproar, the bourbon doing battle with the Black Angus burger and my own jitters about how the cast and crew will handle my reappearance.

The answer is immediately apparent: not well. Most avert their eyes as I pass them in the corridors. A few favor me with a cursory nod or a mumbled hello, but no one stops to talk, much less welcome me back. It's as if I'm exuding a toxic miasma that might prove fatal to anyone in my vicinity. I won't bother trying to describe the atmosphere in further detail – it's too depressing even to think about. Instead I'll cut to the most critical scene – my reunion with Abby. I wish I could gloss over this one too, because it's more painful by far, but I realize I need to confront it.

As always, she looks strikingly beautiful, but today it's a haunted, troubled beauty. Her luminous brown eyes are awash with unshed tears, and despite the best efforts of the makeup artists, I can glimpse the dusky shadows below them. There's a new fragility about her. Her cheeks are more hollowed, and the worry lines creasing her forehead are more pronounced. It's only a day and a half since she drove off into the night after saying her farewells to Mick, but she seems to have aged ten years overnight. She's wearing a black silk cocktail dress trimmed with jet beading, and though the effect is supposed to be sexy and seductive, it comes across as funereal.

We're perched on barstools, nearly knee to knee, and as fate would have it, we're talking about Mick. When he failed to show up this morning, the writers made some last-minute script revisions to account for his absence, and we're doing the first read-through.

"Mick was due back tonight," Abby says. "I went to meet him at the airport, and I even got this new dress to surprise him, because he loves me in black. But when the flight got in, he wasn't on it. His name wasn't even on the passenger list. I'll bet he never intended to catch that plane. He's probably shacked up in some Vegas hotel with Eleanor." Her tears spill over. With a sob, she buries her head in her hands.

"Hold it," shouts Hank, the director. "Abby, that's not the mood we're going for. You suspect Mick is getting it on with his ex-wife, and you're furious. Come on, give me some of your trademark feistiness."

Her shoulders shake as her sobs intensify.

"What's wrong, did you have a bad weekend? Should we take a break?"

"No, that's okay. I can do it." She straightens, squares her shoulders, then wipes her eyes and takes it from the top. This time, per instructions, she draws on inner reserves of anger I've never before seen in her. Her eyes are ablaze with hatred as she stares into mine.

"I'm going to kill that bastard when I see him," she says. The words are scripted, but the passion is all her own.

We finish the run-through, then power through the scene in a single take. We're both wired and a little raggedy, and there's definitely room for improvement, but the director calls it a wrap, no doubt sensing the potential for another meltdown if he pushes Abby too hard. Fortunately our moods mesh perfectly with the script – palpable attraction held in check by caution on my part, anger on hers.

"Let's go somewhere we can talk," I murmur as we slide off the barstools. "How about my dressing room?"

Her face reddens beneath the layers of pancake. "Not a good idea," she mutters. "Surely I don't have to spell out all the reasons."

She's right, of course, but I refuse to give up. "How about if I call you tonight? We shouldn't be seen together, but that way we can fly under the radar."

"I can't, Jonah. Not now, maybe not ever." Her eyes are misting over once more. "As the old saw goes, don't call me, I'll call you. But don't hold your breath." She whirls away and walks briskly out of the bar scene into the shadows beyond.

Chapter Twenty-Five

Intellectually, I know Abby's right: we should definitely keep our distance. But emotionally, her departure hits me like a ton of bricks. I can barely catch my breath. It's as if by walking out, she's sucked out all the oxygen in the room. That's absurd, I know, because I'll see her tomorrow when we shoot the next scenes, but we'll be following someone else's script, powerless as marionettes yanked around by unseen puppeteers.

I'm relieved we're done for the day. I'd expected to shoot another scene or two, but Harvey told me the writers need time to brainstorm some plot revisions to account for Mick's unexpected absence. As my breath comes back to me, I amble off the set, down the hall and out of the studio, then stroll aimlessly north as I mull over the situation.

They'll have to play out the fiction that Mick is still alive, because as far as they know, he is. They'll probably string out the part about his ex-wife Eleanor in Vegas, and if that doesn't pan out, they'll write that that he's simply gone walkabout, as the Australians would say. That's consistent with his character, because he's been known to go AWOL before. He's so bottled up emotionally that he'll do anything to avoid confronting his feelings, except of course for anger and rage – those come to him all too naturally. But listen to me, rambling on as if he's still alive.

Chuck and Harvey are bound to be worried, because they'd given Keith Carlton the pay hike he asked for, and he'd told them he would be back today. Still, Abby told me it was rare but not unprecedented for him to go missing for up to a week at a time. James Gandolfini did the same thing, apparently. After he died, it came out that when he disappeared on a bender, the *Sopranos* producers, cast and crew were always afraid he'd turn up dead. He finally did, of course, long after the show ended, but he self-destructed in plain sight, wolfing down so much food and drink that he suffered a fatal heart attack in front of his son while on vacation in Italy.

That's a good way to go, I suppose – certainly less horrific than the way Mick met his end. But he was a fitness fanatic, and a fat lot of good that did him in the end. Anyway, the showrunners are likely to keep up the charade for weeks or even months, telling themselves he's bound to return sooner or later. Of course, that's assuming his body's not found, and that's a big assumption.

It'll be good if I can will myself into a state of denial and expunge my memories of the past two days, the better to blend in with this ongoing farce. I think I can pull it off, but can Abby? And will she want to? The fury in her eyes when we first started running our lines was frighteningly real, and she kept up the same intensity when we shot the scene in a single take. I know she was fed up with Mick – bored with his intellectual limitations, sick of his possessiveness and jealousy, frightened of his drug-fueled potential for violence. Maybe she was even ready to leave him for me. But their relationship lasted a decade, and she's bound to have some residual affection for him, maybe even love. Not to mention the guilt – if she hadn't taken off for our rendezvous in the Adirondacks, and he hadn't followed, he'd still be alive today.

But what if they find the body? Some rock climber or fisherman is bound to stumble upon it sooner or later. And Tony suspects the worst. He might very well go on a fishing expedition up to the cabin, or send Paul

Devane or some other henchman in his stead. Without the GPS on Abby's car, they wouldn't be able to track me to that bluff further up the mountain, would they? What if Mick managed to hide a bug on my car before he came into the cabin?

Tony claims he has enough evidence to bring me down, but whether or not he does, he's staying mum for now. He told me he's used to the suspense of a story line played out endlessly, day after day, week after week. Hardly surprising, since after twenty years in Ferncliff, that's the pace he's used to. On the other hand, he's getting downright antsy about the vampire issue, and I don't know how much longer I'll be able to string him along.

Since leaving the studio, I've been gradually zigzagging north and east, and the sun is low in the sky as I stroll up Fifth Avenue toward Scott's apartment. It's an understatement to say I'm in no rush. Last night we reached a gentlemen's agreement that I could come and go as I please, no obligations, no questions asked, but I suspect he'll be holed up in his upscale retreat, eagerly awaiting my return and the news of my day. Like Garbo, I vant to be alone, except maybe for Sirius, who doesn't insist on conversation. But Scott has promised to walk him, so my pooch can do without me for a while.

I pass the Plaza Hotel, the fountain and the decrepit horses hitched up to their carriages on Central Park South, waiting with their drivers to haul tourists ploddingly along the paths in the park. Walking north, I notice the trees leafing out in delicate spring green, the pink and white blossoms Abby told me about. She was right – this landscape is infinitely more cheerful than the somber clearing ringed by blackish pines at the Adirondack cabin. Damn, I'm missing her already.

I'm still not in the mood to get back to Scott's place,

so I take an unexpected detour into the Central Park Zoo. I've never actually been here, because whenever I'm in Central Park I'm walking Sirius, and I know he'd go ballistic at the sight of all the exotic animals. I wander through, ogling the bears, the monkeys climbing the metal grids of their cages, but I have too much empathy for all the imprisoned creatures and the place is depressing me, so I beat a rapid retreat back to Fifth Avenue.

Where to go? I pull out my Galaxy, check my messages on the off-chance that Abby's had a change of heart and called, but no such luck. I punch in her number, but her phone goes straight to voice mail. I'm about to leave a message when the device buzzes, signaling an incoming call. Reflexively my finger swipes the screen, and Gloria Kemp's name and number show up. As if with a will of its own, my forefinger jerks to accept the call.

"Mark! I'm amazed you picked up." Gloria's voice is breathy, brimming with excitement. "I've been trying to reach you for days. Did you get my messages?"

I stifle the urge to tell her I'm Jonah, not Mark. As I recall, we never did get around to clearing that up. "I'm afraid I haven't been checking my messages," I say. "Forgive me – my bad." No need to tell her I saw her messages and deleted them unheard.

"I understand. You had a few days off, and you felt like going out of communication for a while. I'm jealous. I wish I could get away with that, but I don't dare, not with my show about to launch next week."

"So soon? You must be really psyched."

"Yes, and scared shitless. I'm a bundle of nerves, and there's really no one I can confide in."

"Oh, come on, Gloria. Surely you've got friends and colleagues you can talk to."

"I suppose so, but I feel a little paranoid. I'm afraid

someone will blab to the tabloids, and the last thing I need is a bunch of stories saying I'm having a meltdown. But I feel I can trust you, that you'll keep my secrets safe, especially since I did a little more research."

My breath catches in my throat. "Research? About what?"

"About you, naturally. Don't panic, Mark, I just Googled you a little more thoroughly. No big deal. Anyway, you've got this calm, reassuring presence. It would do me a world of good to see you. Are you free tonight? You could come up to my place, and we can order in. Thai, Mexican, whatever you want."

The old Rosemary Clooney song comes to mind. *Come on a my house, my house, I'm gonna give you everything.* Outrageously seductive for the 1950's – Gloria wasn't even born when it came out. Nor was I, for that matter. So why do I know it?

Her come-hither tone suggests she has more than food on her mind. What the hell, why not? The idea has more appeal than an evening fending off Scott's flirtatious come-ons, and I'm curious – what has she been learning about me? "Okay, you're on," I say.

I take my time strolling to her apartment. No need to seem overly eager, and I need to chill out and collect my thoughts. But within half an hour I've reached her apartment building, a luxury high rise in the Fifties, near the East River. As I pause under the canopy, checking out the art deco embellishments around the entrance, a doorman in a spiffy uniform that echoes the same era emerges to look me over. As promised, Gloria has phoned down to give him my name, so he ushers me in. Crossing the opulent lobby to the elevator, I'm aware of the security cameras that monitor my progress.

When I ring her bell, she takes her time answering, then asks me to identify myself on an intercom. The peephole in the door darkens as she peers through it.

Then I hear the metallic clicks and scrapes of locks disengaging. At last she opens the door.

She's wearing a silk robe in a dusky rose shade that sets off her Titian-red hair. The fabric clings to curves I didn't know she had, and she's exuding a heavy, sensual fragrance I don't recognize, so powerful that it triggers a sneeze.

She giggles girlishly. "Oh, I'm sorry. Are you allergic to perfume?"

"Not usually." I raise my arm to shield my face as I sneeze again.

"I may have gone a bit overboard, but fragrances are a big no-no on the set, so I like to indulge in private. Won't you come in?"

She ushers me through a foyer and into a living room that's smaller than Scott's but more inviting by far. While his is monochromatic and minimalist, hers is awash in color and pattern. Warm colors predominate – deep burgundies, reds and golds – set off by accents of emerald and indigo.

"This place is fabulous," I say. "The way all the colors play off each other, it reminds me of French artists from Delacroix up through Vuillard and Bonnard, and those cozy interiors they painted."

Her green eyes grow even more sparkly. "Wow, Mark. That's the most erudite comment I've ever heard about this place. But then I shouldn't be surprised – you majored in art history, didn't you? At Williams College?"

"Ah, so that's part of the research you've been doing? You had to dig pretty deep to find that out – Mark doesn't usually talk about his Ivy League education. I think he's afraid it would turn off his fans."

She cocks her head and gives me a quizzical stare. "So you're back to talking about yourself in the third person again?"

"Sorry. I shot some scenes today, and I'm still more

into my Jonah persona."

"That's okay, especially if it makes it easier for you to talk."

I feel myself going tense. "What do you mean?"

"When I was Googling you, I learned that you virtually never give interviews. You've been described as a recluse, to the extent that some online columnists think it's held you back in your career. Schmoozing just isn't your thing, and that's why you don't get more publicity in the soap magazines. You don't like kissing up to the media. So why would you talk to me?"

"Maybe because you don't come across like other journalists I've met. Or maybe because I find you so attractive. You're looking especially beautiful tonight, Gloria." I reach out and caress her cheek, trail my fingers through the red waves of her hair.

She gasps and leans into me, her lips parted, practically begging to be kissed, and I happily oblige. Of one accord, we press closer. I trace the contours of her body beneath the rosy silk, feel her nipples come erect at my touch, feel my own erection pressing against the softness of her belly.

"Come, let me show you my bedroom," she murmurs.

"Are you sure this is what you really want? We can take our time, you know. Get to know each other better."

"Maybe that's the way you do it in Ferncliff, but this is the twenty-first century, Mark. We're both adults, both unattached, and there's no need to agonize for months over a simple matter of animal attraction. And you can't deny we're attracted." She grinds her pelvis against mine.

I groan. "It's not that simple, Gloria."

"You're probably right, but who cares?"

Maybe Abby cares. But then again, maybe not. And Gloria has a point. What's wrong with straightforward, uncomplicated sex? As Tina Turner would say, what's love got to do with it? "There's something I need to tell you first," I say as she leads me toward the bedroom. "You've been calling me Mark, and I've been going along with it, but I'm really not Mark Westgate. I'm Jonah McQuarry."

"Frankly, my dear, I don't give a damn." She reaches down to massage my crotch. "Whoever you are, whatever game you're playing, I want you. I'll call you anything you want, as long as you fuck me now."

Chapter Twenty-Six

Next morning, I come awake to the tantalizing aroma of freshly brewed coffee. I open my eyes to brightness so blinding, I squinch them shut again. Stretching languorously, I feel the slippery sensation of satin sheets against my bare skin. The scent of Gloria's perfume, mingled with the pungent odor of recent sex, overpowers the coffee. Aroused, I sweep my arm across the sheets but she's not there.

Cautiously, still blinded by the light, I squint at my surroundings. The room is overpoweringly feminine, awash in shades of pink and coral, so delicate that I feel like an intruder, which of course I am. My watch tells me it's seven-thirty. Almost five hours till I'm due at the studio, and I can't think of a better way to spend them than here in Gloria's bedroom – assuming of course that she joins me once more.

I hope you don't have a prurient interest in what transpired between Gloria and me on these satiny sheets last night, because I'm not going to spill all the juicy details. Suffice it to say that I haven't had sex of this quality or quantity in ages. She has a joyously uninhibited appetite for sex, along with a quirky aggressive side that would no doubt astound the fans who see her perky, ingenuous persona on TV. We made love for hours – and that's all I'm going to say.

Anyway, you're probably accustomed to this level of discretion if you watch *Sunlight and Shadow,* or any other soap for that matter. You see people embracing, falling into bed in the heat of passion, but you never see them consummate their lust. There's always a cut to commercial, and there's never full-body nudity. After the break, you might see them still in bed, basking in the rosy afterglow, cuddling discreetly under the sheets. Or you might see one of them alone, piquing your curiosity about what went down after the censored climax. Did the vanished partner leave? If so, what mood were they in, and will they ever come back? Is she in the kitchen, whipping up a scrumptious breakfast she'll bring back to the bed, or in the bathroom, guiltily scrubbing away the lingering traces of lovemaking and panicking that she might be pregnant?

Right now, aside from the coffee, I can't detect any cooking aromas, but I do hear the sound of a television coming from a nearby room. The volume's low, but judging by the cheerful patter of voices, Gloria's listening to one of those insipid morning shows. Visualizing better ways to entertain her, I climb out of bed, open the door and pad, naked and barefoot, down the thickly carpeted hall in the direction of the sound.

This room is at radical odds with the rest of the apartment's décor. The forest-green walls and rosewood furniture would suit a successful lawyer's office. Floor-to-ceiling bookcases climb one wall, while a media center dominates another. A large desk flanked by file cabinets and piled high with books and file folders indicate that this is a place where serious business gets done, but that message is contradicted by the chaise longue centered in front of the gigantic flat screen TV. Upholstered in mahogany-brown leather, it would have been utterly at home in Sigmund Freud's office in turn-of-the-century Vienna.

Lounging on the chaise, draped in a velvet robe of pale pink, Gloria could well be an artist's model. She's reclining in the pose of the classic odalisque, beloved from Titian to Matisse. Her face is turned away, toward the TV screen, but the curves of her shoulder, her back and her hips are too enticing to resist.

I pad silently across the room, lean over and sweep her luxuriant hair to one side. So suddenly exposed, the nape of her neck is irresistible. Gently, I plant a kiss on her warm skin.

She shrieks and lurches upright. "Goddamn it, Mark! I mean Jonah. You scared the shit out of me."

"Sorry, you looked so beautiful lying there, I couldn't resist. I didn't mean to scare you."

"Like hell you didn't." Her laugh has a touch of hysteria.

"Well, maybe there was an element of revenge involved. Maybe subconsciously I was getting back at you for sneaking out of bed so early. When I woke and smelled the scent of our lovemaking on those satin sheets, I wanted an encore, but you weren't there."

"I was tempted to wake you, but you were sleeping so soundly, I hated to disturb you." She pats the couch. "Come on, sit down. I'd turn off the TV, but I've got this compulsive habit of watching the Morning Show. After all, I was on it for years."

"I didn't realize that."

"Oh yes, and this guy, Don Abercrombie, was my cohost for most of that time. He's looking older lately, mostly because he's going bald, but he's managed to hang in there, God bless him."

Something in her tone gives me the impression he might have been more than a cohost, and I decide to be direct. "Were you involved with him? Aside from the show, I mean?"

Her fair skin reddens a shade. "Yes, after a while. For the first couple of years, we were careful to keep things strictly professional, but we worked so closely together, and the chemistry between us kept getting stronger. Being in the business, you can probably understand."

"I certainly do." I run my hands over her pink velvet

robe. "It's an occupational hazard, and sometimes it's easier just to give in and get it out of your system."

"That's what I told myself too, when I decided a little fling wouldn't hurt. But then things started to get too serious."

I cup her face in my hands. "You fell in love with him."

She shakes her head. "No, vice versa – he fell in love with me. He was on the brink of leaving his wife, and he has two young kids. I couldn't see myself as a home wrecker, so I broke it off."

"That was probably wise. Those kinds of affairs can wreak havoc with your reputation, especially when you have a squeaky clean image."

She frowns. "True, but that wasn't the main factor. Believe it or not, deep down I'm an ethical person, and I believe marriage is sacrosanct, especially when children are involved. And I knew his wife, liked her a lot. When I got the offer to host the evening news on a rival network, it was a perfect opportunity to disentangle myself from a messy situation."

"Are you still in touch with Abercrombie?"

"No, I try to avoid him. Once in a while our paths cross at some professional or charity event, and we're guardedly cordial to each other, but that's it."

"Except you watch him every morning on TV."

"That's just professional." She takes my hands, gazes intently into my eyes. "That's something you need to understand about me. I'm wildly, pathologically ambitious, and I don't let anything or anyone stand in my way. Last night was fabulous, but –"

"Wait. Are you telling me this was just a one-night stand?"

"Not unless you want it to be. You're an incredible lover, and I hope there'll be an encore, but I'm not up for anything serious." She flashes an impish grin. "Friends with benefits – is that what they're calling it these days? No doubt there's a phrase that's more *au courant* –"

"Maybe fuck buddies?"

She giggles. "That's a bit crass. Anyway, I believe we could be more than that. Friends, lovers, confidantes, yes, but I don't want anything that smacks of a serious commitment."

"I can live with that, but it may take some getting used to. On *Sunlight and Shadow* and the other soaps, relationships tend to be all or nothing. Sex is a big deal, and jealousy runs rampant. People don't just casually screw around. One-night stands are rare, and when they happen, it's usually because the woman is drugged or drunk, so she's not truly responsible. That way the viewers won't think she's a slut. Nevertheless, she practically always winds up pregnant. Then of course paternity becomes a question –"

She silences me with a kiss, then gazes into my eyes as she sinks back into her odalisque pose. "Enough talk, Jonah. Why don't you snuggle in beside me? There's just enough room for us to spoon together."

The words evoke the sensory memory of Abby's body curled against mine on the couch in the cabin, the way we were when Mick burst in on us that fateful night. My entire body goes on instantaneous adrenaline alert.

"What's wrong, Jonah? You're so tense all of a sudden." Her green eyes brim with concern and hurt. "Don't worry, we don't have to make love if you don't want to."

"It's not that. I just had a flashback – something I'd just as soon forget."

"Triggered by the idea of spooning? Anything you care to share?"

"No." Willing myself to relax, I move closer, run my fingers through her corkscrew curls. "I do want to make love with you, just not on this couch, in this room. It's too much like an analyst's office."

She smiles. "Ah, so. You're afraid of having your head shrunk?" She reaches down and strokes my cock. "No shrinkage here, I see. Au contraire. You're magnificent, Jonah, and I'd love to go back to bed with you, but it's almost eight. Just let me catch the news at the top of the hour."

"Okay, if you must."

We lean back, our arms around each other. I caress her shoulder, let my fingers trail down to her breast, but her mind is clearly elsewhere. She grabs the remote from the end table, raises the volume. Don Abercrombie, her erstwhile coworker and lover, is delivering the news with an unctuous solemnity that makes me wonder what she could ever have seen in him.

He pulls a solemn face as his voice deepens. "And now, this just in. A man's body found yesterday in the Adirondacks is believed to be that of soap opera star Keith Carlton, who plays the role of Mick Hastings on the venerable soap opera *Sunlight and Shadow*. Police have not officially confirmed the identity or released details about the cause of death, but sources say he appeared to have fallen from a bluff onto the rocks below, beside a creek in an isolated area miles from the nearest town. A hiker discovered the body late yesterday afternoon. Remember, you heard it here first. Stay tuned to this network. We'll bring you further details as they become available."

A wave of nausea washes over me. I pull away from Gloria and bury my face in my hands. As quickly as it arose, my passion ebbs away, drowned by the shock of the news.

Chapter Twenty-Seven

The news jolts me like a thousand-volt shock, and I spring to my feet. Mumbling nonsensical phrases about the call of nature, I make it to the bathroom in record time, lock the door, slide to the floor and bury my face in my hands. Gloria's far too savvy to fall for my pathetic anatomical excuses, and she's bound to have a ton of questions, but I need to buy myself some time. Except for the dim glow of a nightlight, the room is as dark as a sepulcher, and almost as claustrophobic, but for now the cramped quarters are a welcome refuge.

It was inevitable that someone would stumble across Mick's body, but I didn't expect it to happen so soon. Who in their right mind would be hiking in such a god-forsaken location this time of year amidst all the mud and slush? Obviously someone impatient for the coming of spring. Ironically, in a way it makes the death more plausible. It's a treacherous time in the Adirondacks: mud season with lingering patches of ice, as I learned first-hand from my serendipitous fall. Balmy temperatures to lure inexperienced city dwellers up into the mountains, where they're all too likely to learn that a slippery slope is more than a figure of speech. Mick could easily have been in that particular place at that particular time. Supposedly Keith Carlton was out west looking at land, but like Mick, he was such a duplicitous, secretive guy that it would have been entirely in character for him to lie about his whereabouts.

He's been dead less than two days, and no doubt the temperature in the Adirondacks has dropped below freezing at night, so unfortunately the corpse is probably well preserved. Too soon for decomposition to set in. With any luck, maybe some scavenging critters found him before the hiker did. Bears, coyotes, maybe turkey vultures could have feasted on the carcass and obscured the traces of the attack. But the loss of blood would be hard to explain, and of course Tony will be livid when he hears the news. He's got such a short fuse, he could very well try to kill me – either that or rat me out to the cops. For all I know, he already has.

"Jonah, are you okay?" Gloria's voice at the door short-circuits my ruminations. "That news about Keith Carlton is ghastly, and I could see how strongly it affected you. I've been channel surfing, and everyone has the story. It's on QMA, of course, plus Fox, CNN, MSNBC, and I'm sure it's all over the net by now as well. Don't you want to come out and listen?"

I reach out and touch the cool ceramic floor tiles, the granite panels of the walls. The hard, smooth surfaces are unyielding, unforgiving, like the inside of a crypt, and my claustrophobia ratchets up a notch. "I'll be out in a few minutes," I say. "I just want to take a quick shower."

"Sounds good. Would you like some company?"

Her voice is soft and seductive, and I feel a stirring in my loins, but the craving for solitude trumps desire, and I decline. I flip on the lights, cross to the shower and turn it on. The enormous stall is clad in deep red granite that reminds me of top-of-the-line tombstones. I step in while the water's still cold and gasp as the icy pins and needles pummel my skin. Then abruptly the water turns scalding hot. The pain is excruciating. I dodge out of the way and adjust the temperature to a tolerable level. The hot water in Mark's apartment is erratic and usually tepid, and I berate myself for my carelessness – I should have known the water would be hotter in this luxury building.

I grab a loofa sponge, slather myself with lavender bath gel and scrub my body until my skin smarts. The intensity of the shower's stream feels like a million arrows, and I flash on Renaissance paintings of Saint Sebastian, his muscular body nude but for a loincloth, with blood oozing from the wounds where the arrows pierce his skin as he submits to martyrdom at the hands of enemy archers.

Unlike Sebastian, I have no desire to martyr myself. I dread the day that lies in wait for me – the police, the press, the cast and crew at the studio, the questions and innuendos – but if I keep hiding out in this shower, I'll emerge as shriveled as a prune. I've got a scene to shoot with Abby today, probably showing some skin, and I can't afford to look all wrinkly. I turn off the water, step out and select a luxuriously plushy bath towel the color of fresh blood, then grab a hand towel and swab the steam from the full-length mirror. My back hurts like hell, and I swivel to take a look. Damn, no wonder! The skin is red and raw, as if a cat has used me for a scratching post. Last night was intense, but till now I had no idea Gloria's nails had drawn blood. Maybe I'll be showing less skin than I thought. There are a couple of scratches on my neck as well, but some pancake makeup should cover them adequately.

I find a bottle of moisturizer, lavender and chamomile, with a label touting its miraculously soothing effects. I slather it liberally all over my body, then wrap the blood-red towel around my hips, emerge from my steamy stone hideout and go looking for Gloria. Might as well practice my shtick with her before I take off for the studio.

I find her hunkered down on the chaise, clutching the remote and channel surfing. "So," I say with studied nonchalance. "Anything interesting on TV?"

Taken by surprise, she whirls to face me. Her eyes widen and her mouth drops open. "Jeez, Jonah, you startled me."

"At least I gave you fair warning. I could have snuck up on you from behind."

"Good thing you didn't." She flashes a grin. "Maybe I haven't mentioned it, but I'm a black belt in karate."

"What a coincidence – so am I. I hope you weren't planning to try out your skills on me."

"Of course not." The words lack conviction, but her gaze softens as her eyes travel the length of my body. "Jonah, you look so hot in that towel. Is that what they mean by girding your loins?"

"No, I believe that has more to do with getting ready for battle. It's from the Old English."

"You never cease to amaze me. Is there anything you don't know?"

"Yes, I don't know what will happen now that they've found Mick's body." The words are no sooner out of my mouth than I know I've stuck my foot in it.

Her eyes narrow. "Now that they've found it? It almost sounds as if you know something about this. Jonah, were you involved with what happened to Keith Carlton? Or should I say Mick Hastings? I'm confused – this is starting to sound like the Rolling Stones."

I force a laugh. "Yeah, I've heard people kid about that. Keith Carlton is the actor, and Mick Hastings is the character he plays, or rather played. But no, of course I'm not involved. I knew he was out of town, and I thought it was weird that he didn't show up for work yesterday, but this comes as a total shock."

"Really? Maybe it would help to talk about it." She pats the chaise. "Come on, sit down. I'm a good listener, and I solemnly swear anything you say will be safe with me."

I'm tempted, but I remind myself she's a journalist first and foremost. Barely an hour ago, she told me her career trumps any and all relationships. I'd be crazy to take her into my confidence. "Sorry, Gloria," I say, "but I don't feel like talking about Mick. I think I should leave now. I'm due at the studio in a couple of hours, and I need some time alone first, because I'm sure things will be in an uproar."

"Okay, I understand. But call me later."

Leaving her apartment, I hear the clinks and clanks of locks snapping closed behind me. In the hallway and the elevator, I'm acutely conscious of the surveillance cameras tracking my every move, and as I stride across the lobby, the day-shift doorman scans me with suspicious eyes. "Have a good day, sir," he says as he tips his hat in a gesture as robotic as the cameras. With all this security, Gloria's building is like an armed fortress, but with her level of celebrity, it's easy to understand why. In a way, I feel sorry for her, trapped high in her tower like a fairy tale princess.

I head west to Fifth Avenue, north past Rockefeller Center, then west again on Fifty-Third to the Museum of Modern Art. I spend an hour letting the cool, calm shades of Monet's water lilies wash over me, then stroll through the Surrealist and German Expressionist galleries till it's time to leave for the studio.

As I round the corner from Tenth Avenue, I fully expect to see cops on the scene, interviewing the usual suspects and awaiting the arrival of yours truly, but if they were here, they've already come and gone. Mick's body was found a couple of hundred miles north of Manhattan. At first glance the death appeared accidental, or so they're saying on the news, but there's bound to be a thorough investigation. The sudden death of someone so young and apparently healthy will be treated as suspicious until and unless the medical examiner rules otherwise. No doubt they'll run toxicology screens for all sorts of substances, legal or illegal – blood tests, ironically. There'll be enough blood left to test, but maybe just barely. When they learn how much is missing, the vampire hysteria will begin again and the shit will surely hit the fan. How long till that happens? A few days at most.

In the meantime, how are people handling the news? I've got half an hour to kill before I report to makeup, so I meander over to the break room. Chris Giordano and Paul Devane are huddled at a round table in the corner, talking quietly. When they catch sight of me, they fall silent.

After an awkward moment, Paul beckons me over. "Jonah, come sit down. We were just discussing the tragic demise of Mick Hastings. Shocking, isn't it?" His eyes are practically bulging out of his head, and he seems strangely anxious, but then that's his normal demeanor, so I disregard it, take a seat and silently shake my head, waiting for him to continue.

Sure enough, he does. The kid has chronic verbal diarrhea. "Poor Abby – she's absolutely devastated, but she managed to get through our scene this morning. She's such a trooper, it's unbelievable. But then of course they were married for ten years. No children, though I'm not sure if that's a blessing or a curse. She was always ambivalent –"

I cut him off midsentence. "How about Tony? Mick was his right-hand man – I imagine the news has hit him hard."

"That's a big affirmative. He called in sick today, and I can't recall his doing that in all the time I've known him."

Thank god – that buys me a little time. On the other hand, it indicates the extent of Tony's upset. He was riled up when Mick went missing, and now that the body's been found, there's no telling how he'll react.

Devane lowers his voice. "Lieutenant McQuarry, with all due respect, may I humbly suggest you watch your back? My boss has a hair-trigger temper, and if he flies off the handle –"

Chris erupts. "Put a sock in it, Devane. You got no business talking about my father that way."

Devane cringes. "I'm sorry, Chris. It always slips my mind that you're Tony's son. The two of you are so different, you being an officer of the law and he, on the other hand, being, shall I say, a trifle creative in his interpretations of jurisprudence."

Chris lurches out of his chair. "Shut the fuck up, Devane!" His dark eyes are hard and sharp as obsidian, and the family resemblance is more striking than ever.

Time to jump in as referee, before he makes mincemeat out of Devane. "Hey guys, let's cool it," I say. "I realize you're both upset, and you've got valid reasons, but there's no need for fisticuffs." Fisticuffs? I'm starting to sound like Devane. I hope his pretentious speechifying isn't contagious.

The geek slumps back in his chair with relief, but Chris's fists are clenched and his face is an alarming shade of crimson. "I need some fresh air," he says. Then he shoves back his chair and stomps out of the room.

Paul lets out an enormous sigh of relief. "Thank you, Lieutenant. You defused what was escalating into a potential catastrophe. I'm afraid martial arts aren't my forte. I prefer the pen over the sword. Or the mouse, rather, since I'm an avowed computer geek, although sometimes I'm more of a mouse than a man."

"That's okay, Paul," I say in hopes of cutting him off before I become as crazed as Chris. "Please call me Jonah, by the way. Lieutenant sounds too formal. I'm not into gossip, but this whole situation is so weird –"

"You can say that again! And I must admit I'm not

entirely disingenuous, or should I say ingenuous, I'm not sure which is the proper usage. Anyway, I was involved in secreting the GPS on the undercarriage of Abby's car, and I know Mick tracked her to your cabin. But the trail went cold until that fortuitous hiker happened upon the scene."

Damn! Abby, Tony, and Paul – that makes three people who can link me to Mick's death, although Abby may still be the only one who realizes it was murder. I'd better keep Paul talking, since that seems to make him happy. "So you planted a GPS on Abby's car to help Mick –"

"No, not Mick. I did it to help Tony. He's the only one I take orders from. Mick and I aren't what you would call kindred spirits. He never did take to me, I'm not sure exactly why."

"Well for starters, you're much smarter than Mick. I've seen him get awfully tense when I used a polysyllabic word or made some reference he didn't understand."

"Exactly. But he doesn't want to admit to his lack of erudition, so he just clenches his jaw and glares at me." He winces. "Oh, excuse me. I still seem to be talking in the present tense. I suppose it's a form of denial, the first stage of grief, as Kubler-Ross would say, although I must confess I'm not exactly grieving."

"But I imagine Tony is."

"Probably, although I suspect he must feel more guilty than griefy. After all, he's the one who sent Mick to the Adirondacks, and I'm sure he never dreamed the trip would lead to Mick's demise. When we told Mick the location of the cabin, Tony gave him strict orders not to kill you, even if he found you and Abby *in flagrante delicto,* as it were. He said just to scare you, rough you up a little so you'd back off from Abby."

"Hi, guys. Did I hear my name? Because anything

you've got to say about me, you can say it to my face."

Whirling, I see Abby looking dewy and fresh, swathed in a black silk robe, ready for our upcoming scene. My breath catches as she moves closer. "You look beautiful, Abby," I murmur.

She frowns. "That's because I've just come from makeup. And Jonah, I suggest you do the same, because frankly, you look like shit."

Chapter Twenty-Eight

Abby moves closer, the better to study my face in close-up. "I'm sorry, Jonah. You don't look like shit – for you, that's impossible. But you do look exhausted, as if you were up all night. It's a terrible shock, their finding Mick's body." She narrows her eyes. "When did you hear about it? Probably on the morning news, like I did."

She's not sounding all that shocked, but at least she caught herself in time, before saying something incriminating. I reach out but stop short of touching her shoulder. No telling how she'd react. "This has to be ghastly for you," I say. "I'm surprised you showed up today. People would have understood if you called in, like Tony did."

"I'd rather be here, among friends. I've known lots of these people for years, and they're being incredibly supportive, although –" She glances at Paul Devane, who's hanging adoringly on her every word. "Paul, I need a few minutes alone with Jonah to discuss our upcoming scene."

"Of course, milady, I understand. I'll take my leave immediately." He executes an awkward bow and scuttles off down the hall.

"Jonah, we need to go over our lines," she says. "Can you come to my dressing room for a few minutes?"

"I would, but they haven't given me a script yet. Besides, as you so rightly observed, I need to head off to makeup and let them work their magic."

"True, but we've got time. The writers are still off in a huddle, but they gave me a rough draft, and we can look it over together." She leans closer and takes a delicate sniff. "You smell delicious, by the way. Kind of spicy with a hint of lavender. Are you using a new body wash, or did you borrow someone else's?"

The zinger catches me by surprise, and I stare at her, slack-jawed. She reaches out and runs a finger across my throat, right near the jugular. "What are those scratches? You'd better make sure they put some concealer on them."

"Sirius must have scratched me when we were wrestling around. Sometimes we play pretty rough."

"Bullshit! I've seen you with Sirius enough to know you're always the alpha dog. You'd never let him get away with that." She digs her nails into my back and starts kneading like a cat, right where Gloria did her damage.

Not for the first time, I wonder at her psychic abilities. "Jeez, Abby, cut it out. That hurts."

"You just said you play rough. I'll bet Gloria gave you those scratches. You spent the night with her, didn't you?"

"Why on earth would you say that?"

She digs deeper. "It makes perfect sense. It's obvious you two have the hots for each other. It was crystal clear that day in the restaurant when I saw you together."

"We like each other, yes, but it's purely professional, as I've told you repeatedly."

"Horse pucky." Her nails rake the flesh of my neck as she takes a step back and glares into my eyes. "I understand. You weren't getting anywhere with the grieving widow, so you decided to get it on with someone who's more receptive. A female in heat. No use denying it, Jonah. There's a subtle shift in the kind of energy you're putting out, or should I say not putting out. You're sated, satisfied."

"For all you know I was out on the prowl, satisfying

my blood lust."

"No, this isn't the same. Besides, you smell different. Lavender, like I said. A woman's scent."

What the hell. If this scene were scripted, we could string it out for ages, but what's the point? I might as well come clean. "Okay, you're right," I tell her. "Gloria and I were up all night fucking, and it was great. Is that what you wanted to hear?"

Her eyes well with tears, but before she can answer, there's a staccato rapping at the door. "Sorry to interrupt, Abby, but Chuck and Harvey want to talk to you." Devane sounds like a page announcing the arrival of royalty.

"I'll be there as soon as I'm finished with makeup," Abby says.

"Have you seen Jonah? He's not in his dressing room, and they want to see both of you."

"He's right here with me. We've been running our lines." She scrutinizes my neck, gives my cheek a pat and drops her voice to a whisper. "Sorry for the scratches, Jonah. I'm afraid you need that concealer more than ever."

"Actually, our esteemed executive producer and head writer are right here," Paul says in a sanctimonious voice. "I just wanted to make sure you were decent. I mean of course you are, I didn't intend to imply otherwise, but I thought–"

"Never mind, Paul," I say. "We can take it from here." The door opens and Chuck Winslow strides into the room, followed by Harvey Blaustein. The executive producer and the head writer – this is highly unusual. What the hell are they doing here? My heart starts pounding harder. Am I about to be fired? Arrested? No, that's ridiculous.

"Gentlemen, what an unexpected honor," I say as I usher them in with a sweep of the arm. Jeez, I feel like a pompous phony, as bad as Paul.

"Everything around here is unexpected lately," Chuck says. He's wired, twitchy, as if he's been mainlining Red Bull. "I guess you've heard about Keith Carlton, how they found his body in the Adirondacks. It's been all over the news."

"Yes, it's a terrible shock," I say. Abby shoots a guarded glance in my direction but says nothing, and I realize I'd better follow her lead and stifle the urge to blurt phony platitudes about the tragedy of the loss.

"Horrible," Harvey says with a grimace. "And as you can imagine, it puts us in a bind. When Keith didn't show up yesterday, we managed to do some speedy rewrites, but we were acting on the assumption that he'd show up sooner or later. We could have worked around that, but the fact that he's turned up dead throws everything into turmoil. As soon as we heard, I called an emergency meeting of all the writers, and we've been hunkered down for hours, batting ideas around." He rakes his fingers through his thinning hair. "Unfortunately, we've come up with diddly squat. Mick Hastings is a central part of the show's canvas. His absence impacts the arc of several story lines for months to come, and we haven't decided how to handle it yet."

"In part, it depends on how they spin this in the media," Chuck says. "And on what turns up after a full investigation, including an autopsy, a toxicology screen, the whole nine yards. If there were drugs involved, for example –"

"Mick didn't do drugs," Abby says indignantly. "He was a body builder and a health nut, always talking about his body as a temple and how he needed to keep it pure."

Harvey gazes at her. "That's interesting. We could use that. Which brings me to the point of this discussion. Since we haven't come up with a script per se, we thought we could try shooting some improv. The two of you work well together. You have obvious chemistry, and the feedback we've been getting indicates the fans love you as a couple. We could just get you on the set, let the cameras roll and see what happens."

"I don't know," I say. "I haven't done improv in years. I'm not sure I could pull it off."

Chuck frowns. "Worst-case scenario, it stinks, we don't use it and it'll never see the light of day. No harm done."

"Nothing ventured, nothing gained," Abby says with a wicked grin. "I think I could get into it. This is the day after yesterday, right?"

Harvey smirks. "That's generally the way it works."

"I'm talking about soap time, not real time," she retorts. "Yesterday I was royally pissed off at Mick because I thought he'd stood me up and was screwing around with another woman. By today I'd have had time to calm down and think it over, but I'm confused and my emotions are still in an uproar. Under the circumstances, it would be the most natural thing in the world for me to seduce Jonah. Kind of a revenge fuck."

Harvey smiles. "I like it. But remember, when the cameras are rolling you've got to keep it G-rated."

"Of course. I solemnly swear I won't so much as whisper the F-word."

"I'll hold you to that," Harvey says. "Okay, let's give it a go. You guys need time to talk it over, maybe do a run-through first?"

"I'd rather wing it and keep the spontaneity," Abby says. "How about you, Jonah? Are you up for it?" She gives me a blatantly lascivious wink.

After my night of wild abandon with Gloria, I'm not up for anything, especially not Abby, but I'm hardly about to wimp out, so I force a what-the-hell kind of grin. "I'm game."

"Good," Chuck says. "Let's use the bar set, the same as yesterday. But since it's a day later, you'll both need to get something fresh from wardrobe. Jonah, you'd better get over to makeup and have them do something about those dark circles under your eyes. If one of you has had a sleepless night, it would be Abby, not you."

I salute. "Aye aye, captain." His eyes shoot daggers, and I belatedly remind myself he doesn't take well to sarcasm.

Half an hour later, we're back on the bar stools, knee to knee once more. She's wearing a crimson silk mini-dress that clings to her every curve. It's three o'clock by now, but in soap time it's supposedly high noon. I've dropped in to check on Abby, because I'm worried about her over-the-top reaction to Mick's failure to show up yesterday.

The director calls for action and the cameras start rolling.

"Are you okay?" I ask Abby.

"Of course, why wouldn't I be?" She's slurring her words all too convincingly.

I wonder if she's had a shot or two of the Stoli she keeps in her dressing room. "It's a bit early in the day to be imbibing so seriously, don't you think?"

She leans in closer, offering me a spectacular view of her décolletage, and caresses my thigh. "Talk about the pot dissing the kettle! What are you doing here so bright and early?"

"Checking on you, actually." Gently, I remove her hand from my leg. "You were so stressed out and furious about Mick yesterday, I wanted to make sure you're okay, and I had a hunch I'd find you here. Any word from him yet?"

"No, nothing, but I've got a bad feeling about this. Either he's holed up somewhere screwing around with that slut Eleanor, or he's dead."

My jaw drops in shock – I hadn't thought she'd take it so far so fast. In the fictional world of Ferncliff, Mick is still mysteriously missing in action. Ordinarily, he'd probably stay that way for a while, until they decide whether or not to recast him. But since the discovery of Keith's body is splashed all over the news, obviously standing operating procedures don't apply. So Abby and I plunge ahead, and for the next twenty minutes we trade ad lib lines and steamy looks, skating perilously close to the edge of the real-life cliff that threatens our downfall.

"Cut!" the director yells at last. Abby's hands are all over me by now. She's been begging me to come back to her apartment, and I've got the distinct feeling she's not talking about the studio set she's shared with Mick. Despite the warning bells clanging in my head, I'm becoming aroused, and I'm sorely tempted to succumb. The "cut" command comes in the nick of time.

I scramble off my stool and step away from the bar. "Whew," I say to Abby. "That was intense. You were magnificent."

At the edge of the set, Chuck, Harvey and the director are huddled together, conferring. "That was sensational," Harvey pronounces at last. "I'm not sure how much we'll be able to use, but you gave us more than enough to work with. We'll play around in the editing, see what happens."

"We'll definitely have to try more improv in the future," Harvey says. "It could take the show in a whole new direction. My writers might feel a tad threatened, but –"

"As well they should," Chuck says with a smirk. "Maybe we won't need so many of them."

As a heated exchange ensues, Abby slithers off her stool and over to me. "I meant what I said about my apartment," she murmurs. "I've been thinking things over, and I realized it was stupid of me to get so bent out of shape about Gloria. You and I have something amazing going on, and it would be idiotic of me to destroy it because of a mere one-night stand."

One-night stand? The phrase rubs me the wrong way. For better or worse, I already suspect my relationship with Gloria will evolve into more, but that's the last thing Abby needs to hear right now. I force a smile. "Thanks for being so understanding," I say. "You're right, there's something special between you and me, and I don't want to jeopardize that."

She's gazing into my eyes, her lips parted, and I know she's waiting for something more, probably a declaration of future fidelity, but I'm not ready to give her that. She finally sighs. "I'm still upset, but I'm determined to behave like an adult and not go ballistic over your temporary lapse in judgment. Just make sure it doesn't happen again."

I hate making promises I can't keep, so I silence her with a kiss. She melts into me and twines her arms around my neck, and I feel her heart beat quicken against my chest. Gently, I disengage myself and pull away.

"So, Jonah, now that Mick's out of the picture, are you ready to come check out my apartment?"

My body tells me I'm more than ready, but my mind slams on the brakes. Her emotions have been all over the map today – suspicion, anger, grief, lust – and I'm not sure which ones are real and which are acting. But all in all, she's been holding up surprisingly well, considering she's just lost the man she's been married to for years. Her self-possession strikes me as weird, and it makes me uneasy.

I try for a tone of regret. "I'd love to come to your place, Abby, but I think we should take it slow. You've been through a lot, and you're bound to be feeling fragile. I don't want to take advantage of your vulnerability."

Her eyes blaze with anger. "That's bullshit. You're just afraid you won't be able to get it up after all your fun and games with Gloria."

"No, that's not it." I grab her hand, guide it to my crotch. "Come on, feel me, Abby. I'm more than ready for you, but tonight just doesn't feel right. When we make love, it shouldn't be as a distraction from grief and guilt. We should be fully present for each other."

She scowls. "That's pure rubbish. Psychobabble."

"I'm sorry you feel that way. Will you give me a rain check?"

She glares at me. "No, Jonah, this is it. If you won't come home with me tonight, it's over. Up at that cabin, I thought we had something real, something lasting, and if Mick hadn't shown up –" She cuts the thought short. "Forget it, this is it. I can't take the aggravation."

I ponder my next words, but evidently my hesitation rubs her the wrong way, because she turns her back and flounces off the set. Oddly enough, a wave of relief washes over me. Why do I feel as if I've just dodged a bullet?

Chapter Twenty-Nine

Part of me wants to take off full-tilt in pursuit of Abby, but the sensible side of me slams on the brakes. Better to let the leaving be her choice, and to put off talk of our relationship and how it might evolve. And definitely better to beg off from her less than subtle invitation to her apartment. Sexually speaking, her insult hit home — I may not be up for a command performance, not after last night with Gloria. And emotionally speaking, her mercurial mood swings set off alarm bells in my head.

The thought of Gloria awakens sensations that are hard to ignore, and all at once I'm groping for the smart phone in the pocket of my pants. But as I snap it open to find her number, my super ego takes control and I click it shut in the nick of time. Two beautiful women, both intriguing, passionate and eager to welcome me into their beds — a lot of men would envy me, but right now I'm feeling wrung out and confused. Women are so damn demanding, and not just sexually. They want to explore relationships ad nauseam, to yammer on and on and analyze everything to death. Of course that kind of nonstop rumination is what keeps soap operas in business. Women eat it up, and besides, it's faster and cheaper to film than more complicated action scenes.

Why do couples in daytime drama never hang out in companionable silence? Because it makes for boring television, of course. Anyway, for uncomplicated, devoted companionship, no woman can hold a candle to a dog. Speaking of which, it's high time to check in with Sirius, maybe take him for a brisk walk in the park. I'll have to go incognito, though, maybe use that blond wig I wore when Abby and I went disguised as Midwestern tourists to *Brand New You.* Hard to believe it was only a few days ago. A light-hearted lark, that's all it was, but it triggered the explosive chain of events that's wreaked havoc in my life and so many others.

Seeing Sirius will mean confronting Scott and his inevitable inquisition, but I'm confident I can handle it, and his Fifth Avenue apartment beats any alternatives I can think of if it's privacy I'm after. So I walk over to Eighth Avenue and hail a cab heading uptown. Once inside, I slouch down with my charcoal-gray fedora pulled low over my shades. I've never been big on hats, and I bought it just yesterday in a probably futile attempt at disguise, but I'm beginning to like the look. As the driver weaves his way through the crawling rush-hour traffic, I try convincing myself there's no need to be so skittish and paranoid, at least not yet, but I know I've got a day or two at most until the media start weaving together the tangled threads of Mick's unexpected death. Even worse, the police are bound to pull me in for questioning.

Scott has made sure I'm on the building's list of approved visitors, so I tip my hat to the doorman and cross to the elevator, key in hand. In the twelfth-floor corridor, I start to insert the key in the lock, then realize I'd better announce myself, lest I catch Scott in some kind of compromising situation.

At the sound of my voice, Sirius whines softly. It sounds as if he's just on the other side of the door, and sure enough, when Scott cracks it open, the dog thrusts out his head and muscles his way through, then rears up, plants his paws on my shoulders and slathers my face with sloppy kisses.

I ruffle his thick mane of hair. "I missed you too, buddy," I say as a wave of joy washes over me. Pure, uncomplicated joy, and relief that there's no need to explain or apologize for my absence. Dogs are so forgiving.

"He's been missing you terribly," Scott says. "He's spent most of the time lying here in the foyer in front of the door, and when I talk to him or pet him, he gives me such a mournful look that it breaks my heart. But you've been a good boy, haven't you, Sirius?" He strokes the dog's back.

"I really appreciate your taking care of him for me."

"It's been a pleasure. Miles and I have three dogs, but we keep them up on the farm, where they can run free. I'll bet Sirius would love it there too." He bats his gray eyes, deploying his thick, long lashes for maximum effect. "So would you, as a matter of fact."

"That's right, you were starting to tell me about your farm the other night, but I was too exhausted to take it in. It's up in Columbia County, right?"

"Yes, we've got eighty acres. Miles loves playing the gentleman farmer. We're up to about three dozen sheep and twenty goats, and he's getting into artisanal cheese. But look at me, babbling my head off and keeping you standing in the doorway. I'm being incredibly rude. Come on in, put your feet up and let me get you a drink. I'm sure you could use one after this morning's news. Such a tragedy about Keith Carlton."

Here it comes, the inevitable interrogation, and I've barely stepped over the threshold.

"Yes, it's unbelievable," I say.

"You don't seem exactly shattered. Or even, dare I say it, shocked."

"That's just the poker face I've perfected over the years as a cop. Actually the news hit me hard when I first heard it this morning, but I've had all day for it to sink in, so the shock is starting to wear off."

He grabs my arm and steers me into the living room toward the white leather sofa. "How are the rest of the people at *Sunlight and Shadow* taking it? I want to hear every titillating detail."

I sink down into the cushiony softness. Sirius jumps up beside me, snuggles against my chest and groans with pleasure. I give him a good belly rub, then tell him to get down.

"No, that's okay," Scott says. "Let him be. I love watching you with Sirius. He brings out that tender side you don't let people see. Enjoy your happy reunion. I'll be right back." He goes to the kitchen, returns with a bottle of Glenfiddich Scotch and two glasses. He settles in next to me, a little too close for comfort, but Sirius has me hemmed in on the other side, so I stay put.

Scott pours the Scotch and smiles. "So, back to the news of the day. How did people react when they heard about Keith Carlton?"

"There was a lot of dramatizing, but he was an arrogant, stand-offish guy who pretty much kept to himself, so I don't think most people were as upset as they made themselves out to be. I tried to steer clear and avoid getting pulled in to all the gossip and speculation."

"What speculation? Does everyone buy the story that this was an accident, pure and simple?"

I don't like the glittery look of anticipation in his eyes. "Why wouldn't they?"

"Well, it could have been suicide, or maybe murder. The online gossip sites are abuzz with all kinds of rumors."

I'm tempted to ask for specifics, but I'm better off not knowing, at least for now. Sipping my Scotch in silence, savoring the taste on my tongue, I drain the glass in short order.

"Wonderful, isn't it? Glenfiddich is one of my favorite single malts, and I see you like it too." He picks up the bottle and tops off my glass, no doubt hoping to drown my inhibitions and loosen my tongue. "A few bloggers have resurrected the so-called vampire murders," he says. "They're wondering if there's any connection, speculating about whether the show is cursed."

I take a generous slug of Scotch. It burns my throat on the way down, and I visualize it etching new furrows in the lining of my stomach. By now the first shot is kicking in, and I'm getting light-headed.

"Have the police come calling yet?" Scott asks.

"No, but I imagine it won't be long."

"I guess first they'll have to do an autopsy and determine the cause of death, at least on a preliminary basis. See if there are any signs of foul play."

By now my innards are turning somersaults. "I suppose so."

"Maybe this would be a good time for you to get away, take in some good wholesome country air."

Just then the Galaxy vibrates in my pocket, and I lurch upright. Startled out of a doze, Sirius shakes himself awake and shifts position. The phone's display tells me it's Gloria Kemp.

"Are you going to get that?" Scott asks.

"No need." I let it go to voice mail.

"So as I was saying, maybe you should get away while you still can."

"Why? I haven't done anything." Yeah, right. If he believes that, he's more gullible than I thought.

"That's immaterial. Jonah, no offense, but you're looking and acting wasted. If people see you falling apart, that will just fan the flames of the rumor mills. A few days in the country would do you a world of good. You could stay at our farm. Then when you come back, assuming you want to come back, you'll be well rested, calm and collected, ready to deflect all the shit that's bound to come hurtling your way."

"You've got a point. I'll think it over."

"Better think fast. Sleep on it tonight. Then tomorrow, if you want to go, I'll let Miles know you're coming. He's extremely discreet, and I guarantee no one will know your whereabouts for the duration."

"What about Sirius? He's a city dog. I don't know if he can adjust."

"Are you kidding? He'll be in heaven, with acres to run around on."

"He might get in trouble – get lost or get shot."

"Don't worry, we'll get him a collar to go with our electric fence. It circles the entire property. Cost a fortune, but it's worth it not to have to worry about our own critters getting away."

By now Sirius is on full alert, his big ears swiveling back and forth in response to our voices. "You know we're talking about you, don't you, boy," Scott says. "What do you say? You want to learn to herd sheep? With your shepherd heritage, I'll bet you'd be a natural."

My Galaxy vibrates again. Gloria again, so soon? Or maybe it's Abby. I know I should keep my distance from both of them, but I can't resist taking a peek. I flip the phone open, and the screen shows an unfamiliar number. Probably no one I want to talk to, so once again I let it go to voice mail. But after the caller disconnects, curiosity gets the better of me, and I decide to listen.

The voice is instantly recognizable. "Mark, this is Harvey Blaustein. I'm still on the set. All hell's been breaking loose around here, as you can imagine, and we need to talk. I'll be here by seven a.m., and I hope you can make it in by eight at the latest, so we can have some privacy. Thanks, see you then."

The message is cryptic, the tone clipped and formal. Whatever he wants to talk about, I have a feeling I'm not going to like what I hear.

Chapter Thirty

I reach for the Scotch to top off my glass again, but my hand is shaky and whiskey splashes onto the white leather. Sirius licks it up, then gives me a reproachful look.

"Whoa!" Scott exclaims. He's studying me intently. "Take it easy, Jonah. Don't waste the good stuff on the dog – I don't think he appreciates it. I gather that message wasn't exactly easy listening. Who was it?"

"The head writer. He wants to meet with me first thing tomorrow morning, before everyone else gets in."

"About what? Is this a good thing or a bad thing?"

"From the tone of his voice, I suspect the latter. He's usually pretty laid back, but he sounded awfully uptight." I slug down more Scotch. The burning sensation ratchets up a notch, but I welcome the distraction.

"Are early-morning meetings his standard operating procedure?"

"I wouldn't know. Not with me, anyway. Scott, if you don't mind I'd rather not talk about it. I can envision all kinds of scenarios, and I could lie awake all night obsessing over what he's going to say, but for now I think this Glenfiddich is the best medicine. I can already feel it fogging my brain. I'm aiming for oblivion."

"Okay, if you insist. But let me fix you something to eat, something soothing that will help your tummy handle the assault of all that booze." He stands, claps his hands in glee. "I just remembered I've got some fettuccine in the freezer. Kind of like fettucine Alfredo, nice and creamy but tangier, with some sharp Asiago and gorgonzola. The chef at my favorite place on Madison Avenue makes it up for me as take-out. He knows exactly how I like it – piquant with a little bite to it."

My stomach rumbles, and I realize I'm ravenous. I wonder if he has any steaks in that freezer. A blood-rare T-bone would be perfect, but I don't want to be too demanding, so I smile. "That sounds wonderful, Scott."

And in truth it is. He brings me a heaping portion on a stoneware plate, and I consume it avidly while he picks daintily at his smaller serving, watching me all the while. "Isn't this fabulous?" he says. "I love the way it slides down my throat, so smooth and creamy." He licks his lips lasciviously.

The double entendre is obvious, but I feign innocence. "Yes, it really hits the spot," I say.

He smiles. "It reminds me of the macaroni and cheese casseroles my mother used to make, but in a racier, more adult version."

I dredge my mind for mac and cheese memories but come up empty. Hardly surprising – whatever Mark recalls of his childhood, he hasn't shared it with me.

"You poor darling, you look exhausted," Scott says. "Go to sleep. I'll take care of you, and I solemnly swear I won't do anything naughty."

The rest of the night is a blur. I dimly remember staggering to the guest room and collapsing onto the bed, semi-comatose. Next thing I know, my Galaxy is chiming its melodious New Age alarm, replete with lapping waves and bird calls, evoking the sounds of a tropical island. For all I know, I set it in my sleep. In any case, I'm instantly awake, alert enough to make it to Harvey's office by seven sharp.

His clothes have a rumpled look, and I'm guessing he slept in them. There's a tray of lox and bagels on his desk, along with two steaming cups of Starbucks coffee. "I thought we might break bread together," he says.

My stomach rebels at the sight and scent of food, but I grab a coffee and take the chair in front of his desk. He's splayed back in his green leather chair, hands clasped atop his burgeoning pot belly, looking as exhausted as I feel, with bluish circles under his eyes.

"Thanks for the offer," I say, "but my appetite hasn't kicked in quite yet. Mind if I wait a while?"

"Not at all, but I think I'll help myself." He picks up a bagel, splits the halves and slathers them with cream cheese, piles the pink salmon slices on top and takes an enormous bite, then begins to masticate slowly and thoroughly. The bagel's evidently tough, and several minutes pass before he's finished the first half.

This bit of stage business is driving me crazy, and when he reaches for the second half, I decide to interrupt. "Harvey, you said we need to talk, but your message was pretty cryptic, and the suspense is killing me. What's this about? You've never treated me to breakfast before."

He clears his throat, dabs at his face with a napkin. "Mark, we've worked together for years, and I've always been a huge admirer of your work, dating back to the beginning of *Oak Bluff.* You were outstanding as Jeremy Lowell; no one's ever inhabited the soul of a vampire better. And when that show folded, you transitioned so smoothly to the role of Lieutenant Jonah McQuarry on *Hope Dawns Eternal.* The network should never have shut that down, but then –"

"Excuse me, Harvey. No offense, but I'm familiar with my own curriculum vitae."

"Of course. The point I want to make is that I've always been there for you, and I'm profoundly grateful for the contributions you've made to all three shows."

"But – that's what you're going to say, isn't it? But,

however, unfortunately – something along those lines. Why not come right out and say it? You're firing me, right?"

His face reddens. "No! Absolutely not! Not now, at any rate. There are people who'd like to see you fired, but I'm not one of them. What I'm suggesting is that you take some time off. Just a few weeks, until things calm down."

"By 'things,' I assume you mean the recent deaths associated with QMA."

"Yes, unfortunately."

"But why? True, the police have interviewed me, but they haven't come up with anything they can use against me. They've interviewed lots of other people too, so why single me out?"

"The police we can cope with. We're certainly not going to cave because of some vague suspicions. That smacks of witch hunts and the McCarthy era. But members of the cast are worried. Frightened, even. Your presence makes them uncomfortable, and some say they don't want to be in scenes with you. A couple are even threatening to quit if we don't let you go."

"Who? I'll bet Tony Giordano is one of them, right?"

"I'm not going to name names."

"But the show's ratings have never been higher."

"True, but unfortunately for all the wrong reasons. The media thrive on scandal, and they've been having a field day at our expense. The top management aren't amused. They wanted a scapegoat or a sacrificial lamb, and they thought you'd make a nice juicy one. Chuck and I managed to convince them that would backfire big-time because of your huge fan base, and make them look even worse, so you're safe for now."

The mention of goats and lambs reminds me of Scott's farm, which is sounding pretty damned appealing right about now, and I smile. Harvey smiles back, no doubt relieved that I've seemingly bought his argument. "So we're definitely not firing you. We're just putting your storyline on the back burner for a while. That happens all the time, with lots of actors, so it shouldn't be a big deal. If anyone in the media asks if you've left or been fired, we'll flatly deny it."

He shoves himself out of his chair, edges around his desk and envelops me in a bear hug "Thanks for being such a mensch about this." He pats my back awkwardly, then takes a step back and gazes into my eyes. Behind the tinted aviator glasses, his are moist with unshed tears.

"Jeez, Harvey, don't go getting all sloppy and sentimental. It's not like you. You're making me feel like you've already killed me off."

"We wouldn't do that. Or at least I wouldn't, unless they really force my hand. Even then, we'd write it so they never find your body. That way we can always bring you back."

"Unlike Mick Hastings." The words slip out unbidden.

He swallows hard. "Right. Unless we decide to recast him – that's always an option."

I realize I'd better leave. I'm not feeling like a mensch, far from it. Part of me wants to fall to my knees, beg and plead for a reprieve, but that's Mark trying to take over, and I can't let him. Adrenaline anger is surging through my body, but I don't want to take it out on Harvey. Don't kill the messenger, as they say. Find a more worthy target.

I back away, clasp both his hands in mine. "If you need to, you can reach me on my cell," I say. Then I turn away and leave, hoping it's not for the last time.

Out in the corridor, I pause, at loose ends. Where to go, what to do? In all my years at *Oak Bluff* and then at *Hope Dawns Eternal*, I never took a break of more than a couple of weeks, and those were scheduled well in advance, with a definite return date. And in the periods of enforced idleness between shows, my mind went AWOL. I have no idea what Mark did all that time, but I'll bet he was climbing the walls. Without a scripted story arc to keep me in line, who the hell am I? Like it or not, I guess I'm about to find out.

The Galaxy vibrates in my pocket. Oddly reassuring to know someone actually wants to talk to me, but who? I check the screen, and it's Gloria Kemp. This time I decide to take it.

"Jonah, I'm so glad you picked up. I've left several messages. I've been worried."

I start ambling down the hall. It's still deserted. "Sorry. Things have gotten a little crazy."

"I can imagine, with that news about Keith Carlton. Have they found out anything more about his death?"

"Is that why you've been calling? Hoping for an inside scoop?"

She chuckles. "No, actually I've been calling to see whether you'd like to come over again. Maybe tonight?"

I pause, sorely tempted. But no – I've been cut loose, and it's time to split. "I'd love to, Gloria, but I'm going away for a while." I give her a brief recap of my meeting with Harvey.

"I get it, I really do," she says once I've finally wound down. "When your life and your work are one and the same, and the work is stripped away, it feels like the end of the world. But you can bounce back – I did, and I guarantee you will too. But it takes time. You need some place to hide out and heal, like an animal licking its wounds."

"You may be right."

"Jonah, you could come stay with me for a while. I promise you'd have all the privacy you need. I'll be starting my new show next week, so I won't be breathing down your neck all the time."

"That's a wonderful offer, Gloria, but I've already got a place in mind. It's out of town, and I can bring my dog Sirius. I wouldn't want him trashing your apartment and shedding black hair all over the place."

"I guess you've got a point. But can you at least tell me where you're going? That way I can visit you when you're up for it."

"I'm sorry, but I think it's better for both of us if you don't know. Just for now. I definitely do want to see you again."

"Right. I understand." The phone goes dead, and the red "call ended" box pops up. In a way, I'm sorry she gave up so easily, but it's probably for the best.

By now I've reached the men's room. I don't need to use the facilities, but it's a calm, quiet place to cool down. I'm still riled up from the meeting with Harvey, and the talk with Gloria left me confused and conflicted. She obviously wants me, but why did she have to hang up so abruptly? In a way, I'm insulted – she could have tried harder.

I push open the door, cross to the sink and start scrubbing my hands vigorously with the liquid soap, like a doctor prepping for surgery. Then I splash cold water on my face, pump out more soap and start washing my face, beginning at the hairline and working my way down. Soap gets in my eyes. It stings like crazy, and my vision goes blurry. I grab some paper towels, soak them and start dabbing at my eyes, cursing under my breath.

It's only when my eyes clear and I look in the mirror that I realize I'm not alone. Tony Giordano looms behind me like a malevolent shadow. He's dressed in black from head to foot, with his hands a few inches from my neck. In his right hand he clutches a knife.

Chapter Thirty-One

As our eyes meet in the mirror, Tony springs. In a split second, the knife is at my throat. With his left arm, he's pinning my body against his. The steel blade caresses the skin of my neck.

"So we meet again, Jonah," he says. "One move, and I'll slit your throat. Then I'll drink your blood. Nice role reversal, don't you think?"

I take a slow, deep breath, willing my heart to stop its hammering. His dark eyes gleam with predatory expectation. Is this an act, or is it for real? Either way, I've got to play it cool. "Wow, you're fast," I say. "I've seen that move a million times, but I've never seen anyone so speedy."

He chuckles. "You're not going to buy your way out of this with flattery."

"I realize that. But Tony, could you ease up a little with the knife?"

"Sorry, no can do. Not unless we come to an understanding."

"What kind of understanding do you have in mind?" I know perfectly well what he wants. If I turn him into a vampire, I'll get out of this bind. Or maybe he wants revenge for Mick's death. Or maybe both. In any case, I've got to keep him talking if I want to survive.

"You know damn well what I want. I want you to turn me into a vampire. Right here, right now."

I breathe an explosive sigh of relief. In terms of motivation, this beats the vengeance scenario, because Tony will have to let me live. There's just one niggling problem. "That's what I thought," I say. "But even if I am a vampire, and I'm by no means convinced I am, I don't have the foggiest idea how to turn people. I've never tried."

"I know. You've limited yourself to blood sucking. Time to expand your skill set, wouldn't you say?" He ramps up the pressure of the blade against my neck.

I try not to show my terror. "Okay, we can discuss it. But only if you ease up on the knife."

"It's a deal." He moves the blade away, breaking the contact with my skin. "I've been doing some research online, and there are a lot of contradictory theories. Traditionally, in places like Eastern Europe, a simple bite is thought to be enough, but of course that only works if you don't kill the victim by draining all their blood. Other authorities believe there has to be an exchange of blood. The vampire must drink from the victim, but the victim must also drink from the vampire."

I shudder. "That's disgusting. It sounds like a good way to get AIDS."

"Hasn't that occurred to you before? You've been drinking so much blood lately."

"That wasn't me, it was Jeremy. Anyway, you wouldn't get AIDS by swallowing blood, not unless you've got some kind of lesion in your digestive tract." Which I very well may have, considering the way the whiskey's been burning my stomach recently. Ulcers would make a great pathway for pathogens.

"I can assure you I'm HIV-negative," Tony says. "I get tested every few months, and whenever I fuck a new woman, I make her get tested too. Same goes for my ex-wives if they get nostalgic and want to get it on with me again. My blood's probably a hell of a lot purer than some you've been drinking."

I'm feeling queasy, regretting the Starbucks I

slugged down in Harvey's office, picturing pathogens worming their way through my blood stream. "Let's shift the focus away from digestion," I say. "Assuming there's an exchange of blood, what quantity are we talking about?"

He relaxes his hold, drops the knife to his side, then sidesteps till we're face to face. "I can't believe you're not up on this stuff, given your situation."

"I haven't exactly been in the mood for research. Call it denial if you want, but a part of me keeps hoping this will all blow away like a bad nightmare in the light of day."

"Fat chance. Anyway, there are lots of theories, and it's hard to separate fact from fiction."

I can't suppress a guffaw. "Tony, can't you see it's all fiction? You and me, we're fictional characters, strictly speaking, even if we don't like to see it that way. We're played by actors."

He drops the knife. As it clatters onto the hard tile floor, he grabs both my shoulders and shakes me. "But Jonah, don't you see? That's exactly what gives us such power. We're much stronger than Mark Westgate and Andy Danko. Without us, they're nothing; we took over both of them years ago. We don't need a team of writers telling us what to say. We can make our own rules."

His teeth are clenched, his black eyes drilling into mine. I'm struck silent, not by fear of the violence I know he's capable of, but by the realization that he may be right. Why follow the writers' directions, when we can create our own scripts?

"You get it, don't you," he says. "I can see it in your eyes – those ice-blue eyes the ladies swoon over. I can see clear into the depths of your soul, and I know you want it as much as I do."

My heart pounds harder as I wrench away from his grasp. "Tony, are you hitting on me? I told you the first time we talked, in this same goddamn bathroom – I don't swing that way."

He scowls. "I'm not talking about sex, you idiot. I'm talking about something infinitely more exciting, more adventurous."

We're both breathing heavily now, both acutely aware that we're on the verge of venturing into uncharted territory. Still, I hold back.

"The time for hesitation's through," he croons, channeling Jim Morrison. I can't resist chiming in, and we're halfway through "Light My Fire" before I come to my sense and stop short.

"I've got to admit I'm tempted," I say, "but there are still things we need to discuss."

"You mean the how-to technicalities? I don't think there are any definitive guidebooks. We just need to experiment."

"You're probably right, but I'm thinking more about the ethical questions. Suppose for a moment I did have a hand in those recent killings – and I'm not admitting I did – those people deserved to die." With a twinge of remorse, I flash back to Gene Gentry, the host of *Brand New You*. He was basically harmless, and he didn't deserve to die. "Most of them, anyway. They were evil, and they preyed on or exploited others in one way or another. We're not talking about a random serial killer here."

He frowns. "What about Mick? He wasn't evil. That man had a heart of gold."

"Are you kidding? He was your enforcer for years. He must have killed a dozen people at least."

"Those were work-related killings, strictly professional. And they all had it coming."

"Just like the vampire victims. But I see your point. Mick died in man-to-man combat, in a classic love triangle situation, but it was his choice to go on the attack. That's why he had to die."

Tony folds his arms, begins tapping his foot with impatience. "So when it comes to ethics, I'd say we're pretty evenly matched. I never offed anyone who didn't deserve it."

"Okay, supposing that's true, how can you be sure you'd feel the same if you gained vampire powers? How can you guarantee you wouldn't go off on a killing spree and murder innocent people?"

"I can't be sure. And Jonah, neither can you." He flashes his serpent smile. "We could go on haggling endlessly, but like the lizard king sang, the time for hesitation's through. Time to light the fire, baby."

He's on me in a flash, his hands throttling my neck. I fight back but his strength overpowers mine, and he wrestles me to the floor. Then with both hands, he grabs my head and knocks it against the cold tiles. Ten times, I know, because he's counting aloud. My vision blurs and everything goes fuzzy, but I don't pass out, not totally.

"I'd call that a TKO," he says. "I'm not going to kill you, or even knock you out. I want you fully conscious, fully aware of what I'm about to do." Like a rattler, he strikes with dizzying speed, and I scream as his teeth pierce the skin of my throat. I writhe beneath the weight of his body, but he has me securely pinned, and his strength is superior to mine. With horror, I feel his lips nuzzling my neck, his tongue probing the wound as the sucking of blood begins.

My body convulses in shivers, but strangely enough, the sensation is almost painless, and soon I feel myself fading, sinking into a torpor that feels a lot like the aftermath of sex. But just before I fade into oblivion, he pulls away, rolls off my body and onto his back. His black shirt is already unbuttoned at the neck, but to make his intentions crystal clear, he undoes two more buttons. Then with both hands, he spreads the collar, exposing the delicate tracery of his black chest hair.

Slowly, inexorably, the red mist envelops me, and I feel Jeremy's presence within me more vividly than ever before, urging me to rise up and drink my fill from the throat Tony's so temptingly displaying. But this isn't the violent blood lust that overwhelmed me and robbed me of all self-control during the other kills. The loss of blood has weakened me, and I lie immobilized in a state between wakefulness and sleep, hypnotized by the steady thudding of my heart as it pushes my blood through my body. I drift in and out of consciousness, but at last, when I feel my strength returning, I roll onto my side to face Tony, then push myself up until I'm positioned over his chest, my mouth above his throat.

His obsidian eyes lock on mine. "Go for it," he says in a guttural voice. "You know you want it. Go on, dig in. Savor every sip."

He's right, resistance is futile. I have no choice but to obey.

Chapter Thirty-Two

The moment my teeth pierce the skin of Tony's neck and I taste his blood, I realize this time is different. The liquid jolts my senses; it's fuller, richer. I take a sip, then swish it around my mouth and roll it over my tongue as if tasting a fine red wine. Compared to this savory burgundy, the ones who came before were cheap Chianti. I drink deeper, and my thirst intensifies with every swallow. It takes all the willpower I can muster to slow down and pace myself. Draining Tony to the point of death would be a betrayal of our dark bargain.

My thoughts flash back to all the dieting advice I've read over the years. They say it takes about fifteen minutes for the appestat to kick in and let the body know it's reached the point of satiation. Until then, it's all too easy to gorge mindlessly and consume so many calories that you start packing on the pounds.

I've never thought about the calories in blood. I'm guessing it's about a hundred calories an ounce – that seems to be the magic number for the most delectable foods and drinks, like beef, cheese and whiskey. But what if blood bypasses the usual digestive route and transmutes directly into pure energy? I visualize the holy communions Mark must have experienced as a child, and all at once it's as if I'm experiencing them too. *This is the body of Christ . . .*

Jeez, I'm losing it. This is Tony's blood I'm drinking, and if anything, he's the Anti-Christ. Strange how my thoughts drift toward religion and the holy sacraments, not to mention food and drink, but at least it's better than thinking about sex. Still, there's undeniably something sensual, even sexual, about the taking of blood – the joining of two bodies in an act of the ultimate intimacy, the tastes and smells, the surrender to animal instincts.

But no, I don't dare surrender completely. Deep inside of me, Jeremy is urging me on. His voice is echoing in my head, telling me to bite deeper, gorge myself, take it to the limit and beyond, but some higher power pulls me back and away from Tony. Then all at once I'm floating, hovering above our two bodies and looking down. I've got to admit the two of us look damn good together. Is this what they mean by a near-death experience? I've read about the phenomenon but never before have I lived it.

The vision fades, leaving me strangely energized yet exhausted. Slowly I drift off to sleep, and when I awaken, Tony's gone.

I lie there woozily waiting, wondering if my strength will come back, until my consciousness clears and I realize I can't afford to wait any longer. I hear footsteps and voices in the hall, and I don't want anyone to find me in such a pathetically passive state. Unsteadily, I lurch to my feet, splash myself with cold water and lean forward to study myself in the mirror. Nothing's changed, so far as I can tell, except for my skin tone. It's unmistakably ruddier, with the rosy glow that emerges at twilight after an afternoon spent at the beach, soaking up sun – something I avoid like the plague so as to avoid premature aging. No worries on that score today, though – the skin on my face is taut and satiny smooth.

Will others perceive a change in me? Just in case, leery of looking anyone in the eye or engaging in conversation, I don my dark glasses before leaving the men's room. But as it turns out, I needn't have worried. The few people I encounter as I stroll down the hall to the elevator treat me as though I'm invisible. Has word already spread about my involuntary sabbatical? Probably not yet, but their studied indifference confirms what Harvey told me: I'm persona non grata around here.

I phone Scott as soon as I hit the street, and he's overjoyed when I say I'm taking him up on his offer. "I know you'll love the farm," he says. "And I've even got a get-away car for you. It's an Audi sedan I keep at the garage near my apartment, for those occasions when I want something less conspicuous than my BMW convertible."

"Are you sure? I was going to rent something."

"My dear, why bother? And why leave a paper trail if you can avoid it?" He giggles. "I'm delighted to be a part of your ongoing adventure. I'm afraid the Audi doesn't have much in the way of cargo space, but there'll be plenty of room for Sirius in the back seat."

"That's fine – I'll be traveling light."

I swing by Scott's place to pack and pick up Sirius. Then the three of us walk over to the garage. The Audi's an elegant little car, steel gray. As Scott hands over the keys and directions he's printed off Mapquest, Sirius paws impatiently at the door. I yank him back and away. "No! Sirius, down!"

Scott grins. "Not to worry. This car already has a few dings on it." He opens the door, and Sirius bounds up onto the shotgun seat, panting with excitement.

"Guess we're ready to roll," I say. "Just a quick stop at Mark's apartment, and we're out of here. Thanks for everything."

Scott grins. "This isn't goodbye, you know. See you soon. Give Miles a big kiss for me. Bon voyage!"

I head west to Fifth Avenue, then south a couple of blocks. As we cut across Central Park to the West Side, I crack the front windows to let in the glorious spring air.

Sirius thrusts his nose out through the opening, sniffs, then sneezes. "Hey, boy, are you allergic to something, maybe spring pollen from all the trees? I hope not, because there'll be a lot more of that where we're going." I ruffle his ears. "I hope it's just the pollution, because that we can leave behind."

What else am I leaving behind? A mountainous mess of unfinished business and a tangle of loose ends that are rapidly unraveling: conflicted relationships, murder and mayhem. No doubt I'll be shouldering this burden far into the foreseeable future, but maybe the geographical distance will give me some perspective.

I leave behind practically everything in Mark's apartment. There's so little I need or want – a few books and CDs, a duffle bag of miscellaneous clothes, and of course the vampire cape. That's about it. After all, with any luck I'll be coming back sooner or later – if I want to, that is. As I double lock the apartment's scruffy old door, I'm not at all sure.

By high noon we're cruising up the Taconic Parkway. As I tick off the counties – Westchester, Putnam, Dutchess – the city gradually falls away, yielding to open countryside. The venerable old parkway is winding, narrow by today's superhighway standards, and I set the cruise control to the fifty-five speed limit that Scott warned me is rigidly enforced. With every leisurely mile, I feel the tension ebbing from my body.

By the time we cross the northern border of Dutchess into Columbia County, the panoramic views are magnificent, with rolling farmland in all directions. I pull over at a scenic overlook, grab Sirius's leash, and we climb out for a long overdue break. He tugs me toward the low stone wall that borders the rest area, sniffs, then lifts his leg to mark this unfamiliar territory.

I flash back to the rest stop on that deserted

mountain road in the Adirondacks the morning I pushed Mick's body over the edge of the trail. That landscape was so dark, so foreboding compared to this sunny vista alive with the dazzling greens of spring. To the west, I catch glimpses of the Hudson River, with the Catskills beyond. This is the land that inspired the great nineteenth century landscape painters like Thomas Cole and Frederick Church, who made their homes here.

Apparently I'll be making my home here too, at least for a while. The head honchos at the network have banished me from their fiefdom, forced me into exile. But who knows, maybe they've done me a backhanded favor. Breathing in the pure country air, surveying the gorgeous scene that surrounds me, I feel strangely lighthearted. Even – dare I say it – hopeful.

I check the Mapquest directions Mark printed out for me, but they look pretty wordy, so for extra insurance, I program my destination into the Google maps feature on my Galaxy. As I pull back onto the Taconic, the melodious female voice tells me that just as I thought, I'm approaching my exit. Soon I'll be leaving the parkway and taking a two-lane highway, then another. . .

In case anyone happens to read this, I can't reveal the particulars of my journey from this point on. Doing some due diligence online last night, I learned that Columbia County has 648 square miles, compared to Manhattan's 33.77. That's almost twenty times as much land to get lost in, so consider me lost – for now.

Chapter Thirty-Three

It's been almost two weeks since Harvey cut me loose. I haven't faded away into oblivion as I feared. Nor have I morphed into a ghost or a mindless zombie. No, I'm definitely corporeal, still flesh, bone and blood, and I seem to have all my wits about me. But boredom is making me edgy.

Marooned up here in the boonies, I've been doing a lot of thinking, and I've come to the realization that in essence, I was always a puppet, with the showrunners jerking me around by the strings. I'm finally starting to unwind and come to terms with my newfound freedom. In a way, it's been therapeutic. I'm more relaxed, and I'm not obsessing as much about the string of calamities that befell me in the city. I suppose that's a good thing, up to a point, but relaxation gets old in a hurry, and I'm beginning to wonder if it's time to move on.

The day after I got here, I decided to record everything I can remember about the events of the past few weeks while they're still fresh in my mind, starting with the day I first met Abby in the church. I hoped the writing process would yield some fresh insights into my predicament and what my next steps might be. So far that hasn't happened, but at least I've got a written record for future reference. With time, maybe it will start to suggest some answers.

I've been writing the old-fashioned way, in longhand, in an elegant leather-bound journal Miles picked up for me in Hudson. Using my laptop would be speedier, but I'm afraid I'd be too tempted to log on to the web and start Googling myself. Mark used to troll the Internet in search of good reviews, but the slightest hint of negativity brought him down, and the over-the-top adulation of some of his more obsessive fans made him paranoid, so he quit cold-turkey. God only knows what kind of bile the media is spewing about me now – I'm better off being a Luddite.

Anyway, speed's not an issue, because it feels as if I've got all the time in the world. Right now I'm ensconced in a rocking chair on the wrap-around porch of the beautifully restored nineteenth-century farmhouse Scott bought a few years back. Actually, I stay in the guest cottage a couple of hundred feet from here, but I like writing on this porch, where the view is more expansive and I can smell the delectable scents of whatever Miles is cooking for lunch. He's a serious chef, and although I haven't weighed myself, I suspect I've gained a couple of pounds. I'm hoping it's muscle, from all the laps I've been swimming in the pool and the hours of hiking Sirius and I have been doing, but with Miles's cooking, it takes all the will power I can muster not to wolf down more calories than I can burn.

Sirius is in better shape for sure. With all the free running he does on this farm, he's packed on more muscle. With his heavy fur coat, he's always looked larger than he actually is, and to the naked eye he's still the same, but I can feel the difference when I stroke him. Right now he's curled at my feet, keeping a watchful eye on the sheep grazing in a gently rolling meadow that's bordered not only by the invisible electric fence, but by the old fashioned white-painted rail variety.

Every day my dog and I spend hours exploring the land. Miles loves riding his John Deere tractor, mowing curving trails through the acres of wild meadow. Sometimes we follow those, and sometimes we venture further afield. I got Sirius a collar that's synched to the electric fence that circles the property. The first time I let him off the leash, he bounded over to the herd, barking wildly, but when they moved uneasily away, he stopped short, no doubt realizing he was outnumbered. It took only a couple of zaps from the electric fence to teach him his boundaries. After a few laps, he bounded back to me, panting happily, doing the downward dog bow to entice me to join him. And so I did.

Day by day, we're building up the strength and stamina that had been sapped by the constraints of city living. He's already decided he's in charge of the sheep, and his instinctual talent for herding is coming to the fore. The goats in the far pasture are another matter, more rambunctious and unpredictable. He's studiously ignoring them for now, but I'm sure he'll take them on any day now, when he's ready for a new challenge.

I'm on a strict media deprivation diet. When my Galaxy ran out of juice, I didn't recharge it, and I haven't been tempted to turn on my lap top, watch TV or read newspapers. Ignorance isn't bliss, exactly, but I've found a measure of tranquility in dropping off the grid. Best of all, since I left the city, my doppelganger Jeremy hasn't resurfaced. Nor has my lust for blood.

Miles has talked me into giving up meat. He's a strong proponent of a lacto-ovo-vegetarian diet – dairy, eggs, fruits and veggies. He believes the consumption of meat heightens anger and aggression, especially if it comes from factory-farmed animals and is tainted by traces of the terror and violence that attend their deaths. The sheep and goats on this farm, in contrast, live a placid, peaceful life, and he's convinced the cheeses made from their milk embody the essence of their bucolic existence. For the sake of population control, he occasionally sells a few lambs and kids to a restaurateur in Hudson whose patrons pay premium prices for locally sourced meat, but the man assures him they're treated humanely and gently right up until the end.

Anyway, aggression isn't my problem at present — wimpiness is. Day by day I can almost feel the testosterone leaching from my body. I'm not a sexless eunuch, far from it. The thought of Abby still gets my juices flowing, but I'm trying not to dwell on what might have been. She may never forgive me for killing Mick. And if by some miracle she decides to take me back, what then? She's not the type to screw around — she'd want a serious commitment, and I know I'm not ready for that.

Gloria, on the other hand, has made it clear she wants to avoid the entanglement of a serious relationship, and that's a definite plus. In some ways, I have more in common with her than with Abby. But she's an investigative journalist at heart, and for her, a big story will always trump whatever feelings she might have for me. The bottom line is, I can't trust her.

And speaking of trust, what about Tony Giordano? I'd be crazy to trust him. I have no idea if our blood exchange that morning in the men's room at QMA had any lasting effect. If it did, and he's now a bona fide vampire, how is he going to use his newfound powers? Will he lord it over me, maybe try to take me down? He's a mob boss, after all, so I wouldn't put it past him.

For that matter, am I a bona fide vampire? Frankly, I have no idea. Or maybe I should say I have too many ideas, all of them ricocheting around in my overcrowded brain. For all I know I may never get a call-back from Chuck and Harvey. And I'm willing to bet the cops are hard at work building a case against me, trying to nail down enough evidence to arrest me.

There's no point in obsessing about the future and the things I can't control, but staying in the present moment doesn't come easily to me. Miles swears by meditation as a way of reducing stress and quieting the mind, but I've given it my best shot, and it drives me up the wall. Watching my thoughts float past like little white clouds and letting go of them seems absurd, and whenever I try tuning in to my breathing, I start to hyperventilate.

Just kicking back and focusing on this idyllic landscape works pretty well, but I'm getting a little too fond of drinking while doing it. Maybe I should take up painting as a distraction. But what medium? Oils, acrylics? Or what about sculpture?

All at once Sirius jumps up barking, shattering my artsy reveries. What the hell? An unfamiliar car is cruising up the drive. A red convertible – could it be Scott's? No, there's a woman at the wheel. Wearing enormous dark glasses and a scarf wrapped around her head, she conjures up images of Jackie Onassis. Sirius dashes to the car as she pulls up and parks, then whips off the scarf, revealing luxuriant red curls.

Speak of the devil – it's Gloria Kemp, in the flesh. I propel myself out of the rocker, across the porch and down the steps. As she climbs out of the BMW, the dog makes a beeline for her crotch, sniffs, then wags his tail. Laughing, she pushes him away, then rubs him behind the ears. "So this must be the famous Sirius," she says with a grin. "What a magnificent beast!"

I slam my journal shut and clutch it to my crotch to conceal the evidence of how excited I am to see her. "You're looking pretty magnificent yourself," I say, relieved that my fears of becoming a sexless eunuch are unfounded. "But how on earth did you find me?"

She smiles. "I'm an investigative reporter, remember? I always keep my sources confidential. Although I may make an exception just this once, because I'm privy to some information you should know."

"What kind of information?"

She furrows her brow, and her green eyes go

serious. "All in good time. Don't worry, I won't keep you in suspense for long." Moving closer, she twines both arms around my neck and presses her hips against mine.

My erection swells against her belly and I pull her into an embrace. "Whatever it is, I guess it can wait. Lately I've been practicing slowing down, just being in the moment and savoring the here and now. And right now I want to savor you."

"The feeling's mutual." She tilts her face up for a kiss. As our lips meet and I drink in the taste of her, a warning bell goes off in my head, and I pull away. "Sorry, Gloria, you caught me off guard and I got my priorities scrambled there for a minute. What is it you have to tell me? It sounds important."

She leans in for another kiss, runs the tip of her tongue around my lips, then thrusts it into my mouth. We're both breathing hard now. "Making love with you is my number one priority," she murmurs. "The rest can wait." Taking a step back, she grabs the hem of her green sleeveless sheath and yanks it off over her head, revealing a sheer silky slip in a shade of pink that suggests the pearly insides of a sea shell. She's wearing nothing beneath it, and her erect nipples and thatch of curly red pubic hair are on full display.

I gasp. "God, you're magnificent, Gloria. You take my breath away."

Grinning, she caresses the silky fabric that clings to her curves. "I can take this off too if you want. We could make love right here on the porch, on that loveseat over there. Or on the grass if you'd rather."

I laugh. "Clever. That's an old sales strategy — offering two options, and refusal isn't one of them. 'Would you like the gray sedan, or the teal? You can think about it while I start writing up the order.'"

She reaches for the hem of her slip, gives it a tug.

"No need to waste time thinking about it."

I grab her hand. "Wait, I've got a better idea. See that cottage over there?"

Her eyes follow my gaze. "That one with the blue siding? It's adorable – like something out of a Thomas Kincaide painting."

"Well, for now it's my home away from home. Would you like to see the inside? We can have more privacy there."

"It looks like you already have plenty of privacy, if you don't count Sirius and all those sheep. But if you insist –"

I silence her with a kiss. "I do. I insist." I scoop her up into my arms, cradle her against my chest. She feels surprisingly light. I've made this particular move a few times before the cameras, but it never felt so effortless before.

As I descend the steps, Gloria twines her arms around my neck. "Jonah, it feels heavenly having you hold me like this, but I'm perfectly capable of walking."

"I know you are. You're one of the strongest, most independent women I've ever met, but now that I've swept you off your feet, I'm going to carry you all the way to my bed and ravish you into surrender."

Chapter Thirty-Four

When we reach the cottage, chaos ensues. Still cradling Gloria in my arms, I crouch enough to grab the handle and open the door, whereupon Sirius shoves past us, bounds across the floor and takes a flying leap onto the bed. I set Gloria down, then shoo the dog off and out the door. Laughing, she beats me to the bed and plops onto the cushiony mattress. In seconds, I'm beside her.

True to my words, I ravish Gloria into surrender, but she gives as good as she gets. We come together explosively, then make love again, more slowly and with surprising tenderness. We slake our desires to the point of exhaustion, finally falling asleep in each other's arms. By the time we awaken, the late afternoon sun has given way to twilight, and the bedroom is steeped in shadows.

Gloria is stroking my hair, my face, trailing her fingers down my chest, past my navel, arousing me all over again. She cuddles closer, nuzzles my neck with her lips, and I'm mightily tempted, but then I remember we have unfinished business.

"We've scarcely said a word since we stepped over the threshold," I murmur.

She smiles. "I know. Isn't it marvelous? I could stay here with you forever."

"Me too, but we had a bargain, remember? You said you had some important information and you weren't going to keep me in suspense. What were you going to tell me?"

"It can keep a while longer, can't it? Till morning,

for example?" She flashes her trademark grin, but I'm getting impatient, and it fails to work its customary magic.

I extricate myself from her roving hands and pull myself to a seated position, back against the headboard with its plushy pillows. Lest she get too distracted, I plop a pillow across my hips to hide my nakedness. "No, Gloria, it can't wait till morning," I say. "You gave me the impression it was something critical, so out with it."

"I hardly know where to begin."

"Don't tell me you're at a loss for words – that doesn't sound like you. Suppose you start with how you managed to find me. I've been off the grid for nearly two weeks. No cell phone, no Internet, nothing. I thought I was in the clear."

Gloria forces a smile. "I'd love to say I found you thanks to my stellar skills as an investigative reporter, but actually Tony Giordano deserves the credit."

The name is like a punch to the pit of my stomach. Since our blood exchange in that bathroom, I've tried my best to banish Tony from my mind, but I should have known I couldn't shake him off so easily.

"Jonah, you look as if you've seen a ghost." Her luminous green eyes are aglow with curiosity. "Tony really gets to you, doesn't he?"

Damn! The woman has an uncanny ability to zero in on my most vulnerable areas. "I wouldn't say that." I'm hedging, and I know she knows it. "Tony and I have a lot in common. On the show, we're supposed to be enemies, but in many ways we're on the same wave length."

"So he told me. For one thing, you're both vampires."

"Tony said that? It's totally ridiculous."

"Is it? He told me about how you turned him, how you drank each other's blood that day in the bathroom at QMA. His story was pretty convincing."

"He must be delusional."

"Possibly, but delusional or not, he doesn't strike me as the kind of guy who's imaginative enough to create a story like that out of thin air. And he told me exactly where to find you. He was right about that."

"Did he explain how he found out?"

"Yes, he had a couple of his henchmen tailing you. They knew you were staying at Scott Van Vliet's suite on Fifth Avenue, and they knew when you left in Scott's Audi sedan. When you stopped at your apartment, one of them planted a bug on the undercarriage."

Damn! That sounds all too plausible. It's the same M.O. they used so Mick could track me to the cabin in the Adirondacks. Gloria doesn't know that, of course, and I'm not about to tell her, so I pursue a different direction. "If Tony knew where I was all this time, why did he wait so long to contact me? And why did he send you in his place?"

"What a sexist thing to say! Tony didn't send me. When it comes to my personal life, I'm my own boss and nobody gives me orders. As a matter of fact I sought him out in hopes he'd know where you are. He was delighted to oblige, but as far as he's concerned, New York ends north of the George Washington Bridge, so he had an assistant print out the directions from MapQuest. A peculiar little guy with buggy eyes who talks a mile a minute."

Her description cracks me up. "That would be Paul Devane," I say. "He's an acquired taste, but he kind of grows on you. I suspect he's the brains behind Tony's outfit."

"That wouldn't surprise me. Actually, I was relieved he was around, because Tony scared me. He's wound awfully tight, with a lot of pent-up energy. I get the feeling he could go ballistic in an instant if someone rubs him the wrong way."

"You're right about that, but I don't think you have anything to worry about. Tony is quite the ladies' man, and he has this chivalrous kind of Italian machismo about him. I'm pretty sure he'd never hurt a woman."

Gloria grins. "Machismo is a Spanish word, not Italian, but I see what you mean. You're wrong about his not hurting women, though. There's a woman he's threatening to hurt right now, as a way of luring you out of hiding and back to New York City."

A chill comes over me, and I'm stunned into silence. I'm positive she's talking about Abby, but I can't bring myself to speak her name.

Gloria says it for me: "It's Abigail Hastings, or rather the actress who plays her, Catherine Reynolds. Tony referred to her as Abby, though."

"Yes, he would. That's how he knows her. But what did he say about hurting her?"

"Hurt is hardly the word. He's planning to turn her into a vampire and make her his slave. He says you're the only one who can stop him, but time is running out, and he's not going to wait much longer."

"But if he already knew where I am, he could have come after me days ago."

"That's what I thought too, but when I asked him about it, he said he needed the time to practice and perfect his powers." She shudders and wraps the comforter around her body. "Is it just my imagination, or is it getting colder in here?"

Her nervousness is contagious, and I shiver. "Maybe both. Did he say what powers he was talking about?"

"No. When I asked, he just flashed this reptilian grin and started chortling in a really fiendish way. He stared at me with those beady black eyes drilling into mine and said I'd find out all in good time. He was creeping me out, so I said my goodbyes and left. There's something profoundly evil about that man, and I knew I had to get away before I totally lost it."

"Wise decision." I turn to face her. "Tony's totally aware of the power he projects with that bad-guy persona, and he can turn it on and off at will, or at least I've always thought he could. But maybe he's crossed the line." I pause, take a deep breath, wondering how much to say. "Like I said, I've been off the grid, and I've been on a strict media deprivation diet. But I need to ask: have there been any more unexpected deaths at QMA since I've been gone?"

Her eyes widen. "No. I'm sure I would have heard if there had been."

"What about the city in general, and Manhattan in particular – any grisly murders in the news?"

She sits up, and the comforter slips from her shoulders. "You mean vampire-style murders, don't you?"

"I guess so, yes."

"Nothing comes to mind. But Tony's a mob boss, right? He should have the expertise and the connections to make a body disappear without a trace, unlike his unfortunate enforcer Mick Hastings."

I'm sure she's conjuring up memories of that morning in her apartment when we heard about Mick's death, and I don't like the quizzical look she's shooting my way. "It's true, there are all sorts of ways to dispose of bodies," I say. "People go missing all the time on soaps, although they have an uncanny ability to reappear alive and well months or even years later if it suits the story line."

"Kind of like vampires."

"Yes, or cats with nine lives. Only rarely is someone well and truly dead."

She leans closer, takes my lower lip between her teeth and gives me a nip.

"Ouch! What are you doing?"

Her eyes narrow, and she bites again, harder this time. "Jonah, I vant to drink your blood. Vampires turn me on."

"Cut it out, Gloria. This isn't a joke." I pull away, climb out of the four-poster bed and start retrieving the clothes I threw on the floor.

"Wait, Jonah – slow down. We haven't finished talking."

I've already got my briefs on. "As far as I'm concerned, we have." I yank up my jeans and start zipping my fly.

"God, Jonah, you're so gorgeous. You look so sexy in those jeans, I want to pull them right off again and entice you back into bed."

"I'm flattered, but I have to take a rain check. I need to get back to the city tonight."

"You're taking this awfully seriously, aren't you? A little while ago you said Tony was delusional when he talked about your turning him into a vampire, but were you being straight with me? Maybe he was telling the truth."

A sudden stab of pain shoots straight through my head. I take it as a sign and decide to level with her. "Gloria, I genuinely don't know what to believe, and I'm having a hard time separating fact from fiction. Am I actually a vampire? Is Tony? Maybe I've been hallucinating the events of the past few weeks, or maybe it's a nightmare. The problem is, I can't seem to wake up and shake it off. I'd hoped this time in the country would bring some tranquility, maybe even some insight, but that was an illusion too. I'm more confused than ever. My brain feels totally fried."

She climbs off the bed, retrieves the silk slip from the floor, pulls it over her head, then smooths it over her curves. She does the same with the green dress. Slowly, sinuously, putting on a show.

"Jonah, I hate to see you suffer like this," she murmurs. "Maybe I can help you sort things out and get to the truth. I could offer a fresh perspective and my investigative skills. And since I'm not involved with *Sunlight and Shadow,* I'd be more objective than you could ever be."

"Objective? After what happened between us over the past few hours? You've got to be kidding."

She steps toward me, detangling her hair with her fingers. Her emerald eyes are aglow, but they're the eyes of a hunter, not a lover. "Remember that morning at my apartment, when I told you my career will always take precedence over personal relationships?"

"Of course I remember. But speaking of your career, you're starting your own show."

"Yes, on Monday."

"Immersing yourself in my problems would be a major distraction. You don't need the aggravation."

"Au contraire, Jonah. I'm a workaholic, and I'm good at multitasking."

"What about Abby? She's the reason I'm hell bent on getting back to Manhattan tonight. Doesn't that bother you?"

She grins. "I've got pretty good self-esteem, and frankly, I don't see her as much of a threat. But I know she's important to you, and I won't get in the way of your relationship."

"At this point Abby and I don't have a relationship. I'm not sure we ever will."

"Even so, you need to keep her safe. Go on, jump in your car and ride to the rescue of your damsel in distress. I'll catch up with you in the city tomorrow."

Outside, Sirius breaks into a sudden salvo of barks with the frenetic edge he uses to announce the arrival of a stranger. There's the sound of a car drawing closer, then the engine shutting down. "Damn!" I exclaim. "I'm not expecting anyone. Are you?"

"Of course not. No one knows I'm here. Maybe it's just one of the guys who live here."

"Scott or Miles? No, Sirius recognizes the sound of their cars. This is his stranger bark."

A car door slams, and the barking stops abruptly.

"What the hell?" I walk to the window and peer out. Abby's climbing out of the car, and Sirius is jumping with joy. "Speak of the devil," I say. "Damned if it isn't my damsel in distress."

Chapter Thirty-Five

My heart is slamming against the walls of my chest. I step back away from the window and make a bee line for my shirt, which is still on the floor where I dropped it. "I'll handle this," I tell Gloria.

"Never mind, I'll get it," she says. "You finish getting dressed."

"No, really, it's better if I do."

But it's too late. Gloria's already at the door, her hand on the knob. She flashes me a wicked grin. "This should be interesting." She yanks open the door, then strikes a pose on the threshold, every inch the mistress of the manor. She's extending her hand when Sirius barrels past her, emitting excited little yips as he bounces toward me, his teeth bared in a doggy smile.

Abby follows him in, elbowing her way past Gloria and her outstretched hand. "What the fuck is going on here?"

"Abby! Good to see you again!" Gloria's voice brims with fake enthusiasm. She's donned her public persona instantly, like a comfortable old coat. "What a pleasant surprise!"

Abby isn't buying the act. "Cut the crap!" She sniffs, then grimaces in distaste. "Jeez! This room reeks of sex. It's disgusting."

"I suppose that depends on your perspective," Gloria says with a sly smile as Sirius launches himself at the bed.

The smell of sex – that's something they never talk about on soaps, but Abby's right. The pungent aromas of our lovemaking linger in the air. Denial is pointless. Anyway, even if Abby didn't pick up on the scent, Gloria's rosy glow and my hangdog look would be a dead giveaway. Sirius is burrowing among the disheveled sheets, rolling on his back, luxuriating in the smell and feel of the satin, nipping at the slithery fabric with his teeth. "Bad dog!" I say, though I'm glad of the distraction. "Scott will have a fit if you ruin those sheets."

Gloria chimes in. "Yes, they're insanely expensive. Porthault, eight hundred thread count. I have the same ones at home, but in the pearly pink, not the sea foam blue."

Abby's practically snarling. "Enough with the Martha Stewart act." Her eyes meet mine, then drift down, taking in my bare chest, my unbuckled belt, my rumpled jeans and bare feet. "Sorry I interrupted your rendezvous in this charming little love shack."

"Actually, I'm glad you're here," Gloria says. "Believe it or not, this isn't what it looks like. I came here to deliver a message from Tony Giordano."

Abby scowls. "Yeah, right. Please, Gloria, spare me the phony innocence cliché. It's way overused on soaps, and it usually turns out to be bullshit."

"But sometimes it's actually true," I say, flashing back to the night Abby tried it on Mick when he caught us spooning on the sofa in the Adirondacks. If he'd believed her, he might still be alive today.

Abby flashes me a warning look, then falls suddenly silent, and I know she's reliving that fatal night right along with me.

"Okay, Abby, you have a point," Gloria says. "I should have known better than to insult your intelligence. True, Jonah and I ended up in bed, but that wasn't why I came here. Anyway, I understand you two aren't a couple, if you ever were. I heard you had a pretty serious falling out."

Abby's face flushes crimson. "My relationship with Jonah is none of your damn business."

"And my relationship with him is none of yours."

I'm beginning to enjoy this. Both women are beautiful when they're angry, and it's flattering that they're fighting over me, but their claws are coming unsheathed, and the last thing I want is a full-blown cat fight. "Cool it, ladies," I say. "I'd hate to see this turn physical. With those expensive manicures, you could do each other a lot of damage, and it would be a tragedy if you get your faces all scratched up."

Fortunately, they both get the message and back off. "You're right, Jonah," Gloria says. "This is ridiculous. As I was telling you earlier, Tony wants you to get back to the city right away." She turns to Abby. "If Jonah doesn't get back, Tony's threatening to turn you into a vampire. Not only that, he wants to turn you into his sex slave and take you hunting with him."

Abby breaks into a cackling laugh I've never heard before. "No way. That'll never happen."

Her reaction worries me. Is she getting hysterical? "Abby, you should take Gloria seriously," I say as I move toward her. She backs away, out of my reach.

"I had a long talk with Tony at the studio," Gloria says. "I went there to see if he could tell me how to find Jonah. He did, and that's when he told me about his plans for you. He sounded dead serious. Honey, he's a scary guy. He reminded me of some psychopaths I've interviewed over the years, cold and remorseless."

Abby laughs again. "I'm not worried. I've known Tony for years, and I know exactly how to handle him. And by the way, I hate it when people call me honey."

Gloria smiles. "Duly noted. It won't happen again. And now, since I've delivered Tony's message, I'm going to take my leave. I'm driving over to the Berkshires for a long weekend at my favorite spa, and I want to get there before dark. My show debuts on Monday, and I feel in need of some pampering. That way I'll look and feel my best when I face the cameras." She gives Abby an appraising glance. "No offense, dear, but a couple of days there would do wonders for you too. You're looking a little care-worn, especially around the eyes. Those close-ups can be cruel."

Abby shoots her a glare. "Maybe that's true for you, but you're what? Almost fifty? At my age, I don't have to worry yet."

Ouch! That has to sting, but Gloria doesn't even blink. Through all my years on soaps, I've seen plenty of women hurling insults at each other, but these two are threatening to scale new heights of bitchiness.

"It's been wonderful, Jonah," Gloria says "Don't forget to tune in to QMA on Monday at two." Her lips brush mine and she caresses my cheek, then heads for the door. Striding to her snappy red convertible, she doesn't look back.

Sirius jumps from the bed, his jaws clamped down tight on the quilted comforter. He drags it across the floor, drops it at my feet like a trophy, then snatches it up again. Growling, he shakes it violently.

Abby laughs as gossamer down floats around us like a flurry of snowflakes. "Good dog!" she says as she ruffles the fur around his ears.

"No, bad dog!" I say, but my heart isn't in it. Sirius knows it, and he goes on mauling the comforter, shredding it past the point of rescue.

"It's so therapeutic watching him," Abby says. "Too bad he didn't do that to Gloria."

"He'd never attack a woman." I start to laugh, but the laughter dies in my throat as I see the fury in Abby's eyes. "You're joking, right? Or do you really hate her that much?"

"I hate the fact that she's fucking you, but no, I don't hate her as a person. If anything, I pity her. She's got a lot riding on this show, and she'll be out there on her own, not like us with our huge ensemble cast. And she definitely looks older since she lost that job as an anchor. She needs more than a few days at a spa – she needs some work done."

"I'm glad you didn't tell her that."

"No, but I was harsh enough. I was right, though, when I said I don't have to worry about aging skin. Did you ever wonder why?"

"No. I just know you're at the peak of your beauty. You look every bit as young and radiant as Alifair Churchill did back on *Oak Bluff.*"

"How would you know? You weren't there – that was Jesse."

"I've watched reruns – they're all over YouTube. But face it, Abby. Sooner or later you'll start showing your age. It happens to the best of us."

Her eyes take on an eerie incandescent glow. "Not to me, it won't. And not to you either."

Something in her tone makes me uneasy. "Abby, you're in denial," I say. "But cling to your fantasy if it makes you happy. Just take good care of that beautiful fair skin, and don't forget to use sunscreen, preferably SPF 50."

"Believe me, it's no fantasy." Suddenly she grabs my hand and pulls me toward the bed. Her skin is surprisingly cold. "It's time I leveled with you, Jonah. You'd better sit down for this."

Wordlessly I comply, sinking onto the pillowy mattress, my feet planted firmly on the floor. Sirius whines, makes a couple of circles, then settles at my feet with a sigh.

Abby plops down beside me, a few inches away. Her eyes are downcast, and her voice is the softest of whispers. "You know how almost from the day you arrived at *Sunlight and Shadow,* you've been obsessing about whether or not you're a vampire?"

"Yes, but it wasn't right away. It didn't start till after Gene Gentry died."

"Right." She turns, gazes into my eyes, then lays her forefinger on my lips. "Sssh. This is hard for me, but it'll be easier if you don't interrupt. Pretend you're a priest hearing my confession."

"That won't work. Priests don't just listen, they talk. Ask questions, assign penances, that kind of thing. Or so I've heard tell. I've never actually been to confession."

"Jonah, for once in your life, shut up! Pretend you're an old-fashioned shrink, the kind that never says anything."

"You mean a psychoanalyst. That approach has been pretty well discredited."

She flashes a mischievous grin. "Don't say I didn't warn you!" Leaning forward, she takes my lower lip in her teeth and bites down hard.

"Ouch! Damn it, Abby, that hurt!" I wipe my hand across my mouth and look down at my palm. "You actually drew blood."

"Only a tiny taste." She licks her lips lasciviously. "Yum. It whets my appetite for more." She pulls away, takes both my hands in hers and smiles. "Yes, Jonah, you really are a vampire. I know, because I'm the one who made you."

Chapter Thirty-Six

To say I'm flabbergasted would be the understatement of the century, but at least Abby's gotten her wish – she's rendered me speechless.

"What's the matter, Jonah? Cat got your tongue?" Grinning, she leans closer again, but I dodge out of her way.

I take a deep gulp of air and stammer out a response. "You're putting me on, right? About making me a vampire?"

"No, I'm dead serious. Or should I say undead serious." She trails her fingers down my cheek, along my jawline to my throat, and I shiver convulsively. "Don't worry, Jonah. I promise I won't bite, not unless I have to do it to shut you up. Now, are you ready to listen?"

I nod wordlessly.

"Okay, good. Remember our first scene together?"

"That day in the church? How could I forget?"

"You know how we both had a sense of déjà vu, as if we'd met before? I was doing my innocent ingénue bit, but I recognized you instantly. I knew we'd been lovers back on *Oak Bluff.* And we became vampires and hunted together. According to the script, you drank my blood, then seduced me into drinking yours, but actually it was the other way round. I was the one who initiated your transformation, or should I say your transfiguration. I'd been a vampire all along."

"You're confused, Abby. That wasn't you and me, it was Alifair Churchill and Jeremy Lowell."

She grabs my shoulders, digs in her nails and sinks

her teeth into my lip once more, then lets go with a sigh. "I give up. You insist on interrupting my confession, and arguing about it is a waste of time, so we might as well change the rules. But first, you need to realize: I'm not Abby."

What the hell? This conversation is getting crazier by the minute, but I try not to betray the depths of the alarm I feel. "I don't understand," I say.

"I'm Catherine Reynolds. I have been all along. Abby Hastings is just one of my personas, along with Alifair Churchill. You felt instantly drawn to Abby, even more strongly than the script called for, so that's who I became for you, both on and off set. But it was all an act. I was playing the woman you desired, leading you on with my coy, hard-to-get routine, letting the tension build until I got exactly what I planned all along, right from the moment I learned you were joining the cast of *Sunlight and Shadow.* I must say, you played your part to perfection."

"That wasn't much of a stretch. I've been Jonah McQuarry since I came to *Hope Dawns Eternal* more than a decade ago, and when that folded I came straight to *Sunlight and Shadow.* I'm not acting or playing a part. Jonah McQuarry is who I am. Mark Westgate scarcely exists anymore, except as an inner voice that pops up occasionally when I'm feeling insecure. A wimpy, frightened voice I've managed to banish almost completely."

Abby grins. "That's why you were the perfect man to kill Keith Carlton for me. Or Mick Hastings, if you prefer using his character's name."

My heart starts thudding harder, and I can barely breathe. "I had no choice — he could have killed us both. But you were devastated when he died. I'll never forget the way you were kneeling over his body, singing 'Golden Slumbers.' And you were furious at me afterwards. I thought you'd never forgive me."

"My dear, I was simply acting. It was fiendishly difficult staying in role, because I felt deliriously happy. I'm sorry I took off so abruptly and left you with all the messy details to deal with, but I was afraid I couldn't keep up the charade much longer if I stayed."

I shake my head in disbelief. "So in essence you were just using me."

"That's a crass way of putting it, though I suppose there's some truth to it. But I had to get away from Keith, and I knew that could only happen over his dead body. If I so much as hinted that I might leave him or that maybe we should think about divorce, he said he'd kill me before he ever let me go. And I'm positive he meant it."

"Wait, I'm confused. Are you talking about Mick now, or about Keith?"

"Both. In some ways, he had an identity conflict similar to yours, in that Mick dominated Keith, who was a cowardly wimp at heart."

I wince. "That's pretty harsh."

"Sorry." She touches my lip with her forefinger. "Let me finish. Deep down, I believe you have an innate goodness about you. A sense of ethics and morality."

My eyes stray to the rumpled bed linens. "I'm not so sure of that."

She laughs. "Maybe not when it comes to sex, but I'm talking about something deeper than that. You have a basic respect for the sanctity of life. Unlike Keith, you don't get off on violence for the sake of violence, and you don't enjoy inflicting pain."

"How could you possibly know that? I've killed more than once, and I confess the experiences gave me a frisson of pleasure. Completely unexpected, and I'm not proud of it."

"But you killed for righteous reasons, not out of sheer bloodlust. There's a huge difference. Believe me, I know, because I was there with you each and every time."

I gasp. "No, you weren't. That's impossible."

"Not in the corporeal sense, but we vampires have our ways. If you come back to the city with me, I can teach you."

I fall silent, thinking it over. "There are a lot of reasons I shouldn't," I say finally. "First and foremost, I'm still a person of interest in the murders of Gene Gentry and Jeff Herbert, not to mention your late husband. By now they've probably got all kinds of incriminating forensic evidence against me, not to mention Sirius. I'm sure they picked up a ton of dog hair at the crime scenes."

"Not to worry. If the cops had incriminating evidence, don't you think they would have tracked you down and hauled you in already?"

"I'll admit I've been wondering about that."

"As well you should. But when Jeremy took possession, you not only went through psychological changes, you went through physical ones as well. Fangs, fingernails – surely you must have noticed?"

"Not really. I was a little preoccupied."

"Trust me on this, Jonah. Even your DNA underwent a temporary transformation. Your fingerprints too. Then once you were back to yourself again, they reverted back to normal. Or what's normal for you, at any rate. Your dog probably underwent a similar metamorphosis."

"You really expect me to buy into this, Abby? Before I went off the grid up here in the boonies, I Googled vampires and did a fair amount of research, but I didn't come across anything remotely like this."

"It's cutting-edge science. That's why it doesn't show

up in the traditional literature on vampirism. People didn't even know DNA existed until the 1950's, and vampire lore goes back thousands of years, to the dawn of civilization. It's become a canon, like the Bible, and believers are resistant to change."

"So how do you know all this esoteric stuff?"

"Sorry, but I'm sworn to secrecy. If you come back to Manhattan with me and all goes well, maybe I'll get clearance to share more at some point, but not yet. I've already told you more than I should, but I wanted to allay your fears about the forensic evidence. Otherwise I knew you wouldn't come back."

"You've got that right, but what about *Sunlight and Shadow?* I haven't been in touch with Chuck or Harvey, but I assume I'm still officially on leave, and I'm probably still persona non grata around there."

"Maybe not as much as you think. You know how self-involved actors are – they worry about their own contracts and their own story lines, and they're used to seeing characters come and go. People get recast and come back with different faces, get killed off and come back to life months or years later. Those who stick around for the long term have learned to roll with the punches. And speaking of punches, several actors have taken me aside and said they're relieved Keith is dead and gone. They found him intimidating, even threatening, but they were afraid to say anything."

"What about Tony Giordano? I know he was upset about Mick's death."

"He was putting on an act, just like me. In reality, Andy Danko tolerated Keith, but they were never close. Andy always said Keith was the dullest tool in the box. And I've heard rumors they plan to recast Mick, because Tony does need an enforcer. They're wooing an actor from a soap on another network."

"Andy Danko? I practically never heard anyone use

that name. It was always Tony Giordano."

"Andy insists on that. He's into method acting, and he wants to stay totally in character whenever he's on the set."

My head is starting to spin. "But I've spent time with him away from QMA, and he acts virtually the same. You think he's been conning me all along?"

"I wouldn't presume to say what's actually going through his mind. He's a complicated guy."

"He forced me to turn him into a vampire, or so I thought. But maybe he was just faking it."

Abby falls silent. "I have no idea," she says finally. "I haven't seen him lately. I could find out easily enough, but I'd have to meet him face to face."

"You'd be running a terrible risk. Gloria said he wants to turn you – no, wait, I forgot. You're a vampire already."

"Right. I have nothing to fear. I can handle him – no problem."

"Does Tony know you're a vampire?" I ask.

"No, nobody at QMA knows, and I want to keep it that way. You're the first person I've told, and that's only because you've caused such an uproar that I had to come here to warn you to cool it.. You've got a lot to learn about keeping things on the down low, blending in seamlessly so that no one knows the extent of your powers. I can teach you – I've got centuries of experience."

"Centuries? You mean before you were Alifair Churchill?"

"Oh, long before. Some night I'll tell you all about it, but right now I can think of better things to do." She leans close, clasps me in a tight embrace and begins nuzzling my neck.

The touch of her lips is intoxicating and I shudder.

Our mouths melt together in a kiss so luscious that I'm instantly aroused. The sensations build when she explores my mouth with her tongue, reach a crescendo when she bites down on my lip and I taste the coppery tang of my own blood. I return the bite, harder. Is it my imagination, or is her blood a little sweeter? As our fluids mingle, the boundaries dissolve and it's impossible to tell.

I ease her down onto the bed. "I want to make love to you," I murmur as my tongue caresses the curve of her neck.

She sighs. "I know you do, and I want that too, but not right now. The scent of you and Gloria on these sheets is overpowering, and when we make love I want to be sure you're at peak performance. Besides, there are things we can do together, things we can give each other, that far transcend ordinary sex. Would you like me to show you?"

I nod. Wordlessly, we strip the clothes from our bodies, drop them on the floor and fall together. At the door, Sirius sighs, circles twice, then snuggles into his nest of downy feathers to guard us from the outside world.

About the Author

Julie Lomoe has published two mysteries, both inspired by her personal and professional experience. *Mood Swing: The Bipolar Murders* is set in a social club for the mentally ill on Manhattan's Lower East Side. The novel draws on her many years of professional mental health experience and advocacy for mental health consumers. *Eldercide* draws on her experiences as president of ElderSource, Inc., a Licensed Home Care Services Agency in upstate New York. *Hope Dawns Eternal* is her first venture into paranormal fantasy fiction and the first of a series featuring soap opera characters Jonah McQuarry and Abby Hastings.

A Phi Beta Kappa graduate of Barnard College, Julie received an MFA from Columbia University and an MA in Art Therapy from New York University. She lived in SoHo for many years, exhibiting at the Museum of Modern Art, The Brooklyn Museum, the 1969 Woodstock Festival, and many Manhattan galleries. In 1979 she moved with her family from Manhattan to upstate New York, where she became a creative arts therapist at the now-defunct Hudson River Psychiatric Center. Her full-time immersion in the world of the institutionalized mentally ill inspired her to turn to fiction as a creative outlet.

Julie has published poetry as well as articles on home care, mental health, aging, and women's issues. Check her website, www.julielomoe.com, or her blog, www.julielomoe.wordpress.com to learn more.

Read on to learn more about *Mood Swing: The Bipolar Murders* & *Eldercide.* Both available on Amazon.

Mood Swing: The Bipolar Murders

Julie Lomoe

Suicide can be an alluring option for people with bipolar disorder. So when Erika Norgren discovers Stephen Wright sprawled dead on the asphalt behind WellSpring Club, she assumes the gifted young artist took his own life.

Erika should know. Like Stephen, she has experienced the devastating mood swings of bipolar disorder, so she has a special affinity for the members of the social club she runs as a safe haven for the mentally ill on Manhattan's Lower East Side. But the police seem all too ready to write Stephen off as an insignificant stereotype, and she resolves to investigate further.

Then Jeff Hirsch, another talented artist with bipolar disorder, dies of a drug overdose on the club's front steps. By now Erika is convinced both men were murdered, but the prime suspects are club members she works with every day: the schizophrenic Stan Washington and the edgy, sociopathic Arthur Drummond.

As media scrutiny intensifies, and hostile neighbors including a real estate magnate with mob connections threaten to shut WellSpring down, Erika's own mood swings escalate dangerously. Even so, with only her German shepherd mutt Rishi to guard her back, she steps up her sleuthing, determined to save WellSpring and those who need it most.

Eldercide

Julie Lomoe

When quality of life declines with age and illness, who decides if you're better off dead? Nursing supervisor Claire Lindstrom suspects a killer is making the final judgment call for the clients of Compassionate Care.

A woman with Alzheimer's disease dies unexpectedly in the night. Another is found dead beside a stream. Claire sees the beginnings of a sinister pattern, but Paula Rhodes, her temperamental boss, doesn't want her raising questions. The survival of the home health care agency in upstate New York depends on its reputation for quality care, and a rash of mysterious deaths could kill the business.

Claire antagonizes the county coroner and becomes the prime suspect in the eyes of the police. All the while, from his vantage point near her cottage on Kooperskill Lake, a killer called Gabriel is watching, channeling his obsession with Claire into passionate paintings. Under another name, he's a man she already knows − but which one? And is he part of a far larger scheme of eldercide?

Our society is rapidly aging, our allotted life spans growing ever longer, but at what cost? *Eldercide* explores ethical dilemmas most of us will face − if we live long enough.

Author's Note

Heartfelt thanks to my husband Robb Smith, who inspired me to venture into totally unknown territory for *Hope Dawns Eternal*. Three years ago, the creators of National Novel Writing Month, better known as NaNoWriMo, issued a challenge called Script Frenzy. The goal: to write a 100-page TV or movie script during the month of April

We'd both taken part in NaNoWriMo before. The challenge was to write 50,000 words of a novel during the month of November. Officially, I'd won, but not without considerable copying, pasting, journaling and churning out of gibberish – in other words, cheating. As a writer, I'm simply not speedy enough to turn out upwards of 1600 words a day, because I'm perfectionistic and I prefer to edit as I go.

When Robb suggested I write a script, the idea seemed outlandish, far out of my comfort zone, and I came up with all kinds of reasons to reject it. Then he said, "What about that soap opera you're addicted to, the one with those actors you think are so hot?" Hmm, I thought, that might just work. I dove in and created my own soap opera with its own set of characters. After churning out the 100-page script that April, I realized I'd barely scratched the surface, and that the story was begging to be turned into a novel or still better, a series. Three years later, here's the first installment.

At this point it would be customary to thank the many friends and fellow writers whose feedback helped me shape my story, but in truth, only two people have read it in its entirety – Robb Smith and Carol Bluestein.

I thank them for their perceptive comments and suggestions. Others have cheered me on from the sidelines, including the members of Women Who Write and the local NaNoWriMo group, but in truth, I've been unusually private and possessive about this project. That will change as I launch *Hope Dawns Eternal* on an unsuspecting world and begin its sequel, *Sunlight and Shadow*.

I'm deeply indebted to the many brilliant professionals and devoted fans of daytime drama who have kept the soap opera flame burning brightly through the years. You've been my inspiration and I'd love to hear from you. Please contact me at www.julielomoe.com or at:

Norse Crone Press
P.O. Box 363
Wynantskill, NY 12198

www.ingramcontent.com/pod-product-compliance
Lightning Source LLC
Chambersburg PA
CBHW050015180626
46810CB00002B/434